"You kiss a blue streak, city lady."

"S-so do you," ~~Maxine~~ ... credit's due, sh... ...nt effort to push D... disappointed wh... ...nd she was left alone. "...better not happen again."

"Aw," he said, "don't be such a spoilsport!"

Maxine put on her most forbidding expression. "Sorry, but I'm not here to have fun, and we shouldn't lose sight of that—either of us."

"I wasn't."

She stiffened. "You mean you kissed me hoping to soften me up?"

He scowled. "I kissed you because I wanted to and you kissed me back for the same reason. Don't try and complicate things."

"Things <u>are</u> complicated," she argued. "At least they will be if you...if we form any kind of personal relationship. Not that one kiss signifies anything," she added hastily, anxious not to read more into it than he'd intended.

"So how many kisses would?" he shot back.

Weddings
By
DeWilde

About the author

Daphne Clair, a native New Zealander, has been writing prolifically since the age of eight. She has won several literary awards, including New Zealand's top short fiction prize, The Katherine Mansfield Award, and has produced a steady output of romance novels since 1976, nearly all set in her native country. She was therefore the perfect candidate to bring the Australia/New Zealand background of the far-flung DeWilde empire to life, as she has done in *Wilde Man*, and in her previous DeWilde novel, *Wilde Heart*. She and her husband, a Netherlander, are the parents of five grown children, and live in the 'winterless north' of New Zealand, where she welcomes mail to Box 18240, Glen Innes, Auckland, New Zealand.

Weddings
By
DeWilde

PREVIOUSLY AT DeWILDES

A court date was set to dissolve a decades-old marriage

- ◆ A farewell trip to Kemberly, the DeWildes' English country estate, produced some revealing family history for Grace DeWilde to digest.

- ◆ A six-week enforced residency in Nevada offered some unexpected, and very handsome company!

- ◆ And a surprise visit from her mother-in-law prompted a new understanding of a legendary family romance, and the closely guarded secrets her soon-to-be-ex-husband had no hint of!

As Grace heads for Australia, to attend the wedding of DeWilde general manager Ryder Blake and Natasha, a recently discovered DeWilde, she can't imagine any more shocking news with relation to missing DeWildes and hidden jewels. But more eye-openers await her down under!

Special thanks for help with the research are due to the staff of the Queensland Tourist and Travel Corporation, Auckland; Mr Mark Williams and the staff of Taronga Park Zoo, Sydney; Featherdale Wildlife Park, Doonside, Sydney; Tracie McMichael of Queensland Reptile and Fauna Park, Beerwah; friend and fellow writer Helen Bianchin of Queensland; my wonderfully helpful friend Rosemary Cooke of Bribie Island; and my 'Aussie' sister-in-law Shirley Williams and her family. And a particular tribute must go to the informative and sensitive book *Crocodile Attack in Australia* by Hugh Edwards, which inspired the 'character' of Delilah.

NOTE: There are wildlife parks within two hours of Brisbane, but DeWildes does not represent any of them. It is a fictional place drawn from the above and other sources, and my own experience as a visitor to several similar parks.

First published in Great Britain 1996 by Harlequin Mills & Boon Limited, Eton House, 18-24 Paradise Road, Richmond, Surrey TW9 1SR

Daphne Clair de Jong is acknowledged as the author of this work.

© Harlequin Books S.A. 1997

ISBN 0 263 80101 2

06-9702

Printed and bound in Great Britain by BPC Paperbacks Limited, Aylesbury

Wilde Man

BY

DAPHNE CLAIR

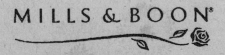
MILLS & BOON®

BARTLETT & FINCHLEY & PARTNERS
Barristers and Solicitors
28A Nerida St.
Sydney 2000

Mr. D. T. Cutter
DeWildes Reptile and Wildlife Park
Goanna Gap
Queensland

Dear Mr. Cutter

We are instructed by the DeWilde Corporation of London and DeWilde's Sydney branch that it has come to their notice that you are trading under the name and logo of DeWildes.

The use of this name may constitute an infringement of trademark rights held by our client.

If these activities do not cease within fourteen days of this date, and we are so informed in writing, we may be obliged to issue proceedings against you on behalf of the DeWilde Corporation.

Please cntact me at the above address.

Yours faithfully

M Sterling

M Sterling

Ph. (02) 179-6290   Fax. (02) 179-6289

PROLOGUE

"*CROCODILE HATS?*" Dev Cutter sat straighter in the creaking secondhand swivel chair and directed an outraged blue gaze across the battered office desk at his cousin Ross. "I know you're the marketing manager, Rooster, and I've gone along with most of your dingbat ideas for publicizing the wildlife park, but I'm not dressing up my crocs in sissy outfits for the tourists." He shook his head definitively, and a sun-streaked hank of brown hair fell across his forehead. "No way!"

Rooster opened his mouth to say something, but his twin sister, Binnie—christened Robina—forestalled him. Sitting on the edge of the desk where she had perched herself immediately after she and her brother had entered the cluttered little office, she wailed, "Aw, Dev! Don't turn it down—they'd look so c-cute!"

Her lips trembled, and even as Dev looked suspiciously at her, Rooster exploded into a shout of laughter.

Binnie joined in, leaning on her brother's shoulder in a fit of giggles, their curly, bushfire-blond heads close together.

Dev's scowl cleared and he settled back to wait tolerantly until the twins subsided and were simply grinning at him, identical blue eyes bright with residual humor.

"Okay," he said with resignation, his own mouth quirking up at the corners, "I can see I misunderstood. So tell me what you meant."

Rooster handed Dev Binnie's sketch pad. Binnie, her bare tanned legs crossed below baggy khaki shorts, leaned across the desk to squint at the page he was studying. "Auntie Maggie likes it," she said encouragingly.

Dev grunted. He doubted his mother liked the idea exactly, but in the six months since the park had opened, she must have learned something about what items sold best in the souvenir shop that brought in a hefty part of their revenue.

"Kids'll love them." Rooster planted both hands on the desk, peering at the picture. "It's a brilliant idea, Dev."

It was a bloody tasteless idea, Dev thought, but no doubt Rooster was right. The picture showed a cartoon kangaroo wearing a baseball cap—but this was no ordinary cap. Unlike the sparely outlined kangaroo, it was carefully detailed and in color. The long peak was a crocodile snout complete with curved teeth and a red tongue in the slightly parted mouth. The crown formed the rest of the beast's head, including yellow crocodile eyes.

"Look on the next page," Binnie urged.

Dev flipped the page and found a back view of the hat, which sported a green sun flap inscribed in flowing red lettering, De Wildes. He just stopped himself from asking why it wasn't shaped like a crocodile's tail. Give these two an idea like that and they'd probably run with it.

"It's a good, practical sun hat," Binnie pointed out. "The Cancer Society would approve. But parents won't have to force their children to wear it."

"The kids'll be begging their parents to buy them," Rooster predicted.

Dev was no expert on children and parents. Not human ones, anyway. But he knew that this kind of thing did appeal to preteens, and maybe to others as a sort of joke. "How are you going to do it?" he asked.

"It's all printed on," Binnie explained. "Scales and eyes and that. We could make the crown in sections with slightly fuller panels on each side to give a hooded look to the eyes, and shape the peak to make the snout realistic. And when the cap is put on, the mouth should gape just a bit—like the picture. It'll look great."

"Won't it be expensive?" Dev suggested hopefully. "People don't want to pay too much for a baseball cap, do they?"

Binnie reached over and took the sketch pad. "Auntie Maggie said she'd talk to some manufacturers about it. The guy who makes the T-shirts for us does a good job and his prices are reasonable."

"We'll get quotes," Rooster promised. "Okay?"

Dev looked at the sketch again and suppressed a shudder. "Okay," he agreed reluctantly.

"WEARING A *CROCODILE?*" Ryder Blake, general manager of Sydney's newest and most exclusive department store, stared across the lovingly polished width of his antique desk at his public relations officer.

"A crocodile *hat*—baseball cap. In Ladies' Wear." Below perfectly groomed silver-gray hair, Lee Bolton's well-bred, handsome face displayed his agitation. "The young man was making a nuisance of himself, peeking into the fitting rooms—"

"Was he, indeed. You called the police, of course?"

"The department manager found his mother—"

"His *mother?*"

"He's about five, I suppose."

Ryder sat back in his chair. "Why are you telling me

this, Lee? Surely the department head could have dealt with it.''

''With that, yes. The point is, I happened to be in the department talking with her at the time. So when the young man—''

''He's a child, Lee. A little boy.''

''When the boy poked his head in under the door of one of the booths, the customer shrieked at the top of her voice. She thought it was a real live crocodile.''

''Is it that convincing?'' Ryder lifted his brows.

''Not really, but she'd taken off her glasses to try on a dress, and when she was pulling the garment over her head and saw this thing coming at her under the door—''

''I get the picture.''

''So of course the salespeople, the department manager and I all went running to see what was wrong—'' Lee cleared his throat, an expression of acute embarrassment crossing his face. ''I'm afraid in the heat of the moment I didn't stop to consider—''

''And?'' Ryder prompted.

''I...er...ran into the area on the manager's heels, so to speak, and several ladies in various...er...stages of...of undress, who had opened the doors of the booths at the first scream, started screaming, too.''

Ryder pressed his lips firmly together and remained silent.

''Of course I got out of there as quickly as I could, but not before I'd identified the culprit.''

''I imagine the poor kid was freaked out by this time,'' Ryder murmured.

Lee said frostily, ''On the contrary, he seemed to be thoroughly enjoying it. If you ask me, he's a little pervert in the making.''

Again Ryder's brows went up, but he said only, ''So

what's the problem? The women want you arrested? The one who saw the 'crocodile' has threatened to sue us?''

''Nothing like that,'' Lee assured him. ''No, it's the *hat*.''

''The hat.'' Ryder nodded patiently.

''The cap. It has DeWilde's logo on it!'' Lee's voice throbbed.

Ryder frowned. ''I don't recall that line of merchandise.''

''No, you wouldn't,'' Lee told him triumphantly, ''because we never sold it. Nor the T-shirt.''

''T-shirt?''

''He was wearing a T-shirt as well, printed with a snake. And also with our logo.''

Ryder's frown deepened. ''Someone's using our name without a license?''

''I assure you, if DeWilde's should ever license this kind of cheap tourist bait it will be over my dead body! Or at least my resignation letter.''

''I understand your feelings,'' Ryder said gravely. DeWilde's Sydney had been in business for little over a year, but the store was modeled on the elegant cosmopolitan tradition of its sister stores in London and Paris, Monaco and New York—an image both he and his PR staff worked hard to foster. ''Did you find out where these things came from?''

''That's why I've brought the young—the boy and his mother to see you. I knew you'd want to know.''

''They're here?'' Ryder glanced at the closed door of his office.

''Waiting in the outer office. I thought I should talk to you first.''

''Ask them to come in.''

Ryder stood up as Lee ushered in a plump, flushed

young woman, holding by the hand a young boy with a belligerent expression, who immediately turned to Lee and stuck out a pointed pink tongue.

Ryder smiled at the mother. "Please sit down, Mrs.—?"

"Mrs. McDonald." The woman eyed him suspiciously and stiffly sat in the chair, the boy leaning on her knee. "You can't accuse us of anything. Timmy's just a normal little boy."

Lee's eyes flickered upward infinitesimally, as though he would have liked to dispute that. The public relations man's relations with this particular junior member of the public didn't seem terribly successful.

"No one is accusing you or Timmy of any wrongdoing, Mrs. McDonald." Ryder resumed his own seat, wrenching his eyes from the striped orange-and-black printed snake circling Timmy's sturdy body, and the remarkable headgear the child sported. He could see why a short-sighted person at first glance might have thought the base-ball cap was a genuine, though smallish, crocodile. "I'm sure he's a charming little boy." Thinking he heard a quiet snort from Lee, he cast him a swift, reproving look.

"Then why did this store detective or whatever he is drag us up here?" the woman demanded.

"I never said I was a detective!" Lee protested. "I *requested* you to accompany me to the general manager's office because I thought he would like to talk to you."

"Well, do you think I don't know what *that* means?" She glared at him.

Timmy, directing a formidable glare of his own at the publicity officer, announced darkly, "That man tried to swipe my cap."

"I merely asked if I could look at it." Lee turned to Ryder. "I hoped to find a manufacturer's label."

"You *touched* it!" Timmy accused.

"And then he wanted to know where we'd got it from," his mother added. "As if there was something suspicious about it. When I told him it was none of his business, he 'asked' us to come with him to the general manager's office." She heaved an indignant breath. "We-'re not shoplifters!"

Lee looked shocked. "The thought never crossed my mind, madam."

"Mr. Bolton is the store's public relations officer," Ryder explained. "We do apologize for any distress we may have caused you, Mrs. McDonald." As her expression became uncertain, though still suspicious, he smiled again. "I appreciate your taking the time to see me. May I offer you a cup of tea or coffee? And perhaps Timmy might like a cola or something?"

Timmy announced, "I don't like cola."

Ryder turned to him. "What would you like, Timmy? With your mother's permission, of course."

If his secretary was surprised at being asked to procure a Rocketship Special from the first-floor café, she was too well trained to blink an eyelid.

Lee almost visibly shuddered at the sight of the tall glass of murky green liquid under a tower of pink cream and marshmallows finished with multicolored sprinkles. But by the time Timmy was sucking noisily at the dregs through his striped straw, the child was quite amenable to removing his precious cap so Ryder could inspect the maker's label.

"Those ladies really scree—eeched when they saw it," he confided proudly. "Like this!" He opened his mouth and gave a bloodcurdling demonstration.

Lee flinched, and Timmy's mother said feebly, "Don't, Timmy."

Ryder's lips twitched. "I'm sure they did, but I'd count it a personal favor if you didn't frighten my customers again, Timmy. It's not good for business, and if I had to close down the store there'd be no more Rocketship Specials. Besides, if you go peeking at ladies in their underwear when you're a grown-up you could be in big trouble. And I wouldn't like that to happen to you."

While Timmy contemplated this, Ryder wrote down the name of the manufacturer of the cap. "Would you mind if I looked at the label on your shirt, too?" he asked, handing back the cap.

Timmy turned and allowed him to do so. "They've got grown-up shirts, too. Dad's got a kangaroo on his, but I like the snake one best. They had neat gear!"

"Really? And where did you buy all this neat gear?"

"At De Wildes, of course!"

Lee gave a quiet snort of disbelief.

Mrs. McDonald said, "In Queensland, on our holidays. It's a wildlife park."

"Do you recall exactly where?" Ryder asked. "You wouldn't know the address, I suppose?"

Mrs. McDonald was vague about that. "It was…we went to so many places…traveled around a lot. I'm not sure exactly…."

"The wild man was there, too!" Timmy said helpfully.

"The wild man?" Ryder queried.

"The De Wildes man," Mrs. McDonald explained.

"He catches crocodiles." Timmy's eyes gleamed. "We watched him feeding them. He holds out meat in his hand and they jump right out of the water and *snap!* Just like me feeding Patch—that's my dog. He wouldn't let me try, though." Timmy looked disgruntled.

"My husband might remember where the place is," Mrs. McDonald offered.

"If he does," Ryder suggested, "perhaps he'd be k
ind enough to phone and let me or Mr. Bolton know. But
I'm sure we can find out. Thank you very much for your
time, Mrs. McDonald—and Timmy. You've been most
helpful. Lee, could you find one of our blue gift vouchers
for Mrs. McDonald to show our appreciation?"

"Certainly." Lee seemed to have recovered his equi-
librium and his usual smooth manner. He even apologized
again to Mrs. McDonald as he opened the door to usher
her out, and quickly suppressed the tremor of pain that
crossed his features when Timmy surreptitiously kicked
his ankle on the way past.

Reaching for the phone, Ryder gave the publicity officer a sympathetic grin and waited for the door to close
before he said into the receiver, "Get Maxine Sterling on
the line for me."

CHAPTER ONE

"OH, YOU LIKE THAT, huh, sweetheart?" Dev grinned as his hand traversed a well-known path from the top of Delilah's head to her chin. He caressed her there and she lifted her head, her white teeth showing in an encouraging smile. Sleepy eyes glinting, she rolled over and invited him to stroke the pale, tender skin of her belly.

Dev laughed softly and obliged, crooning endearments as he admired the familiar beauty at his fingertips.

"Dev?"

Binnie knew better than to interrupt Dev when he was with Delilah unless it was important, and he noted with approval that her quiet tone was calculated not to upset his companion or arouse her temper. But he also noted the controlled tension in his young cousin's voice.

"Sorry, love," he told Delilah regretfully. "Gotta go. See you tomorrow." Giving her a last pat on her stomach, he helped her to her feet and rose without haste from the crocodile's side to cross the grassed enclosure toward Binnie, who was hovering anxiously on the other side of the substantial steel gate.

Delilah made a protesting sound and took a couple of sinuous steps after him, but she'd just been given a feed of thawed fish, and decided she might as well lie in the morning sun and enjoy digesting it.

"What's the problem?" Dev asked as he secured the gate behind him.

Binnie handed him a folded piece of paper. "This must have come yesterday afternoon. I didn't have time to deal with the mail then, 'cause I went on gate duty when Sandy went home sick. Sorry, Dev. I didn't realize it was urgent."

"Not your fault." Besides doing her design and artwork and helping Maggie in the shop, Binnie had taken on many of the routine secretarial tasks that Dev tended to put aside. Dev had no complaints.

He took the letter and unfolded it, frowning at the printed heading across the top.

"They can't do this to us!" Binnie's eyes were bright with indignation, her pretty face flushed. "Can they?"

Dev scanned the single page quickly.

We are instructed by the DeWilde Corporation…you are trading under the name… If these activities do not cease…may be obliged to issue proceedings…

He frowned, said something under his breath and then looked guiltily at Binnie, but she hadn't blinked. "No," he told her, his eyes skimming to the boldly looped signature above the neatly typed "M. Sterling" at the foot of the letter. "Of course they can't."

His instinct was to screw up the piece of paper and toss it into the nearest bin. There were plenty of them around, tin kangaroos with inviting swing-lidded pouches to encourage the park's patrons to use them.

Second thoughts made him stuff the letter into the pocket of his worn jeans. "Don't worry about it, Binnie. And don't mention it to the others, okay?" No point in bothering Maggie and Rooster with this nonsense.

He picked up the empty bucket and went on to check the next pen, full of hungry young crocs falling over themselves and one another to get near the fence as they scented fish. ''Your turn later, guys,'' he told them, and passed on. They would be fed after the visitors began coming through the gates.

He checked the other enclosures, watching for signs of problems among the animals and making sure gates and fences were secure against idiots hoping to take home a live souvenir or showing off to their friends how brave they were.

One of a group of half-grown crocodiles had got injured in a spat with another, and when he'd finished his morning round, Dev and a park worker removed it from its pond, getting covered in mud in the process, to tend the wound. The animal was unappreciative of their attentions and it took half an hour to perform the simple first aid before returning it to its home.

Later Dev showered and stuffed his soiled jeans and other clothing into the washing machine, sprinkled them liberally with washing powder and turned the machine on.

He never even thought about the letter until his mother came into his office ten busy days later.

Maggie Cutter's vivid blue eyes mirrored her son's, although Dev's brown hair, rangy build and broad shoulders were inherited from his father. Maggie's black hair was now highlighted with silver strands, but she was small-boned and as willow-slim as a young girl. Although raised in the outback, she retained an exotic and fragile look that belied a life spent farming.

The Australian sun had weathered a complexion not designed for its rigors, but the smile lines about her eyes and mouth hardly diminished the mellow beauty of her face, which right now was wearing a perplexed expression.

"Dev," she said, "the clothing factory is refusing to handle our order."

"We've got a contract, haven't we? And you and Binnie make sure we pay our bills on time."

"Yes. But...they say they've been threatened with legal proceedings if they continue to manufacture clothing using the name of the park."

"The hell they have!" Feeling guilty, Dev recalled the lawyer's letter he'd promised to deal with. Right now he couldn't even remember what he'd done with it. The thought had never occurred to him that it would affect Maggie's suppliers. "I'll soon sort them out," he promised grimly, and reached for the phone. "No worries."

"Now, Dev." Maggie's cool, unexpectedly capable hand came firmly down on his. "Don't go flying off the handle, will you?"

"You don't trust me." Dev scowled.

"Of course I trust you, dear. I just think you shouldn't be too hard on them. The man was quite apologetic."

"Yeah, all right," Dev agreed reluctantly. "I promise I'll be all sweet reason. Leave it with me."

He kept his temper well under control, but the manufacturer was adamant that he had no intention of laying himself open to legal hassles.

Frustrated, Dev hung up the phone just as Binnie brought in the afternoon's mail and began slitting the envelopes.

"There's another letter from that legal firm in Sydney," she told him a minute or two later. "It says they've had no answer to their previous communication and if we don't reply in writing within seven days, with an assurance that we've complied with their demand, they'll start proceedings against the park and the shop."

"They wouldn't win," Dev growled, renewed guilt nagging at him. "Give me that."

The letter was in legal language but its meaning was clear enough. It was signed with the same bold, looped signature as the first, and it made his blood boil.

He counted to ten before dialing the number on the letterhead. By then he had simmered down enough, he hoped, to conduct a civilized conversation with M. Sterling of Bartlett & Finchley & Partners.

The woman who answered informed him that Ms. Sterling was in a meeting. Could she phone him back?

Dev looked at his watch. In twelve minutes he was due to conduct a busload of overseas tourists around the park and talk to them about Australian wildlife.

"No, thanks," he told the woman. "I'll try again later."

After the tour party had left, he was waylaid by a family who wanted to photograph "the De Wildes man" with their children, and kept him talking for some time. When he finally made it to his office and phoned Bartlett and Finchley again, he was informed that Ms. Sterling was "with a client." Would he like to leave a message?

A message? Where would he start?

"She could call you back," the woman suggested helpfully.

He had things to do. Sitting around waiting for the phone to ring wasn't one of them. "No," he said. "Thanks."

Maybe Rooster was right—he'd been nagging Dev to get a cell phone. But Dev wasn't at all sure that he wanted to be reachable by phone wherever he was.

An hour later, Ms. Sterling was "unavailable." When pressed, the receptionist finally admitted that the lawyer had left the office, and suggested he try again on Monday.

It was not yet four o'clock. Ms. Sterling, he decided snarkily, obviously wasn't above sneaking off work early. High-powered lawyers, he supposed, could do that.

He asked to speak to someone else. After a considerable wait, a Mr. Gordon Finchley informed him that the firm was acting on instructions from the DeWilde Corporation and that he was sure Ms. Sterling would be pleased to talk with Mr. Cutter next week.

Deciding on a different tack, Dev got the number of the DeWilde store from Directory Assistance. He asked for the general manager, only to be told that neither Mr. Blake nor his assistant manager was available. "Perhaps Mr. Bolton, our public relations officer, could help?" the anonymous voice offered.

Dev didn't feel like being fobbed off with soothing words from the public relations officer. He wanted to go right to the top and get this business sorted out once and for all. "No, thanks." He tried not to snarl. The woman was doing her best. "I'll catch up with the general manager another time. Will he be in tomorrow?" Presumably the store would be open on Saturday. But did department store managers in Sydney, unlike wildlife park keepers in Queensland, work a five-day week?

"The assistant manager may be here in the morning, but Mr. Blake's on leave for the next four weeks."

Dev reminded himself that it wasn't her fault her boss had decided to take a holiday. "Lucky guy," he grunted.

"Yes, isn't he?" the woman chirped. "He's getting married, you know."

How nice for him, Dev thought sourly, managing a civil thanks before banging down the phone.

Well, tomorrow Dev would be in Sydney for his weekly spot on TV. Maybe he should check at the store and try to find someone from this DeWilde crowd who seemed to be knotting their knickers over the coincidence of similar names. He could take a later flight home.

DEV'S MODEST TV CAREER had begun when Rooster suggested they try to get a spot on a game show where contestants attempted to guess what the guest participant's occupation was. Dev had rated their chances at next to nil and given him the go-ahead, warning him not to waste too much time on it.

To Dev's surprise, the show organizer had been enthusiastic.

"It's much too good a chance to miss," Rooster had urged. "Great promotion for the park. You can't back out now."

Dev had reluctantly conceded. "Okay, you can take a couple of days to play at being a TV star—"

"Not me!" Rooster interrupted. "It's you they want. The man who talks to the crocodiles, the one who goes out and wrestles man-eating monsters—"

"I only *wrestle* them when things go wrong!" Dev said impatiently. "And it's using words like *monsters* that gives people a totally inaccurate concept of—"

"I know, I know—sorry!" Rooster held up his hands placatingly. "You can see I'm not the right one to do the interview! And anyway, I don't have a degree in zoological sciences. Or experience in the field. I'd get the answers all wrong—it's got to be you!"

Rooster could be very persuasive when he put his mind to it. After ten minutes of arguing, Dev had capitulated, grumbling, "I'd better dig a suit out of my wardrobe—I suppose I'll have to get done up like a sore toe."

"Hell, no!" Rooster protested. "That'd be the wrong image. You oughta look the part—you know, a tough, rugged outback man. Otherwise it's not fair to the contestants.''

"You want to turn me into some kind of Crocodile Dundee?'' Dev asked dangerously.

Rooster's face lit up. "Well, you are in a way—but not exactly,'' he amended hastily as Dev's frown grew thunderous. "You'll be promoting the image of *De Wildes*—'' He sketched the sign in the air with a sweep of one hand.

"I don't know why I ever let you talk me into that,'' Dev told him, thoroughly disgruntled.

"Because it's a great name for a wildlife park,'' Rooster said, not for the first time. "And because you got outvoted by the rest of us.''

He had, too. He'd argued against it, but finally succumbed to the twins' enthusiastic pleading and his mother's endorsement.

Dev might be nominally the boss here, but he couldn't have realized his dream of building a wildlife park without Maggie's generous support and self-sacrifice, and he'd seen how much the idea of calling it De Wildes pleased her. So he'd given in.

He owed a lot to the twins, too. Just out of university, they said they were grateful to have jobs at all, and they'd worked, at first on meager wages, as hard and long as he and Maggie had to get the park opened.

Which was maybe why Dev found himself promising Binnie that for the interview he'd wear the rugged but venerable clothing he normally reserved for his trips to the wild north of Queensland. Before he could stop her, Binnie had ruthlessly torn out the sleeves of the already shabby bush shirt on the grounds that "It makes you look authentic.''

Dev snorted. "If I wore that up Cape York way I'd be

eaten alive by mozzies and sandflies and various other nasties. *Authentic?*"

"Well, macho, then," Binnie insisted. "Anyway, lots of men up there prefer to wear shorts and go sleeveless or even without a shirt at all."

"Yeah, well..." There were two schools of thought about dealing with the rabid insect life in the north. "Some reckon they'd rather see what lands on them than have bloodsucking wildlife sneaking in under their clothes," Dev admitted. Personally he relied on gallons of insect repellent and methylated spirits, and tucked his long pants into sturdy socks and boots. And preferred to have sleeves in his shirts.

"There you are, then," Binnie said, holding up the remains of the shirt. "The women viewers'll love it." Catching his revolted expression, she added firmly, "Trust me, Dev. And wear your Akubra hat."

"I can't wear a hat in the studio."

"Take it off when you sit down," Binnie advised.

"I'm not putting a snakeskin round the band," he'd warned her, his stubborn jaw more prominent than usual.

Binnie cast him an impatient look. "I know that." Her expression changed to hurt. "How could you think I'd suggest it?"

Dev apologized.

ONLY THE FACT that his mother and the twins were looking forward to viewing the program had prevented Dev fleeing the claustrophobic little room where he had waited his turn to be ushered onto the set. During the audition interview he'd been totally relaxed, thinking it would never come to the real thing. But this was it.

When the female interviewer began her introductory spiel, he was pushed onto the set and took his seat at the other end of the studio couch as instructed. He placed the Styrofoam container he carried with him gently down on the floor and removed the wide-brimmed hat from his head to drop it into his lap. The bright lights were hot, and unthinkingly he flicked open three buttons of his shirt.

The interviewer's eyes settled on the wedge of tanned chest he'd revealed, and seemed to glaze slightly before she launched into her first question.

After someone had guessed his occupation and been duly rewarded, the interviewer turned to him again. "Dev, surely crocodiles and snakes are the most feared creatures on earth. And you work with them every day?"

Dev cleared his throat and stooped to remove the lid of the box and take a linen bag from its lining of sphagnum moss. Opening the bag, he carefully drew out a small orange-red snake, its writhing body encircled by black bands. "Now, who could be frightened of this little feller?"

Evidently the interviewer could. She gave a startled shriek, echoed by half the audience.

At least it had taken her mind off Dev's chest. "This is a bandy-bandy, quite harmless. One of these in the garden will get rid of some of those pests that eat up your plants. He likes to eat insects...."

Launched into his favorite subject, Dev got quite a buzz out of the audience's rapt attention and their occasional laughter. Finally he encouraged the interviewer to handle the snake, which she did with much nervous giggling and strangled little screams. When the show was over he allowed members of the audience to do the same, several children clamoring for a turn.

The interviewer detained him for some time afterward, her eyes bright and curious, and he guessed he'd made a convert of her. When he suggested that if she was ever in

Queensland she might like to visit De Wildes, she seemed quite excited, her cheeks flushing under her makeup. She even asked him to have dinner with her and tell her more about his fascinating life.

"I won't be here for dinner," Dev politely told her. "I'm flying out this afternoon." He didn't like the city much, and he'd planned on spending as short a time there as he could get away with.

A COUPLE OF WEEKS after what Dev had fully expected to be his last as well as his first television appearance he was walking toward the house from the park after a lecture in the turtle section, when Rooster came bounding down from the veranda to meet him. "Dev, you know that TV show you were on? The producer wants you for another program!"

Dev pushed back his hat, wiped sweat from his forehead and settled the hat again. "He what?"

"He does this Saturday morning live studio thing with film clips. It's a brunch slot. Their regular gardening guru had a stroke and they need someone to fill his place this week," Rooster explained.

Dev stepped up onto the veranda and turned to walk along it to his office. "I'm no gardener."

Rooster turned and followed him. "No, they want you to do a wildlife segment. Gil reckons—"

"Gil?"

"The producer, remember? He said they'd been thinking of dropping the gardening slot, anyway. There are too many television gardening programs. So it was kind of a blessing in disguise—"

"I'm sure the gardening guru thought so."

"I guess not," Rooster admitted. "The thing is, Gil says you're a natural. If you're as good as you were on the other program, you could get a permanent spot on this one.''

"You seem to have had quite a chat.''

"I am the director of publicity,'' Rooster reminded him as they turned the corner of the veranda, "when I'm not feeding the crocs or cleaning out the snake house. That's why Binnie put him on to me.''

"You mean she put him on to you because she knew I'd say no. Sorry, Rooster. I've had my fifteen minutes of fame already.'' Dev walked through the open side door and tossed his hat onto one of the filing cabinets.

Rooster ignored that. "They'd pay all expenses, as well as the fee. The money's awfully good, and it's brilliant publicity—''

"I'm not doing it, Rooster,'' Dev said flatly, to end the argument.

At the close of that week Dev had found himself on a plane to Sydney, along with a sharp-snouted flap-footed lizard, also known as Burton's flap-footed lizard.

His being there could have had something to do with Rooster's argument that already several park visitors had mentioned seeing the previous program, and that De Wildes couldn't afford to turn down another shot at making the place known outside Queensland. Or Binnie's casual remark that TV was the most effective educational tool of the century.

Or the soft look of pride in his mother's eyes when she said, "You did well last time, son. And Rooster and Binnie are right. Isn't it too good a chance to miss?''

The truth was, he'd grumbled to himself, the "fearless crocodile hunter,'' as the interviewer had—to his chagrin—called him in the closing minutes of "What Do You Do for a Crust?'' was total mush where his family was concerned.

THE GARDENING GURU had retired permanently from the show with the fulsome good wishes of cast and crew, and a segment called Wild Australia had replaced his slot. Dev arrived in the studio every week with a live animal of some kind and chatted to the host about its beauties and virtues and what people might do to protect the species.

The TV crew had spent a couple of days filming at the park for clips to be inserted throughout the series. But when Dev had suggested they video his studio bits in one session as well, Gil made horrified noises about "continuity nightmares" and "immediacy" and "*now* television," and hurt ones about "generous performance fees," and had even held out the promise of "the best accommodation in Sydney" if Dev needed to stay overnight, as though a longer sojourn in the city might be some kind of inducement.

Gil had also been adamant about the clothes Dev should wear. This time the buzzword was *Image*.

"We're billing you as the man from De Wildes. They loved you on 'What Do You Do for a Crust?' You've created a strong TV personality because you looked the part, so stick with the bush shirt and hat."

Binnie had enthusiastically concurred. "We know you're going out there to educate people, but you've got to catch their attention first."

"Otherwise they'll just switch off before you get a chance to put your message across," Rooster added.

After all, what did he know about selling an image? Dev asked himself gloomily. He'd hired Rooster to take care of that side of the business.

And so he had become a TV star—at least to that segment of the population who watched Saturday morning magazine programs.

HE'D GOT USED TO performing for the cameras. The trick was to forget they were there.

This week the show went without any of the major hitches that were a hazard with live television. The baby freshwater crocodile he'd brought along didn't escape into the audience or try to bite the show's host, the right camera focused on the tiny animal at the right moment, and the special weekly guest who followed Dev's spot appeared on cue. Last week's guest hadn't arrived at all, and Dev and the host had ad-libbed for ten minutes to cover the unexpected gap.

The first snag in his day occurred when Dev returned to the room where he'd changed from the presentable clothes he'd worn on the plane and into his "outback" TV outfit.

Fortunately he'd transferred his wallet and plane ticket to the pocket of his battered jeans rather than leave them in the unlocked room—fortunately, because when he looked around, he discovered his other clothes were gone.

The best guess several mystified staff members could offer was that Dev's things had got mixed up with those of a street theater troupe who had been taping in another studio and had also used the room. Trying to trace them seemed fruitless, and he'd already wasted enough of the extra time he'd given himself today. Rather than spend the rest of it shopping for clothes, he resigned himself to traveling home as he was.

His first priority was to find the DeWilde bridal emporium and have a go at tracking down someone in authority and talking some sense into them.

THE TAXI DRIVER was muttering about a holdup that had reduced traffic to a crawl. "Must be some big shindig going on," the man threw over his shoulder in excuse to his passenger. "A wedding or something. Not why you're going to DeWilde's, is it, mate?"

Dev peered out of the window, shading his eyes with a hand. "No, I'm not going to any shindig. Are we nearly there?"

"Down there." The driver pointed. "'Bout a hundred yards. This must be quite a do." He swung the wheel and planted his foot on the accelerator to steer into a gap in the traffic. Unexpectedly a large truck lumbered in front of them, headed for the same spot, forcing him to brake violently.

Dev was saved by his seat belt from being flung forward, but the light Styrofoam box on his lap shot to the floor, the catch flying open, and its occupant vanished under the driver's seat with a flick of its long tail.

The driver was swearing with great efficiency and much imagination at his counterpart in the truck. Dev undid his seat belt and dived to the floor, groping under the seat.

The swearing was broken by a startled yelp, then resumed at a higher volume. Dev briefly closed his eyes. His searching fingers finding no sign of his quarry, he scrambled off his knees and tried to peer over the driver's shoulder. "It's all right, it's only— *Don't open the door!*"

But the man had already thrown his door open and was standing on the road, to the confusion of the surrounding traffic. Several vehicles tooted, the cabbie kept up a stream of extremely pungent words, his eyes white and staring, and Dev glimpsed the end of a tail as the baby croc slithered out of the car. The driver leapt back at least a foot and nearly got himself wiped off the road by a passing limousine.

Dev thrust open his door, and in his hurry to get out kicked the forgotten container forcefully onto the road. It bounced a couple of meters and was promptly crunched into small, flattened pieces by a Parramatta-bound bus.

Dev dived at the crocodile as it was about to disappear under the cab, grabbed it and held it firmly, one hand about its body and one gently circling its neck while the frightened little animal snapped its tiny teeth frantically on empty air.

Still wild-eyed, the taxi driver backed toward his vehicle. "It's a bloody *crocodile!*"

"Only a baby one," Dev told him. "Sorry if he startled you—"

"Startled? It's a bloody *croc!*" the driver reiterated. "*That's* what you had in the esky?"

"That's right. You braked so suddenly—"

"Gee—eeze! You carried a croc in *my cab?*"

"He's a Johnson's freshwater crocodile and completely harmless. Look, don't you think we should get in?" A car swerved past them, the driver leaning indignantly on the horn while his male passenger made a rude gesture.

"*I'm* getting in," the man said, and leaned over to viciously slam the rear door shut before climbing back into the driver's seat. "But I'm not takin' no bleedin' croc nowhere. You're on your own from here, mate!"

"Well, sure. I can walk it now." Dev dug in his back pocket with one hand and awkwardly fished a note from his wallet. "Never mind the change."

The man barely paused to take the note before he gunned the engine and shot forward, leaving Dev standing on the road. Now the indignant hoots and shouted insults were directed at him.

What was left of the crocodile's container wasn't worth rescuing. Dodging between cars, he made it safely to the pavement. Then, ignoring the startled looks of passersby skirting round him, he pulled the leather belt from the loops of his jeans and awkwardly fastened it about his waist over the shirt to make a comfortable pouch. Gentling the little reptile, he searched his pockets for the rubber band he'd slipped over its snout as a precaution when he'd allowed the studio audience to touch the crocodile, but couldn't find it. "You wouldn't bite me, would you?" he suggested hopefully, and tucked the hatchling inside his shirt, where it would be soothed by the warmth of his skin and safe from the foolish behavior of human beings.

Then he walked until he found a big Victorian building with arched windows and carved stone columns, bearing above its imposing green marble entrance an elegantly lettered sign in black and red reading simply DeWilde.

Inside he discovered a long vaulted space lined with boutiques, but opposite the entrance people were piling into and spilling out of a bank of elevators. A uniformed security guard stood in front of one prominently labeled Skyroom Only. And beside him a sandwich board proclaimed, Skyroom Restaurant Closed for Private Function.

As Dev watched, a bunch of women in hats and floating fabrics, accompanied by men in suits and silk ties, swept past him into the lobby. "We're here for Ryder Blake's wedding," one of the women announced in a voice that echoed from the marble walls.

"May I see your invitation?" the guard asked politely, and the woman started to rummage in the small bag she held. Others in the party began hunting through pockets and purses even as a second group arrived and mingled with the first. There was a lot of laughter and cries of "I can't find mine!" and a gilt-edged card fell to the shiny marble floor and skidded across it unnoticed.

Dev picked it up, scanning the group to see who had dropped it. The elevator door was open and the guard held it as the chattering wedding guests crammed in, some clutching their invitations, nobody taking the slightest notice of Dev.

He was still holding the card when the doors closed and the guard turned away, shaking his head.

Casting a dismissive glance at Dev, the man saw the card in his hand and stiffened disbelievingly. "*You* have an invitation…sir?"

At the slight emphasis on the initial "you" and the subtly insulting pause before the "sir," Dev's eyes narrowed and his hold tightened on the magic pass. "Yeah," he said, his easy tone disguising the annoyance in his eyes. Why not go right to the top, after all? "Come to Sydney—" he deliberately drawled out the vowel "—to see me old mate Ryder get himself hitched to a sheila. This is the right place, innit, sport?"

The security man, apparently speechless with shock, nodded as Dev airily waved the invitation under his nose.

Another lot of exuberant guests entered the lobby, and Dev moved aside. As soon as the elevator returned and the door slid silently open he stepped in, courteously holding the door for those following. The guard still looked dubious, but the gilded corner of the white card peeking from the breast pocket of Dev's disreputable shirt seemed to reassure him as he ushered a middle-aged, distinguished-looking couple into the elevator.

Inside Dev's shirt the little crocodile shifted, its scaly skin against his chest. Surreptitiously he soothed it with his palm as the door whispered closed.

CHAPTER TWO

MAXINE STERLING was enjoying herself.

The champagne gently fizzing in the fluted glass she held was the real thing. Come to that, the glass itself was probably genuine crystal. The DeWildes wouldn't serve their guests in anything less. Ryder Blake might not be a DeWilde himself, but he was the general manager of the Sydney store, and apparently his bride was a scion of some long-lost branch of the family tree.

The DeWildes were certainly pulling out all the stops for the happy pair. The champagne circulated freely, as did the reception guests awaiting the arrival of the newlyweds. Under the magnificent glass domes in the high ceiling, the Skyroom tables were dressed with starched cloths, gleaming silverware and exquisite arrangements of fresh flowers; a splendid combination of taste and money.

Maxine counted herself very fortunate to be rubbing shoulders with DeWilde family members gathered from all over the globe, and the cream of Sydney society.

She had already been approached by Jeffrey DeWilde, the head of the DeWilde Corporation. "Miss Sterling," he'd greeted her as he clasped her hand. "Ryder speaks very highly of your excellent work on behalf of our Sydney branch."

"Thank you." Surprised and pleased, Maxine smiled. "He speaks highly of you, too." Ryder, who struck her as an independent type who wouldn't take orders easily from anyone, had a great deal of respect for the man who ran the worldwide chain of DeWilde bridal stores from his London office. In his fifties, Jeffrey DeWilde was quite tall, with penetrating hazel eyes and an authoritative charm coupled with intelligence. During the few minutes she'd spent in conversation with him before his attention was claimed by someone else, Maxine had been stimulated and absorbed.

She was chatting now with an up-and-coming politician, quite handsome and youngish. And he was taking a flattering interest in Maxine. His initial glance had approved her thick mahogany hair, creamy complexion and clear green eyes, and she hadn't missed his covert glance at the long legs emerging from the skirt of her smart—and expensive—bronze silk suit. The jacket hugged her high, gently rounded breasts, and the V-collar allowed a glimpse of the shadowed hollow between them, but the politician was gentleman enough not to allow his gaze to linger there.

"Are you English?" he had asked her soon after they began talking.

"No," Maxine replied without elaboration, but gave him a grateful smile. She had worked hard to eradicate from her voice the tenacious Aussie inflection that she'd seen as a handicap to her career goals.

As her companion expounded on the economics of import and export, Maxine maintained a rapt expression while she wondered if she should have pinned her hair in its usual smoothly groomed weekday style after all, and shifted her weight discreetly from one foot to the other, wishing she'd had more time to break in her terribly smart, genuine Italian leather high-heeled shoes.

Her attention wandered despite herself to snippets of several conversations going on close by.

"Gorgeous dress…beautiful bride…"

"…DeWilde gown, of course…"

"…glad that Grace and Jeffrey DeWilde have buried their differences for the day…"

"Ryder's mother? Over there…blue dress…" Laughter, and then, "I didn't know he had one, either. No, I don't think his father's here…divorced…oh, when Ryder was just a kid, I think…"

"Gabriel DeWilde…the son…wife's expecting, by the look of it. Pity about Grace and Jeffrey splitting up when they're about to become grandparents."

"…hope I look that stunning at Grace's age…"

"Who on earth is that?"

Maxine became conscious of a stirring in the crowd, groups shifting, conversations dying into puzzled silence, heads turning.

The politician broke off in midsentence, staring over her shoulder. Following his gaze, she first saw a silver-haired man in a faultlessly cut jacket gesticulating in a restrained manner that nevertheless betrayed some agitation. Lee Bolton, the store's public relations officer.

Then she discerned the cause of the subdued commotion.

The man was totally out of place—tall, rangy, and wearing the wide-brimmed Akubra hat that was the badge of the Australian outback. At least, Maxine noted thankfully, he hadn't replaced the plaited leather band with a snakeskin. Tanned, muscular arms emerged from the ragged armholes of an ancient khaki shirt that bagged untidily above his waist. One sun-browned hand rested on a broad leather belt that surely ought to have had a sheathed bush knife dangling from it.

He had an aggressively masculine chin with a nose to

match. Below the brim of the hat, very blue eyes shot angry sparks at Lee Bolton's hapless head.

In the spreading silence Maxine heard the publicity officer say placatingly, "Really, this is not an appropriate time. I suggest you secure yourself legal representation, Mr....er..."

"That'd cost a flaming fortune!" The hat didn't hide the fearsome scowl that descended on the man's otherwise rather handsome face. "You lot might have money to throw away on legal leeches, but I've got better uses for mine. We can probably sort this all out, no worries, if you just let me talk to this Ryder Blake for a minute."

Lee Bolton seemed to grow two inches taller. "I'm afraid that's impossible. Our legal representative is dealing with the matter. You can contact Ms. Sterling in business hours at Bartlett and Finchley—"

"I already tried that. Your legal representative went swanning off somewhere yesterday afternoon—and by Monday I'll be back in Queensland."

Maxine stiffened. Just yesterday she'd wrapped up a case that she'd been working on day and night for the past three weeks. After presenting the results to her client, she'd finally taken the time to buy a wedding present for Ryder and Natasha.

"Excuse me," she murmured to the politician, and made her way swiftly to Mr. Bolton's side.

"I'm DeWilde's legal representative," she announced quietly as the PR man turned to her with a flash of relief. "Mr. Bolton, is there somewhere more private where I could speak with this...gentleman...for a few minutes?"

The stranger's face went blank. He blinked at her. "You're Ms. M. Sterling?" he asked, his voice rising.

"Maxine Sterling," she agreed firmly.

"The lawyer?" Obviously he had trouble adjusting to the idea.

"Yes."

She saw the slight movement of his Adam's apple as he swallowed. "Right. Right," he said. "Uh—Cutter. Dev Cutter." He whipped off the broad-brimmed hat, and a lock of mid-brown hair streaked with lighter strands fell across his forehead.

Holding the hat against his midriff with his left hand, he thrust the other toward Maxine, and after a moment she put her fingers reluctantly into his clasp. His palm was calloused and warm, his grip strong, but when she withdrew he released her immediately.

His denim pants were as faded and worn as the bush shirt, and his brown leather stockman's boots showed the creases and scuffs of constant use. Maxine stifled a shudder.

But as her eyes moved up his body on the way back to his face, she couldn't help noticing how the jeans hugged his thighs, emphasizing his masculinity.

Quick heat whispered through her body. She tightened her mouth against the unexpected reaction and willed her eyes to coolness as they returned to his face. It was quite a long way. Maxine was tall and didn't often have to look up that far to meet a man's eyes.

Cutter's lips had hardened, too, and his eyes turned dark and stormy as he stared back at her.

Lee Bolton said, "We'll use the maître d's office." And he led them through the crowd.

It was a small room. Mr. Bolton opened the door and ushered Maxine through, followed by Dev Cutter.

Maxine stood to one side of the big desk that occupied most of the space, not quite behind it. "Perhaps you'd like to explain why you're here, Mr. Cutter?"

The PR man shut the door. "The security people are supposed to be checking invitations," he said. "How did you get in?"

"The guy downstairs is overworked—he can't possibly vet everyone."

"If you didn't have an invitation—"

Cutter pulled a gilt-edged card from his pocket.

Mr. Bolton took the card and frowned down at it. "Miss Flora Webb?"

Cutter laughed shortly. "Someone dropped it. I never gave the security guy a chance to have a proper dekko at it."

"This is most worrying—"

Maxine could see that the public relations manager was not going to let the subject drop. "Mr. Bolton," she suggested, "why don't you go and check on the security arrangements while I talk with Mr. Cutter?"

He looked at her dubiously, then at the big, bronzed man now lounging against a wall, one hand at his belt, the other still holding the hat in front of him. "I don't like to leave you with—"

"I'm sure I'll be quite all right."

"Thanks," Cutter said laconically. "She will."

"Well..."

"Please," Maxine said.

Compromising, Mr. Bolton announced, "I'll station a security guard outside the door."

Cutter's lips twitched, and Maxine said, "Thank you. Though I don't think it's necessary."

"Trusting, aren't you?" Cutter asked as the door closed again behind the PR officer. The slight sneer in his tone and the angry spark in his eyes reinforced her conviction that he had sensed her aversion to his type.

"I can think of no reason why you should want to harm

me, except that you seem to have a bias against the legal profession in general.'' Maxine couldn't help a waspish note entering her voice.

''Leeches?'' Cutter quoted his own epithet. ''Sorry if you were offended. I didn't figure on DeWilde's legal eagle being, um—'' He stopped and started over. ''I mean, I wasn't expecting—''

''A female?'' Maxine finished for him resignedly. She supposed she ought to be grateful that he hadn't—as one reluctant client had—called her ''a sheila in a short skirt.''

Cutter cleared his throat. ''I already knew you were female. Only you look too young and…well, too young to have a law degree, let alone be representing a big outfit like this.'' He jerked his head—indicating, she supposed, the whole DeWilde enterprise in Australia.

''I assure you I have one, Mr. Cutter. Cutter,'' she repeated thoughtfully, the name ringing bells of familiarity. ''The wildlife park that's been using DeWilde's name! You're the operator?''

''Owner,'' he told her. ''One of them. And I'm not using DeWilde's name! For one thing, it's spelt differently. De…Wildes—two words, as in 'the wilds'—get it?''

''The difference is a minor one. Also, the lettering on your products is far too similar to the style used by DeWilde stores throughout the world. I'm afraid they can't allow you to continue to use it.''

Cutter straightened away from the wall. His voice dangerously low, he said, ''Can't *allow* me?''

Maxine found that she had unconsciously moved to stand behind the desk. ''The DeWilde name has been known and respected for a century as a symbol of European-style elegance and sophistication. They have to protect their reputation.''

"Their reputation." His voice sounded flat, giving nothing away.

"Naturally the firm is concerned at any confusion that may arise—"

"What confusion?" The blue eyes flashed at her. "I'm in *Queensland*, for crying out loud! Running a wildlife park! How can anyone confuse that with a swishy bridal store more than a thousand kilometers away in Sydney?"

"Your products have been seen in the store, being worn by people who had visited your…establishment."

"What sort of products?"

"Novelty items, I suppose they'd be called," Maxine explained stiffly. Ryder had reported several more sightings by his staff since the rival wares had first come to his notice. "Customers have even been known to ask in which department they can purchase the articles."

"Well, fine! Why don't DeWilde's staff just tell them to come up to Queensland and see us? Or write. I'm sure we could deal with mail orders. I'd be happy to provide brochures to hand out to anyone who asks. Come to that, maybe we could do a deal with the store about selling some of our stuff—"

Maxine tried to imagine DeWilde's retailing that kind of gimmickry and shook her head almost pityingly. "You may as well stop dreaming, Mr. Cutter. It's precisely to prevent opportunists using the DeWilde name to sell their own cheap, flashy products that the corporation employs people like me."

"Opportunists?" Cutter glowered. "Cheap, flashy products?"

That had been less than tactful. Maxine was rattled, disturbed by the air of raw masculinity this man conveyed. The neat little office seemed too small for him. "Let's just say that your…wares…are aimed at a different—er—sector of the market.''

She wasn't sure what the expression was that flitted across his face, but knew it boded no good. ''The lower sector?'' he enquired softly. The hat came away from his body and swung gently from his fingers. ''I'm surprised that DeWilde's allows such dregs of society into its hallowed halls.''

The bunched fabric of his shirt seemed to quiver suddenly, drawing Maxine's eyes. Disconcerted, she stared for a moment. But Cutter was waiting for an answer, and she forced her eyes back to his. ''I just meant that your park has a different…retail image from the DeWilde bridal stores.''

''Yeah—'' His voice was still soft. ''Sure. You're a flamin' snob, *Ms.* Sterling,'' he said almost sorrowfully. Under stress his accent seemed to get stronger, as much a caricature of ''outback man'' as his clothing, and his underlining of the title before her name was a jibe. ''You can tell your fancy clients that I've got a name to protect, too. *De…Wildes.* I've spent good money on advertising and promotion, and I don't intend to change it now and start all over. I can't afford to. And if they don't like it, they can stick their bloody store—and its elegance and sophistication—back in Europe, where I'm sure they'll be much more comfortable.''

''Can you afford to fight an action through the courts?'' Maxine asked frostily. ''Because I warn you, if you persist in this foolish course—''

''And I warn you—'' He leaned across the desk, planting his palms on it, and the front of his shirt swung away from his body. A button flew open and something wriggled out and plopped onto the polished surface—something long, greenish-gray, scaly and *alive* that immediately started scuttling across to the other side of the desk.

Maxine gasped and jumped back.

"Sorry." Cutter grabbed at the creature, murmuring something to it as he soothed it with his big hand. A number of pale scars marred the tanned skin across the knuckles, and there were several others above his wrist.

Maxine stared, holding herself rigid. "That's...a crocodile!" The man was mad! Stark, staring crackers. A whole herd of kangaroos inhabiting his top paddock.

A spasm of irritation crossed his face. "He's just a baby."

"What on earth are you doing with it—here? Did you just *hatch* the damn thing?" What kind of wildlife proprietor *was* this man?

For a split second she thought he was going to grin. "His container got damaged. Don't worry, he won't bite you."

Maxine hadn't been worried about that, actually. The little crocodile had startled her when it appeared so unexpectedly, but her main fear was for its well-being. "Damaged—how?" Obviously the crocodile hadn't suffered any damage. It had moved pretty fast over the desk.

Cutter slid the small creature back into its hiding place. "It's a long story. You don't want to know."

He was right. Of course she didn't. Maxine swallowed her rampant incredulity. "Mr. Cutter, you would be well advised to reconsider your decision—"

"Your job is advising DeWilde's, not me."

"I'm trying to be helpful—"

"Yeah? Who to?" The front of his shirt moved again, and he placed a gentle hand over the small bulge.

Maxine eyed it worriedly.

"I won't let him go again. Anyway, I told you he won't hurt you."

"I'm not frightened of it," she said impatiently.

Before she could say any more, Cutter gave a sudden laugh. "I can believe that! Well, I've got news for you. *I* don't scare easy, either, dragon lady." He looked at the large silver watch strapped to his wrist. "Hell! Starve the lizards! I've got a plane to catch, and I'll have to find something to put the little feller into first. Look, I gotta shoot through. Just tell the DeWildes to pull their heads in, or they'll find themselves up a gum tree. 'Cause I ain't shifting on this, and that's flat."

He had flung open the door and was brushing past the security guard outside almost before she realized he was leaving.

She caught up with him halfway across the Skyroom. "You know, you really should be sensible about this," she urged him. "Have you any idea how *big* a corporation DeWilde's is?"

He slowed momentarily, glanced around at the heavy chandeliers hanging from the ceiling, the gilt decorating the fluted columns that supported it, the whole impressive, expensively restored Victorian decor, and the formally clad guests, most of them wealthy, many of the faces familiar to anyone who read the newspapers or watched television. "Yeah," he said. "I think I've got some idea, all right."

"Then you must see how futile it is trying to fight them!" She wasn't sure why she was so anxious to convince him, except that she had a guilty feeling she could have handled things better.

"Why should you care?" he asked cynically, echoing her thought. "You gonna do yourself out of a nice fat fee for taking me to court?"

"I don't *want* to take you to court!" she said, exasperated.

The bridal party arrived and the bride's mother, followed by Ryder's, greeted them at the door. Jeffrey De Wilde stepped forward to shake Ryder's hand and kiss Natasha on the cheek. Grace DeWilde stood nearby, inclining her impeccably coiffed blond head to hear something the bride's grandmother was saying to her.

Cutter had resumed his stride, and Maxine caught at his arm, quickly withdrawing her hand when her fingers encountered warm hard flesh fuzzed with wiry hair. "We'd make mincemeat of you, you *stupid* man! I'm trying to save you and your puny little business from litigation that will break you!"

He stopped dead then, and turned to stare her down, blue fire glinting in his eyes. "Is that so?" he asked her, his whole stance radiating angry insolence. "Y'know what I reckon? You know damn well the DeWildes haven't got a leg to stand on, so you're hoping I'll back down without a fight. Sorry, no way!"

He swung on his booted heel and left her standing there.

Fuming, she took three deep breaths and went after him again as he became mixed up in the knot of people milling about the doorway, who turned in surprise at someone leaving rather than arriving. Maxine saw Ryder's questioning look, the uncertainty of the fabulously white-gowned young woman on his arm, the faint lift of Jeffrey DeWilde's brows. And then Grace DeWilde's sudden smile radiating warmth as she held out a slim hand and graciously introduced herself.

Catching up again, Maxine was in time to see Dev Cutter's answering smile as he took the older woman's hand

and spoke to her, shaking his head in answer to some question.

Oh, no! she thought. If he insisted on speaking to Ryder about this after all—disrupting a wedding reception that had been meticulously planned down to the last tasteful detail...

Before she could accost him he had turned to pump Ryder's hand. "Congratulations, mate. I can see you've got yourself a real little beaut, here."

The bride, with a bemused smile, thanked him, and then looked rather startled as he bent and gave her a quick peck on the lips.

At his elbow, Maxine said between her teeth, "Mr. Cutter, if you'd spare me a moment—"

He turned to her, and the glint in his eyes changed. She was closer to him than she'd realized, and for perhaps a second she had the odd sensation that all the noise of several hundred chattering people had receded to some far distance, and that only the two of them remained in the vast room.

"Sure," he said.

As if in slow motion she saw his hands come toward her, one of them still holding his hat, felt them light on her shoulders and give a gentle tug. Her eyes flew wide with astonishment, then instinctively fluttered shut as with a feeling compounded strangely of panic and a sense of inevitability, she found warm, firm lips parting hers, and her heart seemed to leap straight out of her chest.

Her mouth quivered under an unexpectedly gentle persuasion, and fire raced through her veins. She started to lift her hands to touch him—to push him away, she assured herself. But, remembering what he had inside his shirt, she clenched her fists instead, holding them by her sides.

Then it was over. He lifted his head and for a second longer stared into her shocked eyes before releasing her shoulders. "Nice meeting you, dragon lady," he said with spurious courtesy.

She could only stand speechless as he turned away to find Jeffrey DeWilde, with a mildly intrigued look on his handsome face, standing between him and the door.

Cutter cocked an eyebrow at him. "And who are you?" he asked, his tone expressing friendly curiosity rather than insolence.

"Jeffrey DeWilde," the older man answered equably.

Maxine closed her eyes, waiting for disaster to strike. Fortunately the rest of the party had moved farther into the room, where she hoped they were out of earshot.

She heard Cutter say interestedly, "Is that right?"

"And you?" Jeffrey enquired politely.

Maxine opened her eyes and saw Jeffrey, with an amused look in his eyes, take the lean brown hand extended to him.

Then, in that broad twang, the interloper said, "Name's Cutter, mate. Pleased to meet ya." Resuming his hat, he tipped it to a rakish angle before settling it firmly on his head, touched the brim in a careless salute and sauntered out the door.

CHAPTER THREE

RIDING DOWN IN the elevator, Dev reflected that he should have heeded his mother's frequent warnings about acting too hastily, especially when he was angry. Not that he'd known he was still spitting chips, after giving himself nearly twenty-four hours to calm down. Until Ms. M. Sterling had fixed him with those frosty green eyes and all too clearly dismissed him as some brainless drongo from the outback who needed to be removed as quickly as possible before he embarrassed the hell out of the toffee-nosed DeWildes and their guests.

Sheer perversity had led him into an exaggerated Dundee drawl, living down to her obvious expectations. But even as he succumbed to the irresistible desire to aggravate her prejudices, he'd been knocked sideways by the way her chilly, legalistic manner contrasted with the abundant dark brown hair that sparked with fiery lights under the Skyroom's glass domes, the warm, dusky rose flush on her cheeks, and the gorgeous, sweetly contoured mouth uttering those pompous little speeches.

He'd been smitten, in fact, from the moment he laid eyes on M. Sterling. And maddened by the indisputable evidence that not only was she totally unsmitten, she had actively disliked him. At first sight. Unfairly. Because of how he looked.

Ms. Sterling was undoubtedly a snob, and he'd told her so.

Dev winced. His mother would have had his hide for

rudeness. And as for that kiss… He'd better not tell her about that.

Trying to bail up Ryder Blake on his wedding day to discuss this business had not been one of his best ideas. He'd realized that even before Ms. Sterling got into the act. But it wasn't in Dev's nature to back down once he'd embarked on a course of action, so he'd gritted his teeth and tried to see it through.

He'd had a go, anyway, at telling Ms. Sterling where she and the DeWildes could get off. Then, running into the bride and groom and their reception committee at the door, he'd extricated himself as best he could by following convention—congratulating the groom, kissing the bride and shaking hands with the bloke who seemed to be hosting the whole affair.

And then, he thought as the elevator door slid open and he strode past the security guard, tugging his hat farther over his eyes to hide the flush in his cheeks—then he'd turned and found the luscious lady lawyer looking up at him with an expression compounded of exasperation and anxiety. And he'd succumbed to a reprehensible but quite irresistible impulse to find out what those contradictorily enticing lips would feel like, taste like, under his.

They'd been soft and spicy, with an underlying hint of honeysuckle, and at the touch of his mouth, they'd parted in sweet surprise. Afterward, she'd looked at him with eyes that had lost their cool contempt and turned bewildered and defenseless.

He should probably be ashamed of himself, but he couldn't help but feel vindicated in some way. At least it had effectively shut her up.

MAXINE TOOK HER PLACE at one of the tables and tried to appreciate the mouth-watering dishes produced for the wedding guests, and the conversation of her neighbors. But she kept being distracted by the mental image of a pair of angry blue eyes and a voice that, despite the atrocious accent, was like smoke on water.

When the tiered wedding cake had been ceremonially cut, and the bride and groom were mingling with their guests, Maxine left her seat to go and congratulate them.

After speaking to them briefly she stepped back to make room for other well-wishers, and found herself beside Grace DeWilde.

The older woman was staring with an oddly tense expression across the room. Following her gaze, Maxine saw Jeffrey DeWilde talking with a woman of about Grace's own age—the manager of DeWilde's bridal-wear department, Violetta Concetti. A very pretty woman, Violetta had made the most of her curvy figure with a slim-fitting plum taffeta dress featuring a broad, gold-buckled belt. Her dark eyes sparkled with laughter as Jeffrey DeWilde smilingly addressed some remark to her.

Grace turned her head abruptly away from them, and her clear blue glance collided with Maxine's.

"Hello," Grace said after a moment. "You're Ms. Sterling, Ryder's young lawyer, aren't you?"

"I'm DeWilde's lawyer in Australia, yes. My name is Maxine, Mrs. DeWilde. I'm very pleased to meet you." Maxine had never expected to feel sorry for a member of the wealthy and successful DeWilde family, but she'd caught the pain in this woman's eyes before Grace deliberately blanked it out and forced a social smile to her lips. The two senior DeWildes had sat side by side in the church and at the main table. Maxine suspected Ryder had hoped that bringing them together at his wedding might help to heal their relationship.

Grace had smiled a lot and Jeffrey had made a moving speech in which he spoke warmly of the entire family's attachment to Ryder on a personal as well as a business level, and of their pleasure at the discovery that Natasha was related to them by blood. But Maxine had noticed that the older couple had scarcely spoken to each other.

So she was surprised when after a few minutes of light chitchat between Grace and herself they were joined by Jeffrey.

Grace looked about her as if planning an escape, but they were hemmed in by other groups. Jeffrey acknowledged her presence with a brief nod and turned to Maxine.

"Who was that young man who left early?" he inquired.

"Dev Cutter," she said. "We have a problem with him over the name he's given to his business."

Jeffrey looked enlightened. "Ryder mentioned there was a possible legal action pending over the use of our name by another firm."

"Mr. Cutter argues that as it's a different spelling, a different type of business and in another state, there's no danger of confusion."

Jeffrey shook his head. "It's too close."

Grace said, "DeWilde's is extremely jealous of its name and corporate identity, Maxine. Jeffrey gets most upset at any hint of rivalry from other companies—no matter how far away or how insignificant."

Jeffrey flicked a glance at her. "Insignificant?"

Grace's fine complexion colored a little. "Perhaps *fledgling* would be a better word." Turning to Maxine, she asked, "What sort of business is Mr. Cutter engaged in?"

"He has a wildlife park in Queensland—named De Wildes." Maxine emphasized the separation of the prefix.

"That's clever," Grace said, apparently not seeing Jeffrey's look of faint scorn. "I like it. Kangaroos and koalas?"

"And crocodiles." Maxine recalled the one that Dev Cutter had, unbelievably, stuffed down his shirt.

"He also sells tourist trash, I believe," Jeffrey said austerely, "with the name De Wildes splashed all over it."

"What sort of trash?" Grace inquired.

"T-shirts covered in writhing snakes, and baseball caps made to look like crocodile heads, Ryder tells me. That sort of thing…"

Grace laughed. Jeffrey's eyes homed onto her face, and his expression altered subtly, the skin appearing to grow taut.

"They specialize in reptiles," Maxine said.

Violetta Concetti joined a nearby group, flashing a smile at Jeffrey in passing, which he returned. Grace's gaze flickered and then fixed on Maxine. "I may visit this wildlife park while I'm in Australia. It sounds like a lot of fun. I might even buy a T-shirt!"

"Printed with snakes?" Jeffrey inquired. Maxine thought that if he'd looked at *her* with that rather supercilious stare, she'd have been tempted to hit him.

"Why not?" Grace retorted lightly. "One snake, anyway. And the name of…the park. Just to remind me, you know—" she paused there, her eyes meeting Jeffrey's "—of my visit to Australia, and…who I met here."

"Don't you have a *fledgling* business to run in San Francisco?" Jeffrey asked, his normally pleasant English voice turning harsh.

"I'm taking a few days' break. Getting directly back on a plane for another fourteen-hour flight would leave me too shattered to cope with business, anyway. And it's probably a good idea to snatch some real time out after all the stress I've been under lately. My assistant, bless her, almost insisted on it. I can trust her to look after things in my absence.''

Jeffrey regarded her narrowly. "You do look a little tired. What have you been doing to yourself?''

"I haven't done anything to myself! Apart from... personal matters, you may have heard there was a fire at my store. It meant working day and night to get the place back into some sort of order before flying over here— because of course I couldn't miss Ryder's wedding. But we've come through the crisis stronger than ever.''

"We?'' Jeffrey repeated sharply.

"I've employed a wonderful group of extremely capable people. We've all worked very hard to get Grace up and running and keep it going.''

Maxine thought Jeffrey's eyes softened just a little. "You must have,'' he said after a moment. "I congratulate you, Grace. It's quite an achievement, starting a venture like that from scratch.''

He seemed to have taken Grace's breath away. "W-well, thank you, Jeffrey,'' she said finally, seeming cautiously pleased. Then she stiffened as if remembering something. "That's kind of you, considering you did your best to prevent me from going into business on my own at all!''

The merest hint of a smile touched Jeffrey's lips. "Count it as a compliment,'' he suggested. "Knowing your capabilities, I...*the corporation*...had to be worried about any rival store.''

"It was never meant to be that,'' Grace assured him huskily. "I'm not out to compete with you, Jeffrey.''

"But you don't mind supporting other competition?'' he asked dryly.

Grace looked bewildered. "What do you mean?''

"Your plan to visit Mr. Cutter's wildlife park."

"It isn't a *plan*. Just a vague idea." She turned to Maxine. "We're being rude," she apologized. "How far away exactly is this wildlife place? Have you been there?"

Maxine shook her head. "No, I haven't. It's about a thousand kilometers north. The nearest big city would be Brisbane."

"That's near the Gold Coast?"

"Between the Gold Coast and the Sunshine Coast—two great tourist areas."

Jeffrey was staring at Grace. "Are you serious?" He sounded rather peremptory.

"Why not?" She turned a cool blue stare on him. "I've never seen a crocodile except as a handbag. It sounds exciting."

"Does your life lack excitement, Grace?" His tone had changed again, to a low, deadly purr.

Maxine swallowed, shooting a covert glance at the woman beside her.

Grace's chin went up, emphasizing the smooth curve of her neck. "Not at all," she said. "I've had my fair share—as I'm sure you have." Her defiant gaze left Jeffrey's clever, rather forbidding face and lit on the woman he'd been talking to earlier.

The man had a devastating way of using the slightest movement of his eyebrows, Maxine thought. Now they expressed a mixture of surprise and cold amusement before he turned his head without haste and followed his estranged wife's gaze. "Ah," he said softly.

That was all, but it was enough to make Grace's eyes flash with temper. Maxine guessed she was having difficulty restraining herself from saying something really impolite.

Instead she wrenched her attention from Jeffrey to

Maxine, her finely delineated nostrils flaring gently with a deep intake of breath. "I liked your Mr. Cutter." She managed a smile. "His name is Dev. Is it short for Devlin...? Devon...?"

Jeffrey murmured outrageously, "He's too young for you, Grace!"

Grace ignored him, and Maxine decided it was better to pretend she hadn't heard. "I don't know," she confessed. "He's listed in his district telephone directory as D. T. Cutter, Proprietor, under the De Wildes Reptile and Wildlife Park. But as he's never bothered to reply to the letters my firm sent to him, I haven't seen his signature." She paused, thinking she'd have her secretary check Queensland electoral rolls on Monday morning. "Evidently he's one of those people who believe that if you ignore a problem for long enough it'll go away. And he's not *my* Mr. Cutter," she couldn't help adding.

Grace seemed discreetly amused. "I beg your pardon. You don't like him?"

"He's a very pigheaded man! And prejudiced."

Grace looked slightly startled at her vehemence. "Prejudiced? In what way?"

"He doesn't like lawyers."

"Well," Grace said, "if you've been threatening him with legal proceedings on behalf of the DeWilde Corporation, you can't really blame the poor man for being a little...resentful. I know how he feels."

Jeffrey gave a wintry smile with no humor in it. "Grace is remarkably tolerant of those whose sins and omissions affect *other* people."

Grace didn't look at him, but her lips briefly compressed. "I apologize for my—my *former* husband," she said steadily. "We have no right to embroil other people in our differences."

"I'll do my own apologizing, thank you." Jeffrey turned to Maxine. "And I will. I'm sorry if I embarrassed you, Miss Sterling. I'm afraid that while we both wish Ryder and Natasha well, this affair is proving a bit of a strain on Grace and me. Perhaps you're aware that we are very recently divorced."

So the rift was final—and obviously they were both feeling a bit raw. "I understand," Maxine said. She didn't suppose Jeffrey DeWilde often admitted to being in the wrong. And he probably seldom allowed himself to make cutting remarks to his estranged wife—now his ex-wife, apparently—in front of other people.

As if to confirm that, he turned from Maxine to her and said quietly, "And I apologize to you, too, Grace. That comment was uncalled for. We seem to communicate better with an ocean between us than we do face-to-face. If Miss Sterling will excuse us, I think we should continue this conversation on our own."

He took her arm, but she balked. "I don't know that we have anything more to say to each other, Jeffrey."

"Grace—the least we can do is make some show of having an amicable conversation before Ryder and Natasha leave for their honeymoon. I think it would mean a great deal to him, and add a small measure of extra satisfaction to his special day."

"Well...for Ryder's sake, then." Grace capitulated reluctantly.

Jeffrey smiled down at her. "Thank you, my dear."

Grace paused. "It was nice talking with you, Maxine. I hope we'll meet again."

"I hope so, too, Mrs. DeWilde."

"Grace," the older woman said firmly before Jeffrey led her away.

LATER JEFFREY APPROACHED Maxine again. "I've had a word with Ryder," he said, "about your Mr. Cutter. Frankly, I'm reluctant to allow the matter to rest until Ryder's back from his honeymoon. The deputy manager is new and he'll have quite enough on his plate in Ryder's absence. I've told them I'll consult with you, and they're both happy to leave it to us. If you'd prefer not to discuss business here, we can arrange a more suitable time and place—"

"No, I don't mind," Maxine assured him. "I think you're right. We can't afford to let it drag on."

"Good," Jeffrey approved. "I gather Mr. Cutter's rather unexpected visit was simply to inform us he doesn't intend to heed our warnings about trademark infringement?"

"He put it a good deal less politely than that. I don't think it's any use expecting a formal reply to our letters."

Dev Cutter's only response so far had been to gatecrash a society-page wedding reception in an effort to "sort things out"—a totally inappropriate and wrongheaded way of approaching the matter. Mr. Cutter was evidently a simple, if not simpleminded, soul who just didn't understand that not everything could be resolved over a jug of beer or with a few hearty punches.

Well, at least he hadn't thrown any punches. She wouldn't have counted on him not doing so if she'd been a male, though.

She knew his kind—stubborn, righteous in his unshakable and probably narrow beliefs, stuck in a time warp as far as women's rights were concerned, and making up in brawn and beer-induced philosophy for what he lacked in brains. But the toughness and mild contempt for all things feminine that men like him subscribed to had a thread of chivalry running through it that would have restrained him from hitting a woman.

Well, it was time to bring Mr. Cutter into the real world of twentieth-century commerce. He was about to learn that he couldn't just thumb his arrogant sun-browned nose at the DeWilde Corporation and the firm of Bartlett and Finchley.

"I expected these people to see sense before it got to this," she told Jeffrey.

"Who is there besides our rather colorful visitor?"

"Margaret M. Cutter is listed under the same number in the phone book. But he's named the proprietor." Maxine pictured Margaret M. as a downtrodden wife, setting enormous meals onto the table at regular intervals, sewing on buttons without a murmur when required, working in her husband's business for no pay—and putting up with a man who thought nothing of kissing strange women on his visits to the city. "The way he spoke, he seems to be very much the boss."

"I see. Well, you're the lawyer, Miss Sterling. How do you think we should tackle the problem?"

"The next step is an injunction to prevent them using the name until we can take the case to court. Sometimes the injunction itself will frighten people into compliance."

"Hmm. Do you think that will work?"

"Frankly, no. I think Mr. Cutter will fight it all the way."

To her considerable astonishment Jeffrey said slowly, "Perhaps we might try meeting with him."

"Meeting with him?"

"Face-to-face."

"Mr. Cutter and I met face-to-face earlier," she reminded him. "He flatly refused to back down."

"Not the best of venues to choose," Jeffrey commented, looking about them. "He must have felt…out of place. He may feel less defensive on his home ground."

"Queensland?"

"I'm prepared to authorize the expense if you can spare the time to go up there and talk to him. In fact, if it would help to have the CEO of the corporation along, I'd be happy to accompany you."

"That would certainly add…authority," Maxine answered thoughtfully. But she was unable to conceal her surprise. "I thought the corporation would be more than ready to prosecute."

There was a short pause. "Not so long ago," Jeffrey DeWilde said, "I believe that is what I would have recommended. More recently it has been borne on me that an adversarial attitude is often a mistake. How are your negotiating skills, Miss Sterling?"

"You want to negotiate?" Raging doubt must have colored her tone.

"I think it would be a good idea to explore the possibility. You don't agree?"

"I just think that he's unlikely to respond to a kid-glove approach," Maxine warned. "So far he's shown no sign of wanting to negotiate."

"So far, have we?"

"Not…not exactly, I suppose. You aren't going to let him get away with calling his park 'De Wildes,' are you?"

"I'm not in the habit of letting people get away with anything, Miss Sterling. But I thought we could explore alternatives—for instance, we might offer to provide a budget to advertise the change of name."

"That would cost a lot."

"So might your expert services in bringing a suit against Mr. Cutter."

Silently Maxine conceded that. ''I'll abide by your instructions, of course.''

''I don't have a lot of time to spare, but I can delay my departure a few days. I suggest you contact Mr. Cutter and arrange a meeting as soon as possible.''

CHAPTER FOUR

"A MEETING." DEV CUTTER sounded wary, suspicious. Maxine wondered if phoning on Sunday morning—on the logical premise that Sunday for a wildlife park would be a business day—and asking to speak to him in person had been a good idea, after all. She'd thought of sending a fax, but he would probably ignore it, just as he was in the habit of ignoring letters. "Why?"

"Mr. DeWilde would like to talk to you."

"What for?"

"To discuss the matter of changing the name of your operation, Mr. Cutter," she repeated patiently.

"I thought you were all set to take me to court."

"My instructions are to try a negotiated solution first."

"You were bluffing, right? You can't touch me and now the DeWildes are ready to 'negotiate.'"

"I was not bluffing!"

"Are they hoping to buy me off? No go, Ms. Sterling."

Maxine suppressed a sigh of exasperation. "Mr. DeWilde is willing to meet with you."

"With his lawyer by his side."

"As Mr. Bolton suggested to you, Mr. Cutter, you'd be wise to retain legal counsel yourself."

He snorted.

"I'm giving you good advice." Maxine kept her temper with an effort, remembering that her client wanted her to talk with this infuriating man. "If you pass up this opportunity, my clients will have no choice but to issue proceedings against you."

"Proceedings?"

"A tort of passing off, Mr. DeWilde. We can get an injunction almost immediately—"

Cutter made a derisive sound. "You even *talk* like a legal document. What a waste."

"I beg your pardon?" Maxine frowned. "A waste?"

There was a tiny pause. "Of that soft, pretty mouth of yours," he drawled in his smoke-on-water voice.

Maxine gasped, hoping he hadn't heard her. Thank heaven he couldn't see the color she felt flaming in her cheeks.

She'd tried to erase the memory of that audacious kiss from her mind, but now she could almost taste again the warm, male firmness of his lips on hers, feel his big hands gently grasping her shoulders.

"Mr. Cutter." She made her voice as frigid as she could. "On behalf of my clients I must inform you that if you persist in your present course—" she ignored the derisive groan that echoed down the line "—you will lay yourself open to serious legal repercussions."

"If you're trying to intimidate me, I can tell you I'm not easily—"

"I'm trying to *reason* with you, Mr. Cutter! Don't you think this has gone far enough? You can't possibly win—"

"Can't I? We'll see about that, *Ms.* Sterling."

Fighting the temptation to yell at him, Maxine tried a placatory tone. "Believe me, you would be well advised to accept this offer of a meeting. It may be your last chance to avoid very unpleasant litigation."

"Uh-huh." From the absent note in his voice, he

seemed to be thinking rather than concentrating on her words. "Jeffrey DeWilde, huh?"

"He is the most important person in the DeWilde organization worldwide," Maxine reminded him.

"I know that, Ms. Sterling. They're bringing in their big guns. That worried, are they?"

Maxine bit her tongue. "They are not *worried*," she stressed.

The stupid, ungrateful oaf! Didn't he realize how lucky he was that Jeffrey DeWilde was providing him with an opportunity to give in gracefully and privately instead of being whipped in the courts?

No, of course he didn't. He thought the DeWildes were out to get him, and he didn't like lawyers. He wouldn't even hire one himself.

"Mr. DeWilde," she said, making a mighty effort to be conciliatory, "suggests you may prefer us to come to you. He's willing to travel to Queensland."

She didn't know if it was surprise or suspicion that had Cutter silent for all of two seconds. "Okay," he said at last. "Give it a couple of days, though. I'm really busy right now."

Who isn't? she thought. "Mr. DeWilde has only a very limited time in this country."

"I'll get back to you."

"If you're stalling, Mr. Cutter, I should warn you—"

"I've got a business to run here, Ms. Sterling. I need time to make some arrangements, okay?"

It was hours before he called back and suggested a late-afternoon appointment on Tuesday.

"Couldn't you make it earlier?" Maxine demurred, wondering what time the last flight for Sydney left Brisbane.

"Look, this is a popular place, and I don't have enough

staff. We'll be flat out here like lizards drinking for most of the day, but I've worked out a time for you. It's the best I can do.''

"I'll check with Mr. DeWilde,'' she told him.

Jeffrey agreed readily, sounding as though he was quite looking forward to it. Maxine faxed confirmation to the reptile park.

THE NEAREST TOWN to the park, Maxine had discovered, was Goanna Gap, population less than five hundred. Along a side road near the junction of two major highways, the area seemed a good place for a wildlife park, not too far off the beaten tourist track.

A rental car awaited them at Brisbane airport and at Jeffrey's suggestion, Maxine took the wheel. She calculated they should make it to Goanna Gap in about an hour and a half, and the park was about ten kilometers farther on. It was hot this far north, even though winter was supposedly on its way, and she was glad she had worn her hair pinned up off her neck in a businesslike—and cool— knot at the back of her head.

Leaving the city behind, they were soon traveling through rolling farmland covered in tough grasses and gray, jagged stumps left by bushfires and land clearance. Now and then they saw a flock of sandy-fleeced sheep or a small herd of cattle sparsely distributed across a big paddock.

As they crossed a low bridge where a shallow stream lazed along its bed of rounded stones, Jeffrey exclaimed in surprise, and Maxine braked, drawing up the car on the shoulder of the road. ''Something wrong?''

He shook his head. ''Sorry if I startled you—I spotted a kangaroo down there. I've never seen one in the wild.''

"There are probably quite a lot about in this kind of

country." Maxine waited for a few minutes to allow him to watch the creature hopping away into a stand of tall blue gums rattling in a slight breeze, then started the motor again.

Shortly afterward they glimpsed a billboard bearing the words De Wildes—25 Kms and depicting a crocodile under a tree where a couple of writhing snakes, a koala bear with a baby on its back and several varicolored birds seemed happy to coexist.

Considerably less than twenty-five kilometers farther on, Maxine braked again before a gateway in a depressed-looking wire fence bordering the road.

Prominently displayed on the grayed and leaning gatepost was a crudely lettered sign on an unpainted board reading, De Wildes.

Jeffrey looked at her with raised brows. "Surely this can't be it?"

Maxine said uncertainly, "I don't think so, but—" Beyond the gate a rough, dusty track straggled off through a group of trees a few hundred yards away. "Should we investigate?"

Jeffrey shrugged. "Maybe we should."

They arrived eventually at a dilapidated wooden house, the paint that had once graced its walls peeling so badly that it was impossible to guess at its color, the roof rusting and the broad veranda sagging. But it seemed the place was inhabited. At the sound of the car, a man appeared in the shadowed doorway.

A battered and sweat-stained felt hat with an undulating brim and no band shadowed his face, and it was evident he hadn't shaved for days. The half-smoked roll-your-own cigarette dangling from a corner of his mouth released a thin trail of smoke into the warm air. The bush shirt half covering a massive, black-furred chest had lost its buttons, and his army green trousers were tucked into long woolen socks from which two large, hairy big toes protruded.

Jeffrey got out of the car. "Good afternoon."

The man nodded silently.

"We're looking for the De Wildes reptile park."

The cigarette bobbed as the man's lips finally moved. "Cutter's place," he said. "Down the road a bit."

"Thank you." Jeffrey paused. "Your sign at the gateway—I'm afraid it misled us."

The cigarette remained, but uneven, yellowed teeth showed in a grin. "Yer?" the man said. "Gonna take me to court over it, are ya?"

Preparing to reenter the car, Jeffrey straightened. "Why do you say that?"

A gnarled hand slowly removed the cigarette. The man dipped his head to watch the smoke curl about tobacco-stained fingers, then looked up again. "Reckon you're no tourist." He eyed Jeffrey's striped white shirt and dark red silk tie with ironic contempt. "You'd be that pommy joker that wants to close Cutter's place down, and she'll be the fancy lady lawyer." He jerked his head toward Maxine, squinted to see her better and gave a grunt of disgusted confirmation. She supposed if he could have seen the slim jade green skirt and medium-heeled brown pumps she wore with her cream cotton crepe blouse he'd have been even more unimpressed.

"Closing the park down is not our intention," Jeffrey said mildly. "However, I'll be discussing his options with Mr. Cutter. Good day, and thank you again for your directions." He nodded courteously to the man and got back in the car, looking grim as they bumped their way back down the drive. "A pommy joker," he murmured reflectively when they had reached the gate.

"Englishman," Maxine translated.

"Yes, I know. I suppose I should be thankful our sartorially challenged friend didn't refer to me as 'that pommy bastard.' He was really quite restrained."

A few miles along the road another inexpertly hand-lettered De Wildes sign hung drunkenly from a tree overhanging the cattle-stop entrance to a narrow farm track. Maxine slowed, then decided to ignore it.

A little farther on, a makeshift De Wildes banner fastened to a tumbledown shed fluttered defiantly in the breeze.

Several rural delivery letterboxes claimed that they belonged to De Wildes. A red brick farmhouse boasted a neatly lettered board swinging from an elegant wrought iron standard, and the owners of a freshly painted, beautifully restored homestead had placed a blackboard on the veranda roof with De Wildes in roman lettering blocked out in various colors.

Nearing the township, the habitations were closer together, and so were the signs. Every modest homestead or decrepit building bore a hastily manufactured De Wildes sign. When Maxine slowed the car to drive along the main street of Goanna Gap, they passed a De Wildes general store, a De Wildes butchery, De Wildes petrol station, De Wildes hairdresser and De Wildes bakery, handcraft shop, gift and souvenir shop, milk bar and café, even a De Wildes funeral parlor and the De Wildes Hotel—the only two-storied building in the main street. Every business in the tiny town sported a sign proclaiming its name was De Wildes.

Maxine shot a glance at the man by her side, learning nothing from his expression. But he murmured, "I think Mr. Cutter's friends are making a point."

Outside the hotel a crowd had gathered, spilling on to

the road. Several dark-skinned children were chasing about the outskirts, and Maxine slowed the car to a crawl.

"Stop here, please." Jeffrey wound down his window. Looking past him as she pulled on the handbrake, Maxine saw a fair-haired young woman on the broad wooden steps of the hotel. Dressed in a smart suit and holding a microphone, the blonde listened intently to a long-jawed, unshaven man with an antique Akubra hat shoved precariously back on his head.

Waving a pipe in one hand, he was saying loudly, "...Some pansy that makes weddin' dresses for Sydney sheilas tellin' us what to do. Dev Cutter's brung business to this town. Anyone comes poncin' around here tryin' to stop Dev an' Maggie callin' their place what they bloody want, I reckon we can tell 'em what to do with their bloody legal writs—izzen that right?" He appealed to the onlookers, who responded with cheers and clapping.

"Thank you." The woman motioned to her colleague holding a video camera on his shoulder, and turned to thrust the microphone at a bystander. "Would you agree with that statement?"

"Too right! The whole town's on Dev's side. We got a new lease of life here since the park opened. Best thing ever happened to Goanna Gap. An' just when the name's gettin' known, visitors comin' from all over, this lot reckons he's gotta change it. I mean, it's not a fair go!"

A chorus of agreement followed. The reporter looked about for a new target, and spied the hire car. An excited look on her face, she beckoned urgently to the camera operator, starting down the steps through the crowd.

"Let's go," Jeffrey said tersely.

Maxine turned the key instantly and used the horn to clear the way before them.

Jeffrey was frowning. "I'd hoped to resolve this quietly."

No chance now, Maxine supposed, accelerating as they reached the edge of town. Cutter was cleverer than she'd thought.

When finally they reached the real De Wildes, after passing a further dozen or so obvious impostors, there was no mistaking they had found the right place. The sign, right beside a carved life-size crocodile, was large and professionally lettered—in a style all too similar to the DeWilde Corporation logo.

Maxine drove into the car park and found a gap among the vehicles. A van following them shot into a nearby space and the blond interviewer scrambled out, the camera operator and the sound operator at her heels.

As Jeffrey unfolded his long legs out of the car, Maxine retrieved her briefcase from the back seat and scrambled out.

"Mr. DeWilde?" she heard the woman say as soon as Jeffrey left the car.

"I'm sorry, I don't think I've had the pleasure—"

"You don't know me, Mr. DeWilde. I recognize you from your TV interviews when you visited Sydney for the anniversary of DeWilde's opening."

"I see. I'm afraid I don't have time to answer questions just now. I have an appointment—"

"With Dev Cutter," the woman interjected. "We know. Did you come all the way from England to stop him calling his wildlife park De Wildes?"

"I came to attend a friend's wedding," Jeffrey said. "Now, if you'll excuse me—"

He turned to take Maxine's arm, steering her toward a broad gateway shaded by a rustic roof.

They were stopped by turnstiles, and Maxine spoke

quickly to the attendant in the ticket booth. "My name is Maxine Sterling, and this is Mr. Jeffrey DeWilde. Mr. Cutter is expecting us."

"He's expecting us, too," the reporter said.

A young man with a thick mop of red-gold hair came toward them. He was tidily dressed in khaki shorts and a shirt with a "De Wildes" patch on the pocket. "I'll take over," he assured the attendant, and held the turnstile for them. "I'm Ross Cutter." His eyes lingered with interest on Maxine, then shifted warily to Jeffrey.

"A brother?" Jeffrey asked.

"Cousin—and De Wildes' publicity manager. I'll take you to Dev's office." He grinned at the reporter. "You, too. Thought you'd got lost."

The camera team trailed behind with their equipment as he opened a gate marked Private and led Jeffrey and Maxine a short distance along a path through overhanging trees, then across a lawn. Tall gums and birches shaded what must once have been a farm homestead. Big and sprawling, the basic one-story square with a corrugated iron roof and broad veranda had obviously been added on to at different times.

Ross Cutter took them along the veranda to an open French door at the side of the house and knocked on the wooden frame. "Visitors, Dev." Then he stood back to let them enter.

Jeffrey ushered Maxine in first. Coming from the brightness outside, she could barely see the shadowy figure rising from behind a battered desk, which held a laptop computer and a litter of papers.

When her eyes adjusted, she saw that Dev Cutter wore a freshly ironed khaki shirt exactly like his cousin's—with short but intact sleeves, the open collar folded back from his throat. He stepped out from behind the desk and she

noted that the shirt was tucked into matching trousers with
a leather belt. He looked cool and tidy and even more
handsome than she remembered. His eyes homed in on
her and his gaze lit momentarily on her mouth—almost
like a physical touch. Her lips tingled in response, and she
drew in a breath, willing away the sudden color she felt
rising in her cheeks. She tightened her hold on her briefcase and assumed her most businesslike expression.

As Maxine stood to one side, Jeffrey remained just inside the doorway, blocking the entrance. "Nice to see you
again, Mr. Cutter," he said. "I understand that you may
feel you require some moral support, but I really don't
think there is room for your television friends in this discussion, do you?"

Cutter looked at the crew hovering behind Jeffrey, then
gave a short laugh and strode across the room. "Excuse
me."

Jeffrey let him step outside to engage in a low-voiced
discussion with the reporter. Maxine saw the woman
touch Cutter's bare arm, her long, pink-tipped fingers lingering as she spoke.

Cutter looked down at her, then his hand closed briefly
over hers and he smiled. He said something to his cousin
before leaving him with the TV crew, and turned to come
back inside, latching the door behind him.

"They'll wait," he said briefly. "Sorry—why don't
you both sit down?"

He indicated two chairs before the desk and went to
adjust an electric fan sitting on one of the filing cabinets
behind the desk. Then he glanced at his watch. "You're
a bit early. I'll just go and find my mother."

"Your *mother?*" Maxine regarded him with sly mockery. He needed his mother to hold his hand?

Already on his way to the door, he looked back at her,

and his mouth quirked with sudden humor. "She likes to stay in the background and insists the park is my operation, but legally she's an equal partner. I think she ought to be here."

"Certainly," Jeffrey agreed.

Maxine stared after Cutter as he left. "I thought Margaret M. Cutter was his wife."

"I'm no expert," Jeffrey answered thoughtfully, "but somehow I doubt that our Mr. Cutter has a wife."

"You're most likely right," Maxine decided. "No woman in her right mind would have him."

Jeffrey looked amused. "You don't think the rather glamorous young lady out there with the microphone…?"

"Not for a husband," Maxine amended. "Anyway, he'd probably bring a crocodile to bed." Then she blushed as Jeffrey's amusement deepened, although the signs were subtle—the merest movement of his mouth, a dancing light in his hazel eyes.

Fortunately his attention was diverted as Cutter returned, ushering a slim woman with black, silver-lit hair and vivid blue eyes into the room. He introduced them and gave his mother the worn office chair behind the desk while he leaned against another filing cabinet, his arms folded, one ankle propped over the other. A blatant power play, Maxine deduced crossly, calculated to make her and Jeffrey feel at a disadvantage.

Jeffrey leaned back in his chair and looked up at the younger man with an expression of extreme tranquillity. He was, Maxine guessed, far too astute and assured to be disconcerted by being physically looked down on.

He was also a master of the controlled silence. After a few seconds Dev Cutter succumbed to it. "You asked for this meeting," he said, his jaw jutting. "I don't know what you hope to get from it, but I can tell you right off, we're not changing the name of the park. We've put too much into it to start mucking about with it now."

Jeffrey nodded. "We appreciate your position, Mr. Cutter. Perhaps you'd allow me to state ours."

"Your Ms. Sterling has already done that."

"In legal terms? I'm sure she has, most adequately." Jeffrey gave Maxine one of his restrained smiles. "But you see, there are more than legalities concerned here." He cleared his throat. "The DeWilde name has a proud tradition behind it—from the time my forebears were diamond merchants in Amsterdam over a century ago. We've spent considerable time, effort and money building up an image that conforms to the concept our business reputation depends upon. I feel a very personal interest in anything that might affect that concept. The business, after all, carries my family name."

Jeffrey paused there, and Maxine saw Cutter's mouth open, but his mother's head turned slightly and, meeting the blue eyes so very like his own, he remained mute, only shifting his position against the filing cabinet as if to ease his shoulders.

Jeffrey went on. "I'm sure your choice of title for the park was purely coincidental—a clever little play on words. But I'm afraid we feel obliged to ask that you change it."

"I've already said no."

"Really," Jeffrey said gently, "we must insist, Mr. Cutter. But we are not unaware of your difficulty."

He looked at Maxine and she picked up the ball, speaking briskly. "The DeWilde Corporation is willing to consider a financial arrangement to help you publicize the new name."

Cutter stirred, scowling. "How many times—"

Margaret Cutter intervened. "That's generous of you, Mr. DeWilde. Isn't it, Dev?" She looked up at her son.

There was exasperation in the slight shake of his head. "How do we know? They haven't said how much he's offering."

Maxine took the opening and named the lowest figure she'd discussed with Jeffrey DeWilde.

Cutter looked unimpressed. "You're wasting your time."

Maxine allowed herself a discreetly skeptical smile. He was hoping to raise the price. It was her job, of course, to keep it as low as possible. "Mr. Cutter, I feel I should remind you that we still have the option of issuing proceedings against you."

Jeffrey said swiftly, "An option we'd be most reluctant to use."

Margaret Cutter cast him a grateful look.

Her son was glowering at Maxine. "Speak for yourself, Mr. DeWilde. Your lawyer lady here is just dying to drag me to court."

"That's not true!" Stung, Maxine felt her cheeks grow hot. "I've been doing my level best, if you only had the sense to realize it, to save your stupid, stubborn hide!"

Both older people turned to stare at her, Jeffrey with mild interest, Cutter's mother with frank astonishment.

Cutter just stared, without any expression at all that she could see.

The fan whirred in the sudden stillness, while a kookaburra cackled harshly somewhere not far off and a child shouting in the park was answered by a deep male voice.

I'm losing it, Maxine thought, and took a deep breath. Maybe it was the heat. "I mean," she said carefully, "my clients really don't want this to end up in court. And if you persist in refusing all offers, you could lose your business. That's the truth." She fought to keep her voice steady and cool. "No hidden agenda, no bluffing, believe me!"

She held Cutter's eyes with hers, willing him to listen, to understand that he might get badly burned—even lose his business—and that she didn't want that to happen. And he looked back at her with a dark flare of sultry challenge in his electric blue gaze.

His mother broke the silence. "Son?"

He turned his head. "The trouble is," he said, switching his attention to Jeffrey, "you and your family aren't the only ones with a sentimental attachment to the name."

Maxine, remembering she was here as DeWilde's lawyer, said swiftly, "You can hardly compare six months' usage with over a century of recognition."

"But it's *his* name!" Margaret Cutter looked from her son to Maxine, and then at Jeffrey DeWilde. "The name I gave him when he was christened. It's one word, really, like yours, only Ross thought two was better for the park. Dev's birth certificate says he's DeWilde Thompson Cutter."

CHAPTER FIVE

"YES, WE KNOW THAT," Jeffrey said patiently.

We do now, Maxine thought. When her secretary had presented her with the evidence, she'd perceived that the obvious had been staring her in the face the whole time. People did use surnames as forenames quite often; only it hadn't occurred to her that any normal Australian parents would saddle their son with a name that was so exotic and unconventional.

"Everyone calls him Dev," his mother said. "Even me."

"I suppose that's why you're here now," Cutter said. "You found out you're on shaky ground and decided it's best to back down."

Maxine shook her head, her lips tightening. "Mr. DeWilde asked me to set up this meeting before we uncovered your full name." She'd felt sick at first, blaming herself for not digging deeper in the first place and turning up the information earlier.

Miserably she'd apologized to Jeffrey. "I'm not usually so…careless."

"I'm sure you're not." He hadn't disputed that she'd been less than efficient on this occasion, though. But before telephoning the CEO with her confession, she had conducted a hasty hunt through some case law.

"The thing is," she informed Cutter crisply, "it doesn't really make a great deal of difference."

The young man finally straightened from his casual pose. "You can't tell me I don't have the right to use my own legal first name!"

"A court may still judge that a new business trading under a similar name and logo to one of world renown constitutes an infringement of the corporation's rights as protected by patent."

DeWilde's Sydney might have opened its doors little more than a year ago, but the family had traded under the name for generations. The wildlife park had been operating for barely six months before she'd sent the first letter.

Dev raised his eyes briefly to the ceiling. "You never give up, do you?"

"If giving up isn't in my client's interests," she said crisply, "then no."

Margaret Cutter looked troubled. "Is it really so important? Dev—"

"You wanted it," he growled. "It's important to you."

"I'd be very disappointed if we had to give it up, but—"

"Then it stays," her son insisted. "No arguments." He glared at Jeffrey DeWilde. "Sorry, you're wasting your time."

Jeffrey looked back at him with equanimity and then stood up, transferring his gaze to Margaret Cutter. "Perhaps you'd like to think things over," he said, ignoring both Maxine's look of surprise and Dev Cutter's negative movement of the head. "We'll give you a call."

"It won't do you any good," Cutter told him.

"Well, we'll see." Jeffrey gave him a bland smile and laid a light hand on Maxine's arm, leaning forward to open the door.

Brushing aside the eager TV crew and not seeming to

hear the reporter's pointed questions, he guided Maxine
down the steps and over the tree-shaded lawn. Behind
them the reporter and her team rushed up the steps.
"Dev?" Maxine heard the woman's eager voice. "What's
happening? Are they still threatening to take you to
court?"

"A TACTICAL WITHDRAWAL and regrouping of forces,"
Jeffrey explained as Maxine started the car again, although she hadn't said a word to question his decision.
"Pushing that young man into a corner is likely to make
him more set in his views. But Mrs. Cutter may be prepared to listen to reason, and she is a partner. I wouldn't
be surprised if she persuades him to be sensible."

He could have a point, Maxine conceded. Jeffrey must
have a great deal of experience in business negotiation.
His position as CEO of the DeWilde Corporation might
be mainly on account of being born into the family, but
the firm had certainly consolidated and expanded under
his leadership.

The weather had changed. As she drove toward Goanna
Gap, huge clouds rolled up from nowhere, tumbling
across the sky, and great coin spots of rain splashed the
dust from the windscreen and puddled the road.

The downpour became so heavy that the windscreen
wipers couldn't clear the glass fast enough. In the now
deserted main street of the little town, water had already
filled the gutters, and several of the De Wildes signs were
either disintegrating or blurring into undecipherable blobs
and streams of color.

After a few miles more, Maxine gave up, drew into the
side of the road and waited.

"Is it often like this?" Jeffrey asked, watching the water flow down the windows. The sound of the rain was so

loud on the roof of the car that Maxine had to ask him to repeat the question.

"In summer," she answered him, raising her voice to be heard, "quite often. But usually the rains are over by the end of March. Winter is supposed to be the dry season here."

Jeffrey's brows lifted, and he shook his head in bemusement.

After a couple of attempts at conversation, he gave up competing with the rain and leaned his head back, folded his arms and appeared to sink into a reverie.

It was twenty minutes before Maxine judged it safe to drive on. The downpour hadn't stopped completely, but visibility was much better and she was able to make reasonably good time. Until they got to the bridge where Jeffrey had spotted the kangaroo earlier.

Or where the bridge should have been.

It was under water.

Maxine stepped on the brake and her hands clamped on the steering wheel. She bit her lip hard to stop herself from shocking Jeffrey DeWilde with the extent of her vocabulary, then sat and contemplated with unreasoning fury the surge of muddy water swirling around the pale, peeling trunks of the gum trees that lined the now invisible banks.

"What now?" her passenger asked.

"We wait," she managed to reply. "And hope it goes down."

As if to mock her, the rain intensified. When they could see again through the windscreen, the water was still rising. Maxine reversed the car away from it.

Another vehicle stopped behind them, waited a few minutes, did a U-turn and sped off. Later a battered pickup arrived. The driver, wrapped in a yellow hooded raincoat but bare-legged above a pair of boots, got out, went to look at the flood, then came back and knocked on the window next to Maxine.

"She's not going down tonight," he warned when she opened it. "Where're you headed?"

"Brisbane."

"Better take the detour," he said. "Got a map? I'll show you."

It looked like a lengthy route back through Goanna Gap and down another minor road that would eventually lead them to the highway a good deal farther north. "They reckon we might get a new bridge in here sometime this year," the Good Samaritan said. "'Bout time, too." Then he left them to talk to the occupants of another car that had shot past the two parked vehicles and slithered to a halt at the sight of the flood.

Maxine looked at her watch. "I hope we can still make our flight." In good weather the distance would have been easy to cover, but if the rain slowed them too much...

Somewhere they must have taken a wrong turning, despite the map. They ended up on a muddy track that obviously wasn't going to lead them anywhere near civilization, and had to turn back, slowed by the slippery conditions and the deep, bone-rattling hollows lying in wait for their wheels. When they found the road to Goanna Gap again, it was obvious that even if they made it back to Brisbane, they were going to miss their flight.

"We could find a hotel in Brisbane," Jeffrey suggested. "In fact I've been thinking that I may stay in the area for a day or two. I would rather like to have a chat with Mrs. Cutter."

"Mr. DeWilde," Maxine said hesitantly, "I feel bound to advise you that it may be unwise to discuss the issue without a legal representative present."

"I appreciate that, Maxine—I'm sorry, Miss Sterling."

"No, it's all right. Please call me Maxine."

"Thank you. Er…Maxine…it seems a long way back to Brisbane by this alternative route, supposing we are able to find it, and if we are to return tomorrow to the wildlife park…"

"We?"

He smiled. "You just said it would be inadvisable for me to proceed without you, and I'm quite anxious to see some resolution of this matter. Would it inconvenience you a great deal if you were not to return to Sydney immediately?"

"No…" Maxine answered slowly. For a client of the importance of DeWilde's, Bartlett and Finchley would put up with a great deal of inconvenience. Someone would ensure her appointments for tomorrow were looked after.

"Do you have any objection, then, to spending the night at the hotel in Goanna Gap?"

"Not at all." She hadn't been prepared for an overnight stay, but she always carried a toothbrush and makeup kit in her briefcase along with her laptop computer, and she supposed she could wash out her undies and blouse and hope they'd dry before morning.

"Good. Then perhaps we should head back there with all due speed. If there are more stranded travelers, rooms may be at a premium."

When they arrived at the hotel, even the quick dash from the car to the open door of the lobby resulted in a wetting.

The carpet was shabby and the high ceiling fly-speckled. A stale smell of beer and cooking hung about. Maxine couldn't imagine that Jeffrey DeWilde would have contemplated patronizing this establishment in normal circumstances.

The old, high desk, its dark varnish pitted and scratched, was unattended. Perhaps the rain prevented anyone from hearing when Jeffrey lifted the small brass bell and shook it into life.

Voices and laughter floated from behind a frosted glass door, but no one came. "I'll go and see if I can find someone," Jeffrey said.

Maxine followed him into the big, noisy room, filled with smoke and the smell of beer. As Jeffrey cleared a path through the crowded tables and the groups of men standing about with brimming schooners of beer, the babble of talk gradually died until the place was uncannily hushed.

At the bar, a dozen or so patrons drank leaning at the stained counter, each resting one foot on a low brass rail.

Hostility hung palpably in the air. Maxine felt the back of her neck prickle. She stiffened her spine and stared down a bare-chested young man with a salacious grin on his face who was busy undressing her with his eyes, making her conscious that her damp blouse clung to her skin and revealed the lacy pattern of her bra.

Behind the bar, a solid middle-aged woman glanced at the newcomers as she opened the till for change and handed a few coins to a bearded customer.

Jeffrey addressed the older of the two men with her. "Are you the proprietor?"

The man glared back suspiciously. "Yeah."

"Do you have two rooms available for the night?"

The proprietor put down the jug of foaming beer he'd just poured. "You're not booked."

"No," Jeffrey said patiently. "We had intended to return to Brisbane, but the road is flooded. Do you have two rooms?"

The man picked up a ragged gray cloth and wiped a

spill on the counter, then gazed about the room at large as if hunting for inspiration, or possibly gauging the silent opinion of his clientele. Finally he said, "Ask the missus."

The woman came to stand beside him. "We're booked out," she said flatly.

It's a lie, Maxine thought. "That must be unusual," she said clearly. "It's a big hotel for a town this size."

The woman looked back at her with scarcely hidden hostility. "Yeah, well, with the rain...you're not the only ones got stranded, you know."

It could have been true, but Maxine didn't believe her. Especially when her husband chimed in too quickly with, "Yeah, that's right. We're full up."

Jeffrey looked at the pair consideringly, then fished inside the pocket of his jacket and brought out a leather wallet, holding it in his hand. "You're sure you can't fit us in somewhere?" he said quietly.

Maxine touched his arm. "It's no use. We might as well go."

Jeffrey took the hint and replaced the wallet. "Perhaps, then, there's another place in the town that could put us up for the night?"

The proprietor shook his head. His wife said, "We're the only hotel in Goanna Gap."

Jeffrey nodded. "I see. Good evening." And to Maxine's relief, he turned to go.

They were almost at the door when a new voice said, "You could try the Cutters. Maggie might fix you up."

Sarcasm? Maxine thought wearily. But Jeffrey stopped and turned to the speaker, a thin, balding man wearing a plaid shirt and leaning with several others against one of the tables.

"They have accommodation there?" Jeffrey asked.

The atmosphere had changed. Everyone was looking at the man as though he were a traitor, their expressions condemning.

He cleared his throat. "Maggie used to run a guest house at the homestead before they set up the park. They don't advertise it now, but they still take a few backpackers." He looked defiantly round at his fellows. "She can decide for herself. Personally, I reckon Maggie wouldn't turn away a dog on a night like this."

There was a ripple of movement around the room, and a couple of grunts that might have denoted agreement or merely an attempt at thought. No one was looking at Jeffrey and Maxine now.

"Thank you," Jeffrey said. "We appreciate that."

Back in the car, Maxine found she was shaking. She clutched the wheel with both hands and took a couple of deep breaths to steady herself.

"Are you all right?" Jeffrey asked.

"Yes. Yes, thank you."

"We weren't in any danger, I'm sure."

"Danger? No. It's just…oh, they're so narrow-minded, so *bigoted*. They don't know anything about the issues involved, but they've made up their minds and nothing— *nothing*—is going to change them!" She was burning up with anger. For a moment she even wondered if their Good Samaritan at the bridge had led them astray, although he'd seemed genuine enough.

Jeffrey shrugged. "We needn't concern ourselves with them, after all."

Maxine let out another breath and gave a tiny, choked laugh. How nice to be someone like Jeffrey DeWilde, able to brush off the enmity of a whole town as something that simply didn't matter. Public opinion in places like Goanna Gap had absolutely no impact in his world of privilege and wealth. For a moment, as she turned the key to start the engine, she was sharply envious. "We'd better try to find the detour to Brisbane, after all." They'd wasted a lot of time already, and it was getting dark.

"No, I think not."

"No?" Maxine looked at him in puzzlement. Then light dawned. "Stay at the park? Is that a good idea? Always supposing they'd have us."

"You heard what our friend in there said. Maggie Cutter wouldn't turn away a dog in weather like this. It might be a *very* good idea."

Maxine thought about it. "Infiltrate the enemy camp?"

"If you like to put it that way. Strategy, Miss Sterling—Maxine. What do you think?" He actually smiled at her, his eyes gleaming with something suspiciously like mischief.

She wasn't sure if he really wanted to know what she thought or was merely paying lip service to her part in this. "You could be right," she said cautiously. What was that saying about "Know thine enemy"? From the Bible, if she recalled correctly. "I don't fancy driving much farther in this," she confessed as the rain became heavier again and began pelting the windscreen. She had been quite looking forward to a meal and a clean bed somewhere—anywhere.

THE PARK GATES WERE closed, but a large brass ship's bell hung under the roof sheltering the turnstiles. Jeffrey rang it vigorously, and after a few minutes Ross Cutter appeared, dressed in wet weather gear.

"Better talk to Aunt Maggie," he said rather reluctantly in answer to Jeffrey's inquiry. "Bring the car this way, I'll show you."

They parked in front of the house, and when they had

run up the broad veranda steps, the young man thundered with his fist on the closed door.

It was opened by Dev Cutter, who stared first at Maxine with her sodden blouse and skirt and dripping, bedraggled hair, which had partially escaped its pins, and then at Jeffrey, who, despite the raindrops running down his face and the dampness of his clothes, still looked remarkably unruffled.

"They got cut off at the bridge," his cousin explained.

"There's a detour." Dev was looking at Maxine again, as if her dishevelment fascinated him. He watched a drop of water run from her hair to her cheek, under the curve of her chin and down her neck, finally disappearing into the neckline of her blouse. Maxine shivered, hoping he hadn't noticed the peaking of her breasts under the wet fabric.

Jeffrey explained blandly. "By the time we returned to Brisbane that way, our plane would have left. Besides, I preferred not to ask Miss Sterling to drive in these conditions, and as I'm unfamiliar with your roads myself, it seemed a better idea to find accommodation here."

Cutter dragged his attention from Maxine to Jeffrey. "You could have tried the hotel in town."

Maxine said snappily, "They said they were full up."

Surprise and then comprehension flickered across Cutter's face. A corner of his mouth lifted. "Is that what they said?"

"Isn't it what you wanted them to say?" she flared at him.

"I don't own the hotel."

Mrs. Cutter's voice called, "Dev? Who is it?"

As he turned to answer his mother, Maxine felt Jeffrey's hand on her waist gently urging her forward across the doorstep. Adroitly he managed to get them both inside the spacious passageway.

Margaret Cutter came toward them. "Mr. DeWilde!" She appeared almost as disconcerted as her son, but recovered quickly. "And—good heavens, child!" she exclaimed, looking at Maxine. "You're soaked. Did you get caught at the bridge? Dev, shut the door. Ross, are you coming in?"

"I'll go round the back," Ross said, "and take off this gear. These people reckon they need a bed for the night, Aunt Maggie."

"Two beds, actually," Jeffrey specified. "Someone told us at the hotel that you have backpacker accommodation."

"Yes, in the old shearers' quarters," Maggie agreed. She hesitated. "But that's away from the house, and you've nothing with you, I suppose. I won't send you out there in this weather."

"We already have a houseguest," Cutter said.

He and his mother exchanged a look that Maxine couldn't interpret. "There's still room," Maggie told him firmly. "We can't turn away anyone in this weather."

Jeffrey smiled at her. "We were assured you wouldn't."

"Well, first we'd better get you out of those wet clothes," Maggie decided. "Dev, find a shirt and trousers for Mr. DeWilde and take him to the blue room. And I'll get Binnie to lend the young lady something to wear while we dry out her clothes." She turned, calling, "Binnie!"

Binnie's resemblance to her brother was so striking, even to the khaki shorts and shirt she wore, that she hardly needed introducing. Within minutes Maxine was in her room, stripping off wet clothing while Binnie hunted through her wardrobe.

"I don't wear dresses much." She pulled out a T-shirt and a pair of trousers. "I suppose these'll be short on you."

"That's fine," Maxine said quickly. The shirt was big enough to disguise the fact that she'd taken off her wet bra, and she could use the narrow belt of her skirt to make the trousers a better fit. "I'm not fussy."

Binnie looked dubious. Both the Cutter cousins obviously had reservations about their unexpected and undoubtedly unwelcome guests.

Maxine put on the clothes, rolling up the trouser legs to mid-calf.

"My shoes won't fit you," Binnie said. "But Aunt Maggie's might."

She left the room and came back with a pair of sneakers. Not a perfect fit, but Maxine didn't complain.

"Thank you," she said. "Could I wash these things out? I have to wear them again tomorrow."

"Sure," Binnie said indifferently. "Do them in the bathroom next door, and I'll pop them in the dryer for you."

While in the bathroom, Maxine combed her hair and applied a light makeup, then emerged with her clothes wrapped in the towel Binnie had given her to dry off with.

Binnie rose from where she'd been sitting on one of the twin beds while she waited. "You haven't eaten, have you? You'll want some dinner."

"We're putting you to a lot of trouble."

"No trouble," Binnie said politely. Then, thawing a little, she added, "Aunt Maggie ran a farmhouse kitchen for years before my uncle died. She can always rustle up a meal at a moment's notice. Or stretch it. She's probably putting extra veggies and stuff in the casserole right now." She led the way down the passage and turned to take the towel-wrapped bundle Maxine still held. "I'll take that. The dining room's just along there—go right in. I'll be back in a minute."

She carried on down the passageway, and Maxine turned to the door she had indicated. It was ajar, and she paused at the sound of a voice she knew she had heard before somewhere—low, husky, female.

"...A young woman with you? You seem to have developed a penchant for them, Jeffrey."

Jeffrey's voice grated. "Jumping to conclusions, Grace?"

Grace DeWilde. Had Jeffrey known she was going to be here? Maxine hesitated. Should she announce her presence—clear her throat or something?

"Can you blame me?" Grace was saying. "I'm afraid I'm not going to offer to share a room with your latest mistress."

Maxine's noiseless gasp coincided with a scornful sound from Jeffrey. "What on earth is that supposed to mean?" he demanded.

"Maggie said there's only one room left in the house. She seemed to think that you and...the young *lady* might require two. Or was she trying to save my sensibilities?"

"Perhaps you'd prefer to share a room with me?" Jeffrey asked. "I'm sure it could be arranged."

There was a short silence, then Grace's voice again, low and shaken. "That's a very poor joke."

"*Grace—*"

Now, Maxine said to herself. Before someone else comes along and finds you apparently eavesdropping. Taking a deep breath, she tapped on the door and pushed it wide.

Grace and Jeffrey were sitting diagonally across from

each other at a large table set with several places. They each had a glass of wine before them.

Both of them looked up as she stopped on the threshold just long enough to assume a bright, surprised expression. ''Mrs. DeWilde! How nice to see you again.''

Grace's face went blank with shock, then her uncertain gaze swung from Maxine to her former husband.

As Maxine walked forward, Jeffrey stood up. He looked different and rather less formidable than usual in an open-necked casual blue chambray shirt and a pair of ill-fitting slacks. ''Grace,'' he said, ''you remember Maxine Sterling—the lawyer for DeWilde's, Sydney? She and I had a small business matter to discuss with the Cutters today. We had intended to return to Sydney tonight—until the flood rather changed our plans.''

Grace flushed, but her eyes remained steady on Maxine. ''Of course I remember. How are you, Maxine? And didn't I ask you to call me Grace?'' She managed a painful smile.

''Thank you, I'm very well—Grace.'' Maxine took the chair Jeffrey pulled out for her. ''Did you get caught out by the flooding, too?''

''Yes,'' Jeffrey said to his ex-wife, resuming his own seat. ''What are you doing here?''

Grace flashed him a brief glance. ''I told you in Sydney that I might visit the place. Dev saw me wandering about the park, remembered me from Ryder's wedding and introduced me to his mother. When I asked if she could recommend somewhere quiet to stay for a few days, Maggie offered me a room in the house.''

''Just like that?'' Jeffrey quirked an eyebrow at her.

''Yes. And I was happy to accept. It's very pleasant here. I had half planned to travel to the Whitsunday Islands and have a look at the Great Barrier Reef, but at the moment, rest and a peaceful setting suit me better than rushing about sightseeing.''

Jeffrey frowned. Almost accusingly he said, ''I expect you've tired yourself out at your new store!''

''I've done nothing of the kind!'' Grace said emphatically. ''You know me, Jeffrey—I thrive on that kind of stress.''

A quick smile lit Jeffrey's eyes, and then died to bleakness.

''I just needed some time out from...personal problems. And I didn't expect you'd turn up here! Dev didn't mention they were expecting you.''

''No?'' Jeffrey looked dubious.

''I guess they thought it might upset me.''

Jeffrey cast her a searching stare. ''We didn't come here to upset...anybody.''

Maxine changed the subject. ''Mr. DeWilde, shouldn't we do something about rescheduling our flight?''

''I've canceled for tonight. We can phone again in the morning and make new arrangements.''

Binnie came into the room carrying a tray of cutlery and plates. ''You all know each other, don't you?'' she inquired. ''Dinner's on its way. We were just about to start when you folks arrived,'' she informed Jeffrey and Maxine, putting the tray down and efficiently arranging two extra places.

''I'm afraid we've held you up,'' Jeffrey apologized.

Binnie shrugged. ''That's okay,'' she said offhandedly. ''Ms. Sterling, can I pour you a drink while you're waiting? And would anyone like some nibbles?''

They all declined appetizers, but Maxine accepted a glass of wine. ''And please—my name's Maxine,'' she added. ''It was good of your aunt to take us at such short notice," she said, "and not to house us in the old shearers' quarters."

"It's not bad out there, but the rooms have bunk beds, and people are supposed to provide their own sleeping bags, or linen, and food. The house is much more comfortable. And you get meals." Binnie seemed naturally inclined to chatter, although torn between innate good manners and her distrust of the interlopers.

Maxine smiled at her. "We were told it isn't advertised."

"Since Rooster and I moved in, Aunt Maggie's almost given up the guest house business, except when people come recommended by someone. There are only two spare rooms now, and she's pretty busy with the gift shop. That pays heaps better. Before the park opened, there wasn't really a lot round here to see, so we didn't get many real tourists—just backpackers who spread the word among themselves."

Maggie came in bearing a couple of serving dishes, followed by Dev and Rooster carrying more. "Here we are. If you'd like to sit by Mr. DeWilde, Ms. Sterling..."

"Maxine."

Dev Cutter seated himself at one end next to Maxine, and his mother took the chair at the other.

The lamb casserole and accompanying vegetables were nutritious and well-cooked. Maxine was hungry, but the tension in the room made it difficult to do justice to the meal. Only Binnie and Rooster tucked into their generously heaped plates with youthful gusto.

Jeffrey wore a careful, blank expression, his hostess's efforts to draw him out meeting with exquisitely polite stonewalling.

Maggie, although doing her best to ease the atmosphere, seemed a little nervous. Obviously she wasn't un-

aware of the situation between Grace and Jeffrey; that
would add to the strain of entertaining people who were
battling her and her son on a legal front.

Grace talked animatedly to everyone except her ex-
husband; her eyes kept skittering in Jeffrey's direction but
glancing off his face as if she was almost afraid to look
at him for too long.

Maxine was acutely conscious of Dev Cutter's near-
silent presence, his big hands lifting a dish of potatoes to
offer them to her, or pouring wine into her glass, and his
impatient fingers occasionally raking back the persistent
strands of hair that fell forward when he bent his head
over his plate.

He wore a fresh white T-shirt and blue jeans and he
looked clean and strong and very male. She hadn't missed
the quick appraisal he'd given her when he entered the
room, his gaze sweeping over her loose, damp hair, the
concealing clothes and the few inches of bare leg the
rolled trousers revealed. And she'd seen the warmth of
admiration in his eyes. Even when he'd met them at the
door, his intense stare had been quite different from the
lascivious, dehumanizing stare of the young man in the
pub.

Maxine was perturbed at the pleasure it gave her to
know that Dev Cutter liked the way she looked.

Truth to tell, she liked the way he looked, too—when
he took the trouble to make himself presentable. But that
was as far as it went.

They had nothing in common.

Nothing at all.

CHAPTER SIX

"WHAT HAPPENED TO THE TV crew?" Maxine asked, to take her mind off her wayward thoughts.

Ross Cutter answered her. "They wanted to get their film back to Brisbane in a hurry. By the time they left, the rain had already started, and we told them to take the long way."

"Do people often get cut off by flooding?" It couldn't be very good for the park if visitors found themselves unable to leave the area.

"Not this late in the season," Binnie said.

"When we think the creek's likely to flood the bridge," her brother explained, "we put a sign at the gate advising drivers to take the other route. It's not all that much longer if you start from here. But if you get as far as the bridge on the short cut and find it's covered with water, you've got to come all the way back. You just missed the warning."

"We thought you'd have made it," Cutter said.

Wished it, Maxine guessed. He had hoped he'd got rid of them. "The water was quite high over the bridge," she told him, wondering if he suspected them of making it an excuse. "I wasn't willing to risk it."

"You were probably right," he grudgingly admitted, "not being used to outback conditions."

It was on the tip of her tongue to tell him she was just as capable of driving in the outback as anyone, given the right vehicle, but she restrained herself. Instead she said mildly, "This isn't the real outback, surely—less than two hours from Brisbane and the coast?"

He grinned at her. "Loosely speaking. It's certainly not the city."

He was right there, Maxine thought.

There was fruit and custard after the main course, followed by coffee. No one seemed in a hurry, and the two older women somehow kept the conversation going. Binnie and Rooster, excited about the visit from the TV crew, speculated on the chances of the item making the late news.

"They couldn't guarantee it would be used tonight," Cutter warned them. "It's more likely they'll show it tomorrow."

"But they said they could satellite the film to Sydney. And Gil's going to get onto his newsroom friends about using it on the national bulletin. I know he'll be twisting arms—he really wants you to agree to renew that contract."

"Contract?" Maxine asked. Was this going to add a further complication to the legal issue?

"Dev's on Sydney TV every week," Binnie said proudly. "Haven't you seen him?"

He was? Maxine's heart sank. Was this something else she ought to have found out? "I'm afraid not."

"Saturday mornings," Cutter said. "They're hoping I'll sign for another season. But I've got a bit tired of flying down to the big smoke every week."

"It's a live show?" She hardly ever watched television, and never in the daytime.

"The studio bits are shot live, yes."

"I suppose the money's good," she guessed.

"Extremely."

"We can do with it," Rooster said.

"Especially if we're going to be sued," Binnie added anxiously. "Lawyers cost."

Jeffrey, talking quietly to Maggie, looked around briefly, then turned back to his conversation.

"What sort of TV program is it?" Grace asked curiously, perhaps trying to smooth troubled waters. Binnie turned to her and began explaining, aided by her twin.

"You won't be sued if you agree to change the name of the park," Maxine told Dev crisply, but keeping her voice low. "Why is it so important?"

Cutter's eyes strayed to his mother and softened. "You wouldn't understand."

"You have no idea what I might or might not understand, Mr. Cutter."

He considered her. "My name's Dev."

"Apparently," Maxine muttered with a hint of tartness, "your name is DeWilde. It might have helped if you'd told us that earlier."

"I thought you said it made no difference."

Maxine bit her lip. "Your right to use the name commercially would have to be decided in court, ultimately. We're doing our damnedest to avoid it coming to that."

"Are you? I'm not the one who started this."

At last the meal was over and Maggie pushed back her chair. "Dev, take the visitors into the sitting room while we get the table cleared."

"Binnie and I can do the dishes," Rooster offered. "You go and sit down, Aunt Maggie."

"Can I help?" Maxine lingered as the others followed Maggie.

"No, that's okay," Binnie answered. "We've got a dishwasher."

Dev had paused in the doorway, waiting for Maxine.

"Has my mother told you that you can have Binnie's room?"

"No," Maxine said. "You don't mean Binnie is giving it up for me?"

"I don't mind." Binnie was clattering a heap of dishes together.

"We'll put up a camp bed for her in my mother's room," her cousin explained.

"Oh, there's no need for that! I don't want to turn her out of her own room."

"No probs," Binnie assured her indifferently.

"No, please! Really, I'm happy to share if that's all right with you."

Binnie looked at her suspiciously, then shrugged. "Okay. If *you're* sure."

Dev looked at his cousin with approval. "That's settled, then."

He waved Maxine ahead of him and ushered her into a big, comfortable room furnished with fat, linen-covered armchairs and a couple of long matching sofas. On the walls were several prints of open country relieved by stands of misty gum trees and outcrops of ochre rock, peopled by men on horseback wearing wide-brimmed hats pulled over their foreheads, and with stock whips slung on their shoulders. Opposite the doorway hung a large pastel of lizards, snakes, koalas and birds in natural surroundings, the colors subtle and dreamy, yet with the minute detail of superrealism.

Jeffrey strolled over to the picture, taking a pair of glasses from his pocket.

"Binnie's work," Grace told him as he examined it.

"Indeed?" He turned to the young girl. "It's very good. Have you studied art?"

"I majored in it at university."

''Robina's very talented,'' Maggie said.

As Maxine sank into one of the armchairs, something stirred in a basket in a shadowed corner and started to climb out of it.

Thinking it was a small dog or a cat, she gasped with surprise when an enormous brown lizard left the basket and walked in leisurely fashion across the carpet toward the sofa where Dev sat beside his mother.

''It's all right,'' Maggie said. ''Archie won't hurt you.''

The creature reached the sofa and crawled up the arm, then climbed onto the back and settled there.

''He lives in the house?'' Jeffrey inquired.

''Uh-huh.'' Dev turned to give the goanna a pat. ''Since he was a baby. We tried putting him in the enclosure with his relatives but he sulked—didn't you, mate?'' Dev crooked a finger and scratched gently under Archie's chin. ''Thought he was a cut above them—eh, feller?'' The lizard lifted its head, enjoying the caress. ''We introduce him to the park visitors sometimes. He thrives on a bit of attention.''

''So I see.'' Jeffrey eyed Archie with interest. ''Are there more like him in the park?''

''We have all kinds of lizards and snakes as well as our crocs. You should have a look before you go—see what we're all about.''

Only a slight movement of Jeffrey's mouth indicated that he recognized the implicit challenge.

''It's a wonderful place,'' Grace said.

She seemed to address Maxine rather than Jeffrey, but he answered. ''You obviously find it so.''

Reluctantly she turned her blue eyes toward him. ''Dev's right. You should see what he and the others are doing here. Some of these animals are in danger of becoming extinct in the wild. Australia—the world—needs places like this.''

''Your latest cause, Gracie?''

Jeffrey's smile seemed indulgent, even affectionate, but Maxine saw Grace stiffen. ''I've always supported conservation. Last year in London, I was on a committee raising funds for animal sanctuaries around the world, remember?''

''I remember you wheedling a hefty check from me,'' Jeffrey admitted.

''I do not wheedle!''

She sounded indignant, but when he raised a brow at her, her lips quivered and Maxine was sure she almost smiled. ''Anyway, this is the first time I've had the opportunity to see Australian wildlife close up, and I'm finding it fascinating. Anyone would!''

''Even me?'' Jeffrey asked.

''I think you should make time to see it.''

Dev continued caressing the goanna, but was watching the DeWildes with veiled interest. ''I'd be happy to show you round in the morning.''

Jeffrey's gaze switched to him. ''Thank you. I would appreciate that, Mr. Cutter.''

The younger man hesitated. ''Dev. Nobody calls me mister.''

''Then I hope you'll call me Jeffrey.''

Maxine wasn't sure that it was a good idea for the two men to get too friendly, when there was a possible lawsuit pending. As if he'd sensed her doubts, Jeffrey sent her a reassuring smile.

Grace shot her a glance, then looked uncertainly at Jeffrey, and Maxine thought, *She still loves that man.*

What had gone wrong with their marriage? she wondered. Grace's implication that Jeffrey was a womanizer didn't fit Maxine's picture of him. His attitude toward her had been absolutely professional, and he didn't seem like a man who had a "penchant" for younger women.

Well, the DeWildes' marital problems were no business of hers. Returning her gaze to Dev, she found herself studying the long strong fingers so delicately fondling the goanna.

Maggie asked her, "Have you always lived in Sydney, Maxine?"

"Not always," she answered cautiously, turning to the older woman. "But I prefer it. What about you?"

"My parents had a sheep and cattle station up north that my two older brothers are running now. That's where I spent my childhood, and where I met my husband when he came to work for us for a while. His parents owned this place then, but Phil reckoned he couldn't work for his father—their ideas were too different. After we were married, though, he wanted to come home, so we worked on a neighboring property until his father retired to the Gold Coast, and then we bought him out."

"You must own a share in your parents' property in the north?" Maxine queried.

Maggie smiled. "Oh, no. That was my brothers' inheritance."

Maxine hoped her disapproval didn't show. It was none of her business, but she deplored the medieval mindset that allowed a man to will all his property to his sons and leave his daughter totally dependent on her husband.

"So you were farming here before you decided to make the place a wildlife park?" Jeffrey asked.

Maggie turned to him. "That's right."

Grace leaned forward. "I read a very interesting book recently about life in the outback. You need to be tough to survive.'' She eyed Maggie's slight frame with something like awe.

Maggie smiled with a certain wryness. ''That's the truth!''

Drawn out by Grace's interest, she was persuaded to reminisce about her farming days, a chronicle of relentless, backbreaking work, heart-stopping emergencies and a constant battle against nature.

Maxine's blood ran cold as she listened. ''Why did you stick it out for so long?'' she asked at last. ''How could you stand it?''

Maggie laughed. ''I love this country. It's huge and wild and free. I like to look out and see trees and grass and a wide sky. And Phil...he couldn't live any other way. But we had a few bad years, and then he got sick. Dev wasn't even high school age when his father died. We couldn't manage the place on our own, and nobody wanted to buy it in the condition it was in. The bank wouldn't lend us any more money. In the end I had to walk off the land, lease out what I could and get a job in Brisbane to try and pay off some of our debts. But this place has a hold on me. I always wanted to come back.''

Jeffrey nodded. ''So you turned an uneconomic farm into a tourist attraction.''

''Not just a tourist attraction,'' Dev said.

Maggie looked at her son. ''Dev had started bringing in animals that might otherwise be destroyed or die and keeping them on the place. But providing the right conditions is expensive. Opening it to the public brings in money to help continue his work, and gives him the opportunity to create understanding and support for conservation programs.''

''And you've backed him up.'' Jeffrey looked from her to Dev.

"Couldn't have done it without her," Dev told him. "She even sold the family jewels to get the place out of debt and finance the park development."

Maggie shook her head at him, looking embarrassed. "I'd have sold that thing years ago if your father would have let me. Only he was even more stubborn than you. There was no way I could have made him use the money to save the farm."

"Thing?" Jeffrey asked.

"My one and only heirloom, apart from my mother's Bible."

Grace looked at her inquiringly. "You weren't sentimental about it?"

Momentarily a faint shadow crossed Maggie's face. "In a way. But what use was it? Nobody but the royal family actually wears a tiara these days, do they?"

"A tiara!" Jeffrey exclaimed.

Maggie laughed. "Can you imagine! A real tiara. Diamonds and pearls, no less! When I died, Dev would have got it, and he'd have had even less use for a thing like that than I do. If he had any sense he'd sell it then. So I reckoned, why not do it now and use the money to give us the kind of life-style we both want?"

"Why not, indeed?" Grace approved. "Jeffrey, don't look so thunderstruck. The DeWildes aren't the only family in the world to have inherited jewels. *You* may think it's a crime to sell them, but other people have different priorities."

Maxine peeked curiously at Jeffrey. "Thunderstruck" might have been an overstatement, but then Grace knew him better than anyone else in the room and was surely able to gauge his feelings. He certainly looked pensive. "It's not a crime," he said slowly. "But it could be...a coincidence."

Grace looked at him in surprise, which changed to quick comprehension followed by skepticism.

"When I was little I thought it was a crown." Maggie chuckled. "I used to imagine that I was a long-lost princess and my real parents were a king and queen in some mythical, far-off country. You know how kids are."

"Your real parents?" Jeffrey queried. Both he and Grace were staring at Maggie.

Grace spoke first, almost as though trying to caution Jeffrey about something. "Children often imagine they're from some nobler or more romantic background than their parents. It's a common childhood fantasy."

"Yes," Maggie agreed quickly. "I believe it is."

"But—" Grace paused there, perhaps having second thoughts about what she'd been about to say, as Binnie and Rooster came into the room.

Binnie said, "Your things are dry, Maxine. The blouse needs ironing, though. You can do it in the morning."

"Thanks, Binnie." Maxine smiled at the girl.

Binnie perched herself on the arm of the sofa shared by Dev and his mother, and began gently scratching Archie's head with two fingers, crooning endearments.

"So what was your actual background?" Jeffrey asked Maggie. "Where did your parents come from? What were they like?"

"They were good, solid country people from the Northern Territory. Dad was a bit restless when he came back from the war, I think—took a while to settle down. When I was born they were living in an opal town near Broken Hill in New South Wales. It was a new field and lots of people went there from all over. I don't remember the place at all. Dad was fossicking for opals while my mother ran a boarding house to bring in some sort of steady income. Then Dad got lucky, found a big black stone, worth a lot of money. They went back to the Territory and bought a property with the money they got from that opal and a few smaller ones.''

"And when was that?" Jeffrey's voice was casually interested, but he seemed to lean forward in his chair as though the answer mattered. Grace, too, was regarding Maggie rather intently.

"It was 1948 to '49," Maggie said. "I was just a baby when we left the place.''

"Do you know where your father was born?''

"Same place as my mum, way up north. You wouldn't have heard of it, it's not even a town. They'd known each other all their lives.''

Jeffrey frowned. "All their lives?''

"Since they were kids. They got married quite young. I think my oldest brother was already on the way, and it was a shotgun job, but they were happy together. Mind you, people did marry much younger in those days.''

Jeffrey shook his head slightly as though the answer had been unexpected. "What was your father's name?''

"William. William Wesley Thompson.''

"And how did William Wesley Thompson come by a diamond-and-pearl tiara?''

Maggie seemed confused for a second. "Oh," she said vaguely, "now, that's another story.''

"I should think it might be," Jeffrey agreed smoothly. "Was it a war souvenir?''

Maggie stared at him blankly for a moment. "You mean looted from somewhere when the troops were in Europe?" A flicker of dismay crossed her face. "No! It couldn't have been.''

Maxine saw that Dev was staring fixedly at his mother.

"What did it look like, this tiara?" Jeffrey asked.

"Pretty spectacular," Maggie said. "It had sort of swirls of diamonds and pearls twisted together."

Grace looked sharply at Jeffrey, but his gaze was fixed on Maggie, his face quite expressionless, but his eyes betraying a keen interest. "Did your father ever tell you where it had come from, how he came by it?"

Maggie hesitated. "I'm not exactly sure." She glanced uncertainly toward Dev, then returned her gaze to Jeffrey. "But the Thompsons aren't thieves. My...my father would never have stolen anything."

"It's surely an odd thing for an Australian farmer to have owned. Why didn't *he* sell it to finance his purchase of the cattle station rather than gambling on the chance of finding an opal? And there's something else I'd like to know. Why did you—"

"Jeffrey!" Grace cut in decisively. "You really can't browbeat our hostess this way!"

Jeffrey seemed taken aback. "Was I browbeating you?" he asked Maggie. "I beg your pardon."

"No, that's all right," she said hurriedly, obviously flustered. "But you can't really be interested in my life story. I've talked too much."

"Not at all," Jeffrey denied promptly.

Before he could say any more, Grace added her reassurance. "Of course you haven't. I want to hear more about your early days on the farm. It must have been very difficult having to move to the city when your husband passed away."

Maggie appeared relieved at the change of subject. "I felt as if I'd betrayed him...his memory." Her eyes went sad. "And I didn't like it there, anyway. My brothers helped us out when they could, and Phil's people were always very generous, but I don't like being in anyone's debt. When I'd made a little bit of money and Dev had finished his education, I came back here and turned the house and the shearers' quarters into accommodation for people who fancied something quieter than the hotel in town. It didn't make much, but I could write a book about the experience.'' She gave a small laugh. ''If I ever have the time I might do that.''

Binnie turned to her aunt. ''Tell them about that nutty family you had staying who spent the whole night looking for snakes under the beds!''

Maggie laughed again, and launched into the story. She was an entertaining raconteur. Maxine divined that Dev's easy manner and ability to communicate on television owed something to his heritage from his mother.

One story led to another. Rooster and Binnie chivied Dev to recount a few of the adventures he'd had trying to capture animals that had to be moved for their own protection from the encroachment of civilization or from hunters after their hides.

Even Jeffrey, although he seemed a little preoccupied, laughed aloud at Dev's description of trying to save an ungrateful crocodile from locals who were determined to shoot it after a few dogs and a farmer's pig mysteriously disappeared. And the twins, who must have heard all the stories before, were almost rolling on the floor.

''But it must be terribly dangerous!'' Grace exclaimed, voicing Maxine's own rather horrified thought.

''Crocodiles are wild animals,'' Dev said, ''and they'll try to defend themselves when we go out to capture them. But they're not as naturally ferocious as people think.''

Maxine made a small, skeptical sound. Dev glanced at her, the blue eyes holding a gleam of laughter. ''You don't believe that, but it's true. Most creatures are vicious only when they feel threatened.''

''Or hungry.''

Dev laughed, and Maxine found herself smiling back at him. "Okay," he conceded. His eyes still dancing with humor, he cocked his head to one side, and a fleeting look of speculation crossed his face.

Maxine felt the pull of attraction between them and bit her lip, trying to still the sudden, unexpected warmth, the flutter of delicious apprehension in her throat. *Not this man,* she said sternly to herself. An outback man with his mother's love of wide-open spaces and rural living, he was the embodiment of a life-style she'd been lucky to escape once, and she had no intention of ever going back to it.

Binnie looked at her watch and said, "We should turn on the TV for the late news. We don't want to miss our bit if it is shown tonight."

Rooster backed his sister up. "They might have found a slot for it. Gil has good contacts."

Cutter had been making the most of his, Maxine thought. Had he indicated that he'd be willing to sign the contract for the show if this Gil somehow got the town's protest aired on the national news?

Binnie got up to switch on the television.

Maggie glanced at Jeffrey. "Mr. DeWilde may not want to watch it, Binnie."

Jeffrey shook his head. "I'd be interested to see it."

For the next half hour, conversation centered on the various news items that flickered across the screen.

Binnie was settled cross-legged on the floor, stroking the goanna, which had climbed off the sofa and draped itself over her thighs. Her brother shifted himself sideways in a chair with one leg hooked over the arm. Both of them concentrated on the screen as if afraid that by taking their eyes off it for a minute they'd miss something.

Grace talked mostly to Maggie and Maxine, and Jeffrey

to Dev. Catching the men's conversation while she pretended to be absorbed in the news, Maxine was surprised that Dev seemed as well-versed in world affairs as Jeffrey, and able to explain succinctly the political background to local items when Jeffrey questioned him.

The bulletin neared its end, and Binnie said disappointedly, "Looks like they didn't make it in time."

"No—yes! There it is!" Rooster leaned forward excitedly.

The blond reporter appeared, standing in front of the sign outside the wildlife park. "The tiny town of Goanna Gap in Queensland is in an uproar over a threat to its only tourist attraction," she began. "Local boy and TV personality Dev Cutter is credited with bringing renewed prosperity to a district that had fallen on hard times."

The camera cut to a shot of Dev walking nonchalantly through a grassed enclosure full of crocodiles.

Then came a close-up of Dev speaking to the camera. "Our aim is to save endangered animals and show the people of Australia and the world what a wonderful heritage of wildlife we have in this country. That's what this place is all about."

The camera picked up the reporter speaking into the microphone. "But when he called his park De Wildes— and what else would you call a wildlife park specializing in crocodiles and snakes, folks?—he ran afoul of a mighty commercial enterprise. Threats of legal action were followed by a *personal visit* from the president of the multimillion-dollar DeWilde Corporation—who flew out from London—and the firm's legal representative."

Maggie cast a rather worried glance at Jeffrey. She seemed genuinely concerned that he might be upset by the report.

Maxine caught a glimpse of herself alongside Jeffrey

as he hurried her past the reporter and into the car. "They refused to comment for our camera, but the town had plenty to say."

The scene changed to the pub steps and a short montage of pithy comments from grizzled characters like the man Jeffrey and Maxine had seen being interviewed. "And," the reporter added triumphantly, "the town has a message for the corporation that is hard to miss."

The camera panned around the buildings along the street, lingering on the more bizarre De Wildes signs, before slowly leaving the town, picking up placards, posters and banners along the highway more and more quickly until they were just a blur as the credits rolled for the end of the news, finally fading on a shot of a makeshift signboard that hung crookedly against a gatepost, still dripping red paint.

CHAPTER SEVEN

GRINNING HUGELY, Rooster lifted a fist. "Yay!"

Binnie, flushed and excited, turned to Dev. "That was brilliant, Dev!"

Maggie glanced apologetically at Jeffrey. But it was evident that she too was pleased with the piece. Dev had a small grin on his mouth, but it faded to a quizzical, challenging look as he met Maxine's eyes.

"It wasn't accurate," Maxine said, feeling something was required of her.

Dev cocked an eyebrow.

"They implied that Mr. DeWilde came out to Australia specially to lean on you. And it simply isn't true that the DeWilde Corporation wants to close the park. It was a totally one-sided report."

"If you wanted to put your side, maybe you should have talked to them," Dev said. "They did ask you to."

Grace shook her head at her former husband. "Bad public relations, Jeffrey."

"You know it's not my forte."

She smiled at him almost sympathetically. "Get Lee Bolton to contact them and give them your angle."

Jeffrey regarded her ironically. "Thank you for your advice."

Grace's face went wooden and she looked away from him. A vexed frown appeared between Jeffrey's brows, as if he regretted the snub.

Maggie turned to Dev. "I don't think they were quite fair to Mr. DeWilde. He is here with an offer to negotiate, after all." She looked at Jeffrey again. "You can't blame the children for being pleased with the publicity," she told him. "I'm sure they don't mean to embarrass you."

"Thank you, Mrs. Cutter. But I've got over being embarrassed by the media, especially since..." His gaze strayed to Grace, then slid away. "Well, anyway, I generally make it a policy not to talk to them."

"Obviously Mr. Cutter doesn't have any such reservations," Maxine commented.

Dev grinned at her, and she forced herself not to smile back. He was far too pleased with himself for her liking. "I made the best use of my contacts," he said. "I'm sure Jeffrey would agree that's sound business practice."

Surprisingly, Jeffrey laughed.

Maxine said swiftly, "Certainly better than ignoring our letters. Or was that 'sound business practice' too? Did you wait until you could be sure of maximum dramatic impact and guaranteed publicity?"

Dev blinked, evidently taken aback.

The big lizard Binnie was cradling decided to move, scrambling off her lap and wandering over the floor toward Maxine's chair. "More likely he just forgot," Binnie said. "I guess I should have reminded you, Dev."

"Are you his secretary?" Maxine asked, conscious that Dev was watching her as the goanna sidled closer.

"Sort of," Binnie answered. Archie had arrived by Maxine's chair, where he stopped as if sniffing the air. "I open the mail and type letters and deal with phone calls. I like helping around the park, and I do some of the morning feeds, but my main responsibility is keeping the signs freshly painted and designing items for sale in the shop."

Archie lifted a splayed foot and began climbing up the

upholstery. Maxine felt Dev's gaze on her and looked back at him calmly. If this was a test she was damned well going to pass it.

The lizard reached the top of the chair arm and posed, nose high, perhaps thinking about tackling the back. Maxine turned slightly and stroked it, finding the skin surprisingly warm and almost velvety. Two pale yellow parallel lines along its length merged at the tip of its tail.

The creature settled along the chair arm and dropped its chin.

"He likes you," Binnie said.

Dev was studying her with a guarded respect, and Maxine thought smugly that he'd expected her to scream and run. *Not likely,* she told him mentally. *I'm made of stronger stuff than that, mate.*

Jeffrey said with absent humor, "Do you take a crocodile to bed with you, Dev?"

Maxine flushed, afraid to look at either of the men. Binnie giggled, and Grace said, "For heaven's sake, Jeffrey!"

"I just wondered what other creatures might be wandering about the house or warming the beds."

"Reptiles are cold-blooded," Dev reminded him. "Not much good at warming beds."

"Better than some men, perhaps," Grace said.

Rooster gave a guffaw, and Dev laughed shortly.

Maxine stared at Grace and saw that she appeared rather embarrassed, as though the remark had slipped out unpremeditated, but also a little defiant as she met Jeffrey's narrowed eyes and thin smile.

"Archie isn't cold," Maxine volunteered hurriedly.

"He takes on the temperature of the air about him," Dev explained. Looking up, she found him staring at her with open curiosity. Had he noticed her blushing? "That's why reptiles try to find cool spots in hot weather—they can easily get overheated.'' He dragged his gaze from Maxine and transferred it to Jeffrey. ''But you won't find one in your bed.''

Jeffrey stood up. ''I'll trust you on that and call it a day, if you'll all excuse me.'' He turned to their hostess. ''What time would it be convenient for us to appear in the morning?''

''We breakfast at about eight, after some of the park chores are done, but if that doesn't suit—''

''I'm sure that will be fine. Is it all right for you, Maxine?''

Maxine readily agreed, and stood up. ''I'll go to bed now, too.'' She would have to phone her office in the morning. Jeffrey seemed in no hurry to leave, and she supposed that if she was to protect the DeWilde Corporation's interests, her boss would expect her to remain by his side.

MAXINE WOKE BEFORE SEVEN, to find Binnie moving stealthily about the room, dressed in blue shorts and a baggy white T-shirt. The beating of the rain on the roof must have stopped sometime during the night, and now the only sound outside was the chattering of hundreds of birds.

''I didn't mean to wake you,'' Binnie said.

''You weren't noisy. I guess I was ready to wake up, anyway. Are you starting work already?''

''We have quite a lot to do before the gates open.''

Maxine sat up. ''Can I come along?''

Binnie looked surprised and uncertain for a moment. ''Sure, if you want to.''

Maxine spent five minutes in the bathroom, resumed

the clothes she'd worn last night and slipped her feet into Maggie's sneakers. "Okay, I'm ready."

The air was pleasantly cool at this hour, and still held the metallic smell of the rain. The shrubs all looked newly washed and shiny. Binnie greeted a couple of men raking rubbish and leaves from a pathway and hosing down a paved area near the gate, then led Maxine to a barnlike building, where she filled a couple of containers with dried food pellets and began chopping vegetables and fruit from several bins into small pieces.

The building smelled quite strongly of grains and over-ripe fruit. As she helped Binnie to cut up carrots and apples, Maxine glanced toward a bank of small cages at the other end.

"Better keep away from there if you're nervous of rats and mice," Binnie advised her.

"Rats and mice?"

"Food for the snakes and some of the lizards. They're humanely killed first, of course."

"Of course," Maxine murmured.

"Come on, then."

Maxine took a container and followed her guide outside. Half a dozen kangaroos, apparently freely ranging in the park, had gathered nearby, one with a joey peeking from its pocket.

She helped Binnie hand-feed the animals, unable to resist stroking their soft, dense fur.

"Don't give them too much," Binnie warned. "We sell feed for the visitors to give them, and seed for the birds. This is just to keep them going until the gates open."

In the surrounding trees the brilliant plumage and excited twittering of the birds announced their waiting presence. A large black emu stalked across the grass, its curved neck undulating. "This is Marmaduke," Binnie said. "He thinks he owns the place, don't you, boy?"

The bird cocked its head and nodded as though agreeing. Maxine couldn't help laughing.

"You're up early, Ms. Sterling."

She turned at the sound of Dev Cutter's voice, trying to hide the fact that it had sent a pleasurable shiver feathering along her spine. He wore jeans and a T-shirt and held a lidded bucket.

"Maxine," she suggested. Even Jeffrey had invited Dev to call him by his first name. It would be absurd for her to insist on formality, especially on such a beautiful morning. "And I'm not the only one," she retorted. "You people have a long day."

"He works us like slaves," Binnie moaned.

Dev grinned and tweaked her flame-colored curls. "You love it."

"Yeah, well...we're all nuts in this family." Binnie grinned back at him. "Why don't you take Maxine along to say hello to Delilah? You are going that way, aren't you?" To Maxine she added, "You really should meet her."

"Who's Delilah?"

Binnie's smile grew wider and mischievous. "Dev's girlfriend. A real beauty! He visits her every morning."

Maxine had a strong suspicion she—or Dev—was being teased.

Dev didn't add his persuasion, but there was a subtle challenge in his eyes. "If she's game."

"Lead on," Maxine said lightly. "Thanks, Binnie."

Dev led her across the grass and through a grove of trees, then to a broad path lined with double fences, the outer one waist high, the inner one made of higher, stronger netting framed with sturdy iron pipes. Dev unlocked a gateway and led her along the mown grass path between the two fences.

The first enclosure seemed empty except for some dead logs lying near a murky pond, but when Dev checked the padlocked gate, one of the long gray logs came to life and lifted a menacing snout.

"I didn't see him!" She looked at the clearly painted sign near the gate that read Estuarine or Saltwater Crocodile. Keep Away From Fence.

"That's what makes crocs dangerous in the wild. People don't see them, and get too close for the croc's comfort, or go swimming in its territorial waters."

"And the crocodile attacks to protect its territory?"

"Sometimes." Dev walked on to check the next gate. "But anything splashing about in their larder signals food to a croc. They don't distinguish between animal and human."

He stopped at an enclosure full of smaller crocodiles with longer, narrower snouts. All of them hurried over to the fence, a moving mass, climbing over one another to reach it.

"Sorry, fellers," Dev said cheerfully. "We'll feed you later." He turned to Maxine. "These are a freshwater species, not harmful to humans."

"They still have teeth."

Dev laughed. "They can inflict a nasty little bite if you're careless, but they don't attack people." Having tested the gate, he moved on.

"You can keep saltwater and freshwater crocodiles in the same place?"

"Salties have a gland that allows them to excrete salt. They're actually quite happy in fresh water. Some live in billabongs miles from the sea and estuaries."

"I never knew that."

''Bet you don't know much about crocs at all, city lady.''

Maxine tried to raise her defenses. ''You really needn't do the Dundee act for my benefit. I noticed you almost lost the accent last night.''

Dev grinned. ''Is that right?''

''You know it is.''

He shrugged. ''Maybe. This is where Samson lives. Up north he was suspected of taking a couple of people crossing his river, and the shooters were after him. I wanted to relocate him farther upstream, but the locals weren't having any. They insisted he had to be either killed or caged. So I brought him here.''

Maxine peered through the fence. ''I don't see him.''

Dev cupped his hands about his mouth and began to make a strange sound, a sort of mewing, falling call.

Something erupted from the mud-colored pond in the center of the enclosure, and a huge black crocodile began lumbering toward them.

Dev kept calling, and Maxine held her breath. The creature reached the fence and reared up, its open mouth displaying a fearsome array of wickedly long, sharp teeth.

Dev lowered his hands and began talking in a soft, soothing voice, until the crocodile dropped back onto the ground and stayed poised with its nose lifted and its snaggle-toothed mouth parted, as though it was listening intently. Maxine was almost mesmerized, sensing some kind of communication between the fierce man-eater and the quietly crooning man beside her.

At last Dev stepped back and began to stroll on.

''Where did you learn to do that?'' Maxine asked, trying not to let awe color her voice.

''Calling them? From an aboriginal friend up north. His tribal ancestors are crocodiles.''

And the man had been willing to pass on his eerie, arcane skill to a white man? Despite herself, Maxine was impressed.

"Here's Delilah," Dev said. "Stay here while I go and say hello to her."

"You mean I can't come with you?" Maxine feigned exaggerated disappointment.

Dev's eyes lit with surprised humor. "We wouldn't want to make her jealous."

Jealous. Maxine gave him a disbelieving look and glanced down at her borrowed, ill-fitting and workmanlike clothes. "Maybe you should explain to her that she doesn't have anything to be jealous of me for!"

His hand on the gate latch, Dev stopped and looked at her consideringly, his gaze slipping over the loose T-shirt and rolled-up pants. Hardly glamorous attire, but his eyes held the same smoldering sexual message that she'd seen in them last night. She hadn't had time to pin up her hair this morning, and it tumbled about her shoulders in loose, undisciplined waves. Dev's look lingered on it briefly, and his eyes darkened.

Maxine felt her cheeks warm, but when his gaze returned to hers she met it unflinchingly, trying to keep her expression indifferent.

"No?" Dev gave a tight, slightly rueful half grin and unlocked the gate, closing it behind him when he'd stepped into the enclosure.

Delilah wasn't as big as Samson but she was still an impressive length, and Maxine's heart increased its beat as Dev walked nonchalantly toward the animal. He had a short stick tucked into the back of his belt, but didn't take it out. He opened the bucket and took out several fish, which the crocodile snapped up one after the other as he tossed them to her. Then he walked to the water and rinsed his hands before coming back to the beast and squatting beside her.

The crocodile's upper body was a murky olive color, with wonderful complex gold-and-black markings, but as Dev began rubbing his hand along the underside of her jaw, Maxine saw that the skin there was a rather beautiful golden cream.

"How are you this morning, gorgeous?" Dev was murmuring. "Okay? Oh, you like that, don't you? Yeah, I know. You want your belly tickled, eh?"

The crocodile actually rolled on her back like a playful dog and lay still while Dev stroked her tummy. Half fearful for his safety but also fascinated, Maxine scarcely dared move.

Dev's hand was tanned and lean, the fingers long and blunt-ended. Delilah lay supine under his gentle, admiring caresses. Maxine could almost feel her own skin reacting with little shivers of pleasure.

At last Dev straightened and came unhurriedly back to the entrance. Delilah rolled over and followed at his heels and, when the gate clanged shut, weaved her head from side to side as if mourning his departure.

"See you later, love," he promised, and Maxine followed him along to another gate, which let them out to the public walkway. The sun was rising in the sky now and already the air had warmed.

"So that's your girlfriend," Maxine said.

Dev laughed. "You think she's my type?"

A couple of galahs, pale gray with pink markings, fluttered on whirring wings from one tree to another, distracting Maxine. "I wouldn't know what your type is."

Dev looked down at her. Softly, he suggested, "Tall, long-legged, gutsy—"

"*Gutsy?*"

He went on as if she hadn't spoken. "With dark brown hair that glows with coppery lights and looks alive and warm and silky, as if it would wrap itself around a man's fingers of its own accord—I like it down, by the way—and a mouth to drive a man mad."

Maxine felt a hot shiver pass over her skin. His voice was hypnotic. Heavens, even crocodiles responded to it!

She dipped her head, trying to remain calm and cool. Her normal self. Then she looked up again, pasting a smile on her lips. "Are you flirting with me, Mr. Cutter?"

"Dev." Oddly enough, he seemed almost abashed. "Are you objecting?"

"I don't think it's...appropriate."

He had stopped walking, pausing in the shadow of the trees. Apart from a number of bird calls, everything seemed silent. "Appropriate?"

"Well, we're on opposite sides of the fence, so to speak. Litigation is still a possibility."

He sighed. "And you haven't even had breakfast yet."

"What?" She blinked at the non sequitur.

"Do you eat legal textbooks instead of cornflakes? It sure sounds like it."

"There's no need to be rude."

To her surprise he said almost guiltily, "It just slipped out."

"Like that crocodile you had up your shirt the first time we met." Maxine laughed, only now seeing the funny side of the episode.

"You don't know the half of it," he told her, grinning, and launched into an account of how he'd had a mishap in the taxi, describing the driver's horror when he discovered what his passenger was carrying.

"But it was *tiny!*" Maxine recalled. "I was worried that it might get hurt."

Dev looked quizzically at her. "Worried," he repeated.

"Being carried around in your shirt didn't seem very safe for him."

"They're tough little critters, even at that age." He was regarding her so intently that Maxine turned away in embarrassment to walk on.

"Delilah seems pretty tame," she commented. "I'd never have believed a crocodile could roll over like that."

"They roll in water to drown their prey—the death roll—or to break off bits of their food. On land they roll when they're fighting or if they're caught in a trap or net. Delilah's the only one I've seen do it for fun. But she's different. She was brought up as a family pet."

Maxine peeked sideways at him, wondering if he was joking. "The one you don't take to bed with you."

Dev laughed. "I had a pet possum when I was a kid that used to curl up on my bed. But Delilah came from an old bloke up at Cape York who hand-reared her from a baby. He made me promise to look after her if anything happened to him. So when he died I brought her here. She's used to human company and seems almost affectionate."

"Are reptiles capable of loving people?"

"They're generally regarded as untamable, but Delilah seemed to pine for the old man when he went. He always reckoned she was as gentle as a baby. Though I nearly lost a hand to her when she first came here."

"She bit you?"

"It was my own fault, really."

They had reached a sturdy wooden fence surrounding a pit in which a gum tree stood, stripped of its natural leaves, but a park worker was tying bunches of fresh leaves to the branches. Two sleepy-looking koala bears sat in the forks. Dev looked into the pen. "Okay, Sandy?" he asked.

"Sure, Dev. Do I need to change their water? The rain's kind of filled the troughs. And these guys hardly ever drink."

"The water needs to be clean when they want it," Dev said. "Scrub out the containers and refill them."

"Okay, boss," Sandy said cheerfully.

"How was it your fault?" Maxine returned to their earlier conversation as they passed more koalas and a wombat pen.

"She was so tame I got careless. The old guy used to hold fish out to her one by one and she'd take them from his hand. I was talking to Binnie and Rooster while I fed her, and I dropped one of the fish. Delilah grabbed my hand instead—it would have smelled and tasted of fish and probably she thought that's what it was."

Maxine winced. She glanced down at his hands. That was where the scars had come from.

"I was lucky. A croc's jaws are made to hang on once they've closed on something. Rooster and Binnie started trying to pull me away, but that'd only have torn my hand right off, so I made them stop. With a tap or two on the nose with a stick and a bit of persuasion, I managed to talk Delilah into letting go and having a fish instead." He looked down at his hand, turning it over thoughtfully. "It could have been a lot worse."

Maxine felt quite ill. "And you still go into the cage with her and stroke her?"

"Never had any trouble with her since. Keep calm and use your head. That's what's important."

"You think that always works?"

"It helps."

Maxine pursed her lips. "Is that what you were doing

when you stormed into the DeWilde wedding of the year in Sydney, demanding to see Ryder Blake?''

"I didn't demand, I asked. All right," he admitted, his mouth curving in response to her provocative sideways glance. "Maybe I'm better at dealing with reptiles than human beings."

They crossed a bridge where a bunch of smaller crocodiles basked lazily on the banks of the shallow streambed. "Freshies," Dev told her as she dubiously eyed them.

Soon afterward they reached the snake section. "Want to see something special?" Dev asked her.

"Why not?" She had never been keen on reptiles, but viewing them with someone who knew and loved them was giving her a different perspective. While she didn't see herself ever cuddling up to a crocodile, she was willing to learn more about them.

He unlocked a door to a concrete room. It was very warm, and on a bench stood a couple of glass tanks holding small, leafy branches in a few centimeters of water. Dev went over to them, felt about carefully among the leaves in one tank and lifted out a tiny, writhing, butter yellow snake.

"What is it?" Maxine asked cautiously.

"A baby green python. They just hatched a few days ago. They're not venomous."

"Pythons squeeze their prey to death, don't they?"

"Yeah. But this fellow's too small to be any risk to us. Want to hold him?"

Maxine swallowed and stepped forward, holding out her hand.

The baby snake wound around her fingers. She laughed and looked closely at it, intrigued by the shiny yellow pattern of its scales as it undulated about and wove itself between her fingers. "He's quite lovely, really," she admitted. "But he's not green!"

"He will be when he's bigger." Dev took another identical snake from the neighboring tank and inspected it. "These two look healthy. They can be hard to rear."

"How big will they grow?" She watched the snake crawl up her hand and wrap itself about her wrist.

"Not too big—a meter or so. That looks like a bracelet on you."

Maxine lifted her wrist and tried to make eye contact with the baby snake, laughing when it lifted its tiny head at her. "You'd be a gorgeous one, wouldn't you, sweetie?" she cooed.

Dev laughed. "For a city lady you're pretty brave," he allowed.

"Listen, country boy, don't jump to conclusions. We city folk aren't all wimps, you know."

He put back the snake he held, then carefully untwined its twin from her wrist with one hand, the fingers of his other hand replacing it. Retaining his hold on her, he returned the python to its tank. And then, without warning, he tugged Maxine toward him, pulling her close.

As soon as his lips touched hers, she realized she had been waiting for this. Ever since yesterday, the memory of that brief kiss at the wedding had been lurking at the edge of her consciousness.

This one was longer, more leisurely, and totally devastating. He wrapped her securely in his arms and kissed her with passion and panache. It was openly erotic and tender and demanding, his lips frankly exploring as though he found infinite pleasure in the taste and texture of hers.

At first she made a feeble effort to hold back, to make her head rule her stupid heart, but soon she found herself responding in kind, reveling in the scent of his skin and the tantalizing movements of his lips and the warmth and strength of his hard, lean body against the length of hers.

When he lifted his head to look at her, his eyes alight with overt desire, she stayed in the tight circle of his arms and stared back at him with a mixture of dismay and bemusement.

"I've been wanting to do that again ever since the first time," he said, his voice deep and slow. "You kiss a blue streak, city lady."

"S-so do you," she admitted.. Credit where credit's due, she told herself. She made a reluctant effort to push him away, and was unreasonably disappointed when he allowed his arms to fall and she was left alone. "But it had better not happen again." She'd enjoyed it far too much to let it become a habit.

"Aw," he said, "don't be such a spoilsport!"

He was back to his wild man act. Maxine straightened her spine and put on her most forbidding expression. "Sorry, but I'm not here to have fun, and we shouldn't lose sight of that—either of us."

"I wasn't."

She stiffened. "You mean you kissed me hoping to soften me up?"

He scowled. "I kissed you because I wanted to, and you kissed me back for the same reason. Don't try and complicate things."

"Things *are* complicated," she argued. "At least they will be if you...if we form any kind of personal relationship. Not that one kiss signifies anything," she added hastily, anxious not to read more into it than he'd intended.

"So how many kisses would?" He was staring at her with those mesmeric blue eyes. His smile and the warm light in his questioning gaze were exerting a subtle pull on her senses. "I'll be in Sydney once a week until the end of this TV series. And if I sign that contract Rooster's trying to push me into, I'll be into a new series later in the year. He'd be glad if I found an incentive. Maybe we could get together sometimes on Friday nights, city lady?"

Her eyes widened, warning bells ringing in her brain like a galaxy of burglar alarms. She should turn him down flat, for about a hundred and two very good reasons. Her tongue refused to formulate one.

"Or Saturdays," he said. "You choose. I might even be able to wangle both sometimes."

"For what?" she asked finally, stalling.

His smile grew, and her heart turned over at the tenderness in his eyes. "Dinner," he said. "A date. You know, two people go out together, talk, laugh, have fun, get to know each other a bit. Maybe they kiss now and then. And maybe…" He studied her face, his smile fading to a faint curve of the lips, his eyes darkening. "Maybe, if they like each other enough…there's more."

It sounded so seductive.

But of course it wouldn't do. "No!" she said. "It's not possible."

"Why?"

"For one thing, it's unethical. I can't represent the DeWildes if I'm having a…a relationship with you."

He looked thoughtful. "What about after?"

"After what?"

"This can't go on forever. Can I see you after it's all over?"

Maxine briefly bit her lip. She couldn't say yes. Not without taking leave of her senses. "That could take a long time if you're determined to be pigheaded about things. And you won't want to see me again," she added rather sadly, "when we've beaten you in court."

"You're so sure you'd win?"

"We *will* win, Dev." Maxine looked at him earnestly, trying to get through to him. "People like the DeWildes don't lose. They have the money—and money is power."

Dev frowned. "Are you saying justice is for sale?"

"I'm not saying that. But they can afford to hire better lawyers than me, if necessary. And even if they did lose, they could keep fighting until they bankrupt you."

"You think Jeffrey would do that?"

"I think Jeffrey is accustomed to winning."

Dev looked thoughtful. "Yeah? Well, I don't give up easily. And maybe I don't have his money, but listen, city lady, I'm accustomed to winning, too."

She stared into his eyes and saw the determination in them, and the desire. And felt her body respond, heated and tingling although he wasn't even touching her.

He was so far from being the man of her dreams it was ludicrous. He was her worst, most terrifying nightmare come true. *Why* did she feel this ridiculous, overwhelming attraction to him?

It's a trap, she thought. A trap baited with honey and soft words—and kisses. A trap she'd evaded years ago and wasn't going to be lured into entering now.

He looked at her for a long moment. "Why are you so scared?" he said quietly.

Her eyes fixed on him. "Scared?" She willed scorn into her voice. "Don't be silly!"

"I work with fear," he said. "My own fear, the animals' fear when I take them away from their homes and habitats, the blind fear of people who see predators as monsters. I know fear when I see it. And I see it in you. I don't want to hurt you." He sounded calm and quiet, as he had when he'd talked to Delilah. Maxine thought fleetingly, foolishly that she wished he'd stroke her as he had the crocodile, soothe her with his big, gentle hands.

This man talked the most feared creatures on earth into trusting him. And then he caged them. Oh, all for their own good, of course. But they were caged, nevertheless. He was downright dangerous!

A shiver ran through her body. "If you don't want to hurt me," she said starkly, "you'll leave me alone."

Dev looked at her quite soberly for a long time, and then he gave a nod. "I never go after a frightened creature unless I have to. Sometimes it's necessary, of course, to protect them."

Maxine swallowed. "I don't need any protecting, Mr. DeWilde Cutter. I can look after myself very well. And I'm not frightened of you," she added belatedly.

At last he smiled a little. "Never thought you were."

She didn't want to ask him what he meant by that.

Because she was afraid to hear the answer? Brushing aside the uncomfortable thought, she turned abruptly and pushed open the door and started walking away from him.

When he caught up with her, she said briskly, "I hope you've given some thought to being sensible about the DeWildes' offer."

"Can't you give it a rest?" Dev asked plaintively.

They walked by an open concrete compound where a frilled lizard, a shade smaller than Archie, scurried along a big log and froze, hoping to remain unnoticed. "Have you had a chance to discuss it with your mother?"

"You think she'll agree, don't you? Jeffrey's probably trying to talk her round now. My mother's too soft for her own good, but it won't make any difference, you know. I'll fight it all the way."

"Why?" Exasperated, Maxine turned on him. "For her sake? But if she's willing to compromise—"

"Because I feel guilty!" Dev said harshly. "And this is one way of making it up to her, that's why!"

"Making what up to her?"

"The fact that I hate my name," he growled. "That ever since I was six years old I've refused to answer to the name she gave me."

CHAPTER EIGHT

"AH, THERE YOU ARE!" Jeffrey came strolling toward them, his hands in the pockets of his freshly pressed trousers. "Good morning. Did you sleep well, Maxine?"

"Yes, thank you." Maxine found herself speculating on who had ironed his clothes—Maggie? Or with all the traveling he did, perhaps he'd learned to do it himself. "When were you thinking of returning to Sydney, Mr.—er—Jeffrey? I should contact my office."

"I've booked us on a late afternoon flight," he said. "And contacted Mr. Finchley at his home. I told him I feel it's imperative that you stay on while we continue the negotiations we began yesterday."

"You...did?"

Jeffrey's brows lifted. "Have I presumed too much?" he asked. "Grace rather thinks I may have crossed the boundary of efficiency and strayed into officiousness."

"No, not at all," Maxine said quickly. "Thank you. I didn't know you had my boss's home number."

"It wasn't difficult to discover it."

Not if you were Jeffrey DeWilde, evidently.

"He said not to worry," Jeffrey told her. "All your commitments will be taken care of. I gather you have helpful partners and a very capable secretary."

"Yes." To both. But her standing had risen considerably since Ryder Blake had chosen her, after a chance meeting at a charity dinner, to take over the legal affairs of DeWilde's Sydney. And it would go up more if Jeffrey DeWilde had personally indicated that her presence here for another day was indispensable.

Maxine took a deep breath. If he was showing such faith in her, somehow she must see this thing through to a satisfactory conclusion.

But Dev evidently had other ideas. "You're both welcome to stay as long as you like," he said. "But I thought I'd got the message across yesterday. No deal. No negotiations."

Jeffrey looked at him blandly. "You have promised to show me over the park, though. I'm sorry if I should have got up earlier."

"No. Any time that suits you."

"Thank you. Perhaps after breakfast? Your mother said it would be served about now."

GRACE AND THE TWINS were already at the table with Maggie. Grace had toast and coffee before her, and Jeffrey was soon tucking into bacon and eggs.

There were bowls of fruit and cereal on the white cloth, and covered dishes held hot fare. Dev pulled out a chair for Maxine and she sat down, trying to hide her surprise at the unexpected courtesy. She was, she realized, still influenced by her first impression of Dev Cutter, when she hadn't suspected him of possessing any social graces.

She ladled fruit into a bowl and Dev poured her some orange juice. Maxine glanced at him, wondering where she might find a chink in the armor of his determination. Or should she pin her hopes on Jeffrey, whose handling of the issue so far had been pretty masterly?

Right now Jeffrey seemed to be giving Maggie a potted history of the DeWilde Corporation—from his great-grandfather's apprenticeship to a diamond merchant in

Amsterdam to the evolution of the worldwide chain of bridal specialty shops headed by Jeffrey today.

Maggie hung on his every word, the picture of a good listener. "How many stores do you have now?" she asked.

Dev cast his mother a searching glance as he poured milk on his cereal and fruit.

"Five, at last count," Jeffrey told her. "London, Paris, Monaco, New York, and now Sydney."

"It's...an empire," Maggie commented.

Jeffrey laughed. "So some people say. I prefer to call it a family business."

"Around here," Maggie said dryly, "a family business is the local grocery store, where the owner's wife and daughters help out behind the counter."

Jeffrey smiled. "That's how we began, and how we still function, largely. Although the American branch has been rather different until recently...."

Eventually Jeffrey turned the conversation back to Maggie. "While we're on the subject of families—why did you christen your son DeWilde?" Grace's head lifted in surprise, but Jeffrey didn't seem to notice as he went on smoothly, "It's an unusual name to give a boy, surely?"

Dev gave a snort of laughter. "You bet. Especially around here."

His mother looked at him with compunction. "I'm sorry, son."

He shrugged. "No worries. Taught me how to stick up for myself."

Grace was staring. "You were christened DeWilde?"

Dev grinned across the table at her. "That's right. And everyone round here is called Bill or Tom or Jack, with an occasional Steve or Dave for variety."

"You're exaggerating," his mother chided.

"Not much." He turned an affectionate smile on her. "You can imagine," he went on, pushing away his bowl and reaching for a thick slab of toast, "how the school bullies reacted to a kid with a fancy name like 'DeWilde.' They thought it was sissy and expected I'd be a push-over." He lifted the lid from a platter of bacon and eggs to shovel some onto his plate.

Maxine could imagine only too vividly how it must have been. Her heart ached for the little boy who had been the butt of his schoolmates' taunts and jeers.

"So you changed it to Dev," Jeffrey guessed.

"Not exactly. I wasn't going to be intimidated into changing anything." Dev flashed a glance at the older man, who didn't react visibly to the implied challenge. "No, it sort of evolved after a while—and after numerous playground spats."

"He was forever coming home with a black eye or a cut lip," Maggie interjected, "but he would never tell me why he got into so many fights. The teachers thought *he* was a troublemaker!" she added indignantly. "And he'd always been the gentlest little boy! From when he was just a toddler he collected wounded birds and animals— he'd get upset even when someone killed a snake."

"I still do," Dev said. "Snakes are wonderful crea-tures, and the vast majority of them are harmless to hu-mans if they're just left alone."

"But people do die of snake bites," Maxine objected.

Dev turned to her. "Ninety percent of bites are to peo-ple trying to kill the snake. Wouldn't you lash out if some-one was doing their best to chop your head off or batter you to death?"

"When you put it like that..."

"Don't start him," Binnie warned. "He can talk for hours about snakes and how great they are."

"Tell us," Jeffrey suggested, "how you came by your nickname."

He shrugged. "Eventually the kids tired of tormenting me and started calling me Dev."

Rooster reached for more bacon and dropped a generous rasher on his plate. "It's short for Daredevil," he said. "One of Dev's mates told me he was such a battler he'd take on anyone, even three or four kids at once. And he'd do anything for a dare. When he was seven he climbed to the top of an enormous old red gum in the school grounds. It was about three stories tall and with no branches to well over head height—no one knew how he did it. The teachers just about had kittens. And he used to handle snakes for dares."

Dev shot a reproving look at his cousin. "I was just showing off. Kids are stupid that way."

And he needed to live down his sissy name and be accepted by the other children, Maxine guessed. At that age, being despised by one's peers was a desperate situation.

"And it stuck," Rooster said. "Hardly anyone remembers his real name now."

"And he never uses it," Maxine said slowly. Friends and family knew him as Dev, and everywhere else he went by his initials.

Dev glanced at her. "Yeah, well…"

Jeffrey was looking at Maggie. "Is it a family name? Your maiden name, perhaps?"

She seemed to hesitate. "I just like it. I…read it somewhere." She added firmly, "My name was Thompson."

Dev was looking hard at his mother. Though he said

nothing, Maxine sensed his tension and wondered what was bothering him.

"I didn't realize," Maggie explained, "that having an unusual name would make my boy's life such a misery when he started school." She hurried on. "You told me about the American DeWildes, Jeffrey. What made you decide to open a store in Sydney? Is there another branch of the family in Australia?"

Jeffrey shook his head. "Ryder Blake is my son Gabriel's best friend, and a very gifted young man. The Australian operation was Ryder's idea, and he's in charge of the Sydney store. As far as I know, we have no family born here—but an uncle of mine spent some time in Australia many years ago."

"When was that?"

"About 1948 to '49." Jeffrey paused for a moment. "We lost touch with him after that."

"Oh…really?" Maggie seemed oddly breathless. "That's…a shame."

"We learned just recently that he lived in New Zealand for many years. Unfortunately he died before we traced him. But Ryder's bride, Natasha, is his granddaughter, we have discovered."

Binnie looked up from her bacon and eggs, her eyes shining. "What a great story! Isn't that romantic? But kind of sad, too."

Grace smiled at the girl. "The DeWilde history is full of romantic stories. And sad ones…" Her eyes clouded. She exchanged a glance with Jeffrey, and for a moment the room was filled with an atmosphere of tension and sorrow.

Maggie broke it. "Grace, can I get you some more coffee?" She got up to take her cup and Grace's to the coffee machine on the big old-fashioned sideboard. Jeffrey followed her movements attentively—so attentively that for once Grace was gazing at him openly and unseen, her eyes expressing confusion and curiosity, and perhaps a hint of dismay.

Jeffrey pushed away his plate as Maggie sat down again. "You were going to tell me, Maggie, where you found the name DeWilde."

"Oh, I...as I said, I read it somewhere. In a book."

"What sort of book would that be?" He sounded kind and interested, but Maxine was conscious of a hint of implacability behind his half smile, and Grace was looking faintly anxious.

"Just...one my mother had," Maggie said. "A long time ago."

Dev looked from Jeffrey to his mother. He seemed about to say something, but changed his mind.

Maggie put down her untouched coffee and pushed back her chair. "I'd better be getting along to the shop— I want to rearrange some stock before we open today. Binnie, can you deal with the breakfast dishes? I hope you enjoy your tour of the park, Jeffrey. Dev, you're going to show him round, aren't you?"

"Sure." Dev nodded.

Grace sipped at her coffee, then held her cup in both hands and spoke to Maggie. "I'll join you in a few minutes if that's okay? You said you'd welcome some advice."

Maggie paused, already on her way to the door. "I'd be thrilled. Any time it suits you, Grace."

Jeffrey wordlessly raised his expressive brows at Grace as Maggie left the room.

"I offered a few suggestions for improvements," she said defensively. "Maggie's not experienced at retailing. She's grateful for a little help."

"I'm not accusing you of anything, Grace."

Dev drawled, "I think it's called 'giving comfort to the enemy.'"

Jeffrey slanted a smile in his direction. "I hope there is no need for me to be anyone's enemy. I've found it's a very uncomfortable state of affairs."

Grace shot him a wary and slightly surprised glance.

Binnie finished eating and began stacking dishes with Rooster's help. Dev gulped down some coffee and placed the cup in its saucer. "If you're ready, Jeffrey, I'll take you on that tour."

"Do you want me along?" Maxine asked Jeffrey.

He shook his head. "I don't think that's necessary. Dev and I will take some time out from business discussions. I want to see this park of his."

Which left her with nothing to do. She helped Binnie and Rooster clear up and then ironed her blouse and skirt, but didn't put them on before wandering over to the shop, where Grace was still in consultation with Maggie. Although by now visitors were beginning to arrive, none of them were buying souvenirs as yet.

Alongside an array of garish tourist trinkets there were quite beautiful printed and hand-painted items of clothing featuring scenes of the rain forest and gracefully depicted animals. A series of framed pictures showed the same delicate touch as the big pastel in Maggie's sitting room.

"Most of those are Binnie's work," Maggie confirmed. "And over here we have some designs drawn for us by a local aboriginal artist, based on traditional patterns."

Maxine was unable to resist a silk scarf with motifs reminiscent of aboriginal cave paintings, and a small picture of a monitor lizard on a red rock. She hoped she wasn't compromising her position as DeWilde's lawyer by purchasing them.

Maggie wrapped the items for her in paper with De Wildes printed on it. Looking at it, she sighed. "It will mean a lot of changes if we have to give up our name. Paper, labels, all our invoice books and letterheads, tickets..."

Grace looked sympathetic. "It may not come to that. Jeffrey seems almost willing to compromise." She paused there, as though the idea was somewhat astonishing. "Maybe we could persuade Dev to meet him halfway...." She looked hopefully at Maxine. "What do you think?"

Maxine said carefully, "I'm here to represent the interests of the DeWilde Corporation. I really can't discuss the matter unless Mr. DeWilde is present."

Grace smiled at her. "How very discreet of you, Maxine! Just...don't go away." Turning to Maggie, she said as if Maxine weren't there, "You know, some of these goods are printed with lettering that looks quite similar to the DeWilde logo used throughout their stores."

Maggie looked worried. "But we didn't copy it, honestly. Actually, it's my fault. Binnie thought a rustic style would suit the park, but I took a real fancy to this more flowing calligraphy, and Dev...I know he really didn't care one way or the other—he's more interested in the welfare of the animals than the commercial aspects—but he always comes down on my side."

"You're lucky," Grace said, "that your son is so loyal." Her husky voice became brisk. "Well, supposing he agreed to make the lettering style quite different? Go with Binnie's idea, for instance?"

"I could suggest it to him," Maggie offered. "But...we have a lot of merchandise with this lettering on it."

"You do." Grace looked around. "Some of it is very

good. I think DeWilde's Sydney wouldn't be ashamed to sell those hand-painted Ts, for instance. I wonder..."

Maxine bit her tongue. She was supposed to be pretending not to be here. Grace and Jeffrey DeWilde would have made a formidable team when they were married, she reflected. Their favorite bedtime reading must have been the works of Machiavelli—they'd probably read excerpts to each other on their honeymoon.

Twenty minutes later she left the shop and went over to the house to deposit her parcel. Binnie came outside holding Archie nestled in her arms, his brown body across her torso and his front feet on her shoulder. "I'm taking him to meet a bunch of schoolkids," she said. "Want to come?"

The children were entranced by the lizard. While Archie posed and preened and let himself be petted by gentle little hands, Binnie talked of the importance of caring for wild habitats so that his relatives could live in peace and freedom.

While Binnie returned the lizard to the house, Maxine joined the visitors thronging the paths. She wondered if Dev and Jeffrey were still on their tour.

As she trailed her fingers along a low wall, a broken gray branch with mottled bark inside the small compound startled her by moving.

A sulky slit of amber eye gleamed among the camouflage of feathers that exactly matched the branch on which the tawny frogmouth sleepily perched, its broad, short beak tucked against its chest.

Children were feeding crumbs and seeds to the multicolored birds that flocked about under the trees. At the snake house, Maxine watched the wonderfully patterned bodies sliding against the glass for several minutes before she moved on.

Reaching Delilah's grassed enclosure, she stopped, admiring the intricate latticing of the creature's scaly skin and the fearsome grace of its body.

Delilah sat still for ages, her mouth open in that famous crocodile grin, before slipping silently into the pond in the middle of the enclosure, leaving not even a ripple, then surfaced with only her hooded eyes and the end of her snout above the water. Other people who had been watching walked on, but Maxine stayed.

"Gone for a swim, has she?" Dev's voice said.

Maxine didn't turn. "I thought you were showing Jeffrey round."

"I did." A brown hand appeared on the wooden rail of the waist-high fence beside her. "We've finished."

When she turned he was very close—close enough that she could see herself reflected in his eyes. "I'd better go and see if he needs me."

As she made to step away he brought his other hand up, so that his arms enclosed her against the fence. "I wouldn't."

Maxine stiffened warily. "I—"

"He was talking to Grace when I left," Dev said.

"Grace?" Maxine's voice sharpened. "Have you persuaded her to be your advocate?"

"What a nasty suspicious mind you have. Grace is her own woman. I wouldn't presume to try and persuade the lady to do anything. Jeffrey might, though...."

"What do you mean by that?"

"I mean the two of them obviously have some unfinished personal business to sort out. You can't have missed the atmosphere between them."

"Nobody could!"

"Exactly. So I wouldn't advise you to go barging in on their tête-à-tête."

"Their marriage is over. They're divorced."

Dev shrugged. "Maybe. I still had the impression they'd rather be alone for a while."

It struck Maxine that despite the visitors now strolling about the park, she and Dev were temporarily alone, too. There didn't seem to be anyone about in this particular section.

He was smiling at her, and as his eyes lingered on her mouth, she found herself remembering his kiss that morning, the feel of his mouth exploring hers.

As if he'd read her mind, he leaned forward and touched his lips to hers, softly, persuasively. She felt herself responding.

Dimly she heard a splash, and then there was a loud, metallic crash behind her.

Maxine jumped, and Dev's head jerked back, his hands closing on her arms and pulling her toward him.

For a moment his arms went about her, and her cheek was pressed against the hardness of his shoulder. But his eyes were riveted on several hundred kilos of wet, ferocious crocodile that had just hurled itself at the fence, little more than an arm's length away.

Turning her head, Maxine saw Delilah's pale belly pressed against the mesh, her long, sharp teeth caught on the wire of the inner fence as she tried to bite through it.

Dev grasped Maxine's arms again and stood her away from him. "Don't move!" he ordered her.

"You're not going in there?" Maxine objected shrilly.

"No." He vaulted the low outer fence and stepped toward the inner one, squatted a foot or so from it and began talking in that hypnotic, calmly rhythmic voice. With two fingers through one of the apertures of mesh he stroked the crocodile's belly, and Maxine held her breath. But Dev stroked and talked, and at last the crocodile dropped back to the ground, her head still lifted, her mouth agape.

A bunch of people came along and stopped to watch. Dev kept talking, taking no notice.

''That's the wild man, I saw him on TV!'' a child's voice said.

Everyone stared at Dev, then back at Delilah. A father picked up his little girl for a better view.

At last Dev straightened and climbed back to the path, standing beside Maxine but not touching her. ''Are you all right?'' he asked quietly.

''Yes.''

''Let's go.'' He turned to walk away, and she fell shakily into step alongside him.

They came to a curve in the path under some trees and he glanced back, evidently checking they were out of sight of Delilah's enclosure. Then he grabbed her hand. ''I'm sorry,'' he said gruffly. ''That was my fault.''

Maxine swallowed. ''You weren't kidding about her being jealous.''

He looked down at her. ''Wild creatures have feelings, too.''

''She was after me.''

''Maybe,'' Dev said. ''Maybe she was just pleased to see *me*.''

Maxine ruefully rubbed at her arm.

Dev looked down. ''Did I hurt you?''

''I suppose you got a fright, too.''

Dev loosed her hand and put an arm about her shoulders, his fingers giving a little squeeze. ''You were quite safe, really.''

She ought to move away from him, but she liked the feel of his arm about her, the warm hand cupping her shoulder as they walked.

Dev looked down at her, and suddenly he was walking her off the path and into the trees growing alongside it, dodging under an overhanging branch and pushing aside a rustling flowering shrub.

"What are you doing?"

"Just finishing what Delilah interrupted." And he hauled her right into his arms and kissed her—properly.

Vaguely she heard the flurry of wings as a bird took off from a branch overhead, and the voices of people walking along the path. Then everything faded away and time stood still as he worked some kind of magic with his mouth, capturing her lips and making her blood sing and enchantment shimmer through her body.

His right arm was snug about her waist, while his other hand ran up and down her arm, stroking it as though he loved the texture of her skin. Then he curved his fingers about her nape and supported her head as it tipped back under his deepening kiss.

Her body arched against his arm, and he shifted it, his hand finding the bare skin of her back under the T-shirt and traveling along her spine even while he coaxed her mouth to open for him.

The kiss was long and satisfying, and when their mouths at last reluctantly parted, he touched his forehead to hers.

Her breath was shortened as if she'd been running. She had to take two gulps of air before she could speak, her voice shaking. "Dev, you mustn't. I can't…"

"The hell you can't!" He kissed her again, fierce and sweet and determined.

But this time she summoned all her willpower and pushed him with her hands on his chest until he let her go, a scowl between his blue eyes as they leapt with angry fire.

"Damn it, Cutter!" she snapped, whipping up her own anger to try to drown the treacherous desire that still suffused her body. "You know I shouldn't be doing this with you! I'm supposed to be arguing a *case* against you!"

Dev lifted his hand and struck his forehead. "Can't you forget that for one damn minute?" he demanded, glaring at her in frustration.

"No!" But to her own considerable surprise she heard herself say, "You agree to remove the DeWilde name and logo from your park and your products and then...I'll think about it."

Dev's head snapped back and his eyes narrowed. "What?" He looked positively dangerous.

"You heard me." Her voice shook despite herself. This was recklessness in the first degree. Terminal stupidity, probably. But maybe she could save him—and this place that meant so much to him—from his own stubbornness.

"This is a condition?" Dev asked, his voice grating. "I give in to your boss's demands, and then you'll *think about* letting me near you? I hand you my business on a plate and in return I get you—is that what you're saying?"

Maxine stared at him, her cheeks flaring with rage. She felt like stamping her foot or, even better, slapping him till his head spun. Instead she yelled at him. "*No,* that's *not* what I'm saying, you impossible, bloody-minded man!" She added a few more adjectives and a noun or two that she hadn't allowed to cross her lips for years, and watched his jaw fall in astonishment. To her horror, she heard her carefully cultivated pseudo-British enunciation slip into pure Strine—the distinctively Australian accent that she'd worked for years to eliminate. "What I'm saying, you brainless bushwhacker," she finished, "is that I'd have to be stark, staring *crackers* to get involved with the most pigheaded, pea-brained *drongo* this side of the flaming Black Stump!"

CHAPTER NINE

WITHOUT WAITING for his reaction, Maxine turned and fought her way through the shrubbery back to the path.

In her haste she scratched her arms on some of the twiggy growth, and she reflected bitterly as she headed for the house that between that and the probable bruises left by Dev's hands when Delilah had lunged so unexpectedly at the fence, she'd be looking like the victim of a misadventure.

She felt like one, too. What had possessed her to contemplate even for a moment the prospect of seeing Dev Cutter on a regular basis? The sooner she got out of this place and back to the sanity of Sydney and her job and her relentlessly upmarket apartment the better.

Grace and Jeffrey were sitting at a small table on the veranda, so intent on their conversation that they didn't seem to notice Maxine's approach across the grass.

She heard Jeffrey say, "She's hiding something. It's too coincidental."

"Don't you think you're becoming a little obsessive about this?" Grace asked him. "Hiring a private investigator and—" She broke off as Maxine reached the steps up to the veranda.

"I won't disturb you," Maxine said, about to pass on into the house.

"You're not," both of them assured her, and Jeffrey

pulled out another chair. "Please sit down, Maxine," he offered.

She looked from him to Grace uncertainly.

"Do—please," Grace urged her. "Jeffrey and I were probably about to have another quarrel. We can't seem to help it these days."

Maxine took the proffered chair and Jeffrey turned to her. "You're a lawyer," he said. "Do you think Maggie was being evasive about her reason for naming her son DeWilde?"

"I'm not a trial lawyer," Maxine disclaimed. Since he continued to look at her expectantly, she added, "But...she did seem rather vague about it."

Jeffrey shot a vindicated glance at Grace, who said, "That doesn't mean she's dishonest."

"Dishonest?" Maxine was surprised.

"I wasn't suggesting anything of the kind." Jeffrey sounded impatient.

Grace looked at him accusingly. "You said the tiara must have been stolen."

"Might have. And I didn't say Maggie stole it."

"Who, then? Her father?"

"Possibly."

"He could have bought it legitimately."

"He seems to have been dirt-poor until he found the black opal Maggie spoke of. And the proceeds from that went to buying a property. He wouldn't have had enough left over to purchase the Empress Eugénie's tiara."

"Whose?" Maxine was bewildered.

Grace raised her brows at Jeffrey. "Maxine is the DeWilde lawyer in Australia, and she doesn't know about this?"

"*This* is a family matter," Jeffrey said stiffly. "We don't need advice from outsiders."

Grace went white, and after a moment pushed back her chair. "Well then, perhaps you shouldn't have tried to enlist my help to pump information from Maggie."

"Grace, I only meant—" Jeffrey stood up.

Grace could put frost in her warm, husky voice when she wanted. "I'm sure you and Maxine have things to talk about before you mount your next assault on the Cutters. And I have plans for today. Maybe I'll see you at lunch." She gave Maxine a perfunctory smile and whisked away into the house, the screen door slapping to behind her.

Go after her, Maxine was tempted to tell him. But it wasn't her business and she didn't quite dare. Jeffrey might have unbent a little in the last couple of days, but he was still the head of DeWilde's and a lot older than her to boot.

For a second she thought he might do it, anyway. He stood frowning at the doorway, clenching and unclenching one fist. Then he swept his gaze down to her and said in a perfectly calm voice, "She's right. We need to plan the next step in our campaign." Resuming his seat, he asked, "Do you have some ideas?"

MAGGIE LEFT BINNIE in charge of the shop while she and Rooster carried dishes of food from the park café to the house for their visitors' lunch.

"I hope you're going to join us," Jeffrey told her. "Dev told me he would be here. Maxine and I really have to leave this afternoon, and I had hoped to talk to you both before we go."

Maggie hesitated until Grace said quietly, "Dev may need your opinion if Jeffrey and Maxine have any fresh proposals to resolve matters."

Maggie nodded and took her place at the head of the table.

Dev was late. When he arrived at the table his hair was damp, as if he'd just showered, and he was still buttoning his shirt.

He apologized, sat down and took a bread roll from a basket on the table, then heaped salad and cold meats onto his plate. Maxine was careful not to look directly at him, but she felt his gaze on her. She had changed out of her borrowed clothes and back into her own things, a resumption of her everyday armor that she was sure wasn't lost on him.

Grace was quiet, Rooster attacked his food with intense concentration, and Jeffrey made scant headway in trying to draw Maggie into a real conversation, her reluctance in marked contrast to the night before, when she and Grace had seconded each other's efforts at sociability.

As soon as Dev pushed aside his plate and reached for his coffee cup, Jeffrey reminded him, "You did say you would give us half an hour after lunch."

"Okay," Dev said indifferently. "Shoot."

"Here?" Jeffrey glanced about the table.

"Why not? Rooster's our publicity manager. This affects him, too."

Grace picked up her coffee. "I'll have this on the veranda."

"You don't have to leave," Jeffrey said gruffly.

"I prefer to, really, while you're discussing DeWilde business. It's very pleasant out there." Grace smiled serenely at the rest of them and left the room.

Jeffrey shifted his cup and coffee spilled over the rim into the saucer. He frowned, straightened his shoulders and turned to Dev. "Maxine has some interesting ideas to put to you."

"Really?" Dev looked at her and for the first time she met his eyes. They were very bright and almost hostile. *Convince me,* they seemed to say.

Maxine took a deep breath. She was uncomfortable about accepting credit but, taking her cue from Grace, hadn't dared tell Jeffrey where most of the ideas had come from.

"Mr. DeWilde has asked me to seek a compromise solution. If we agree not to legally challenge your use of the name De Wildes, would you consider changing the style of lettering you use so that it's more distinctive— different from the DeWilde Corporation signature?"

Dev glanced at his mother. "Maybe."

"The offer of financial help to change your advertising and stationery stands, of course. Furthermore, Mr. De- Wilde offers to consult the management of the Sydney store with a view to buying all existing stock that carries a similar design to the DeWilde logo."

Dev's brows went up. "What would you do with it?"

Jeffrey said, "I will have to check with Ryder, but he may be able to sell some of the clothing and artwork in the Sydney store—which could open a new market for your cousin and the young artist who does the aboriginal motifs. Much of the other merchandise, I'm bound to say, will be unsuitable. But that would be our loss."

"We must remind you, however," Maxine put in, "that all these proposals are subject to Ryder Blake's approval."

"Aren't you his boss?" Dev asked Jeffrey.

"I'm not in the habit of overriding my branch general managers," Jeffrey replied. "I'm only standing in for him because we believed that this little problem had become a matter of some urgency. So I undertook to deal with it while Ryder is on his honeymoon."

"It sounds fair to me," Maggie said.

"It'll cost you," Dev remarked, his gaze still on Jeffrey.

"Probably not as much as taking you to court. Besides..."

"Yes?"

Jeffrey looked at the other man and gave him a rueful half smile. "We may find that suing you is not in our best interests, long term. If it was Ross's idea to put the townsfolk up to that publicity stunt you pulled, I think I should suggest that Ryder try to headhunt the young man for our Sydney store."

Rooster blushed. "It just sort of came up when I was in the pub, telling some of the locals we were trying to get on the TV news. They wanted to show their support, and the whole thing was pretty spontaneous, really. But that's what made the reporters come. There've been some phone calls this morning from newspapers. The local rag's running the story, and we even got calls from New Zealand."

"It was masterly," Jeffrey told him. "I'm fairly sure Ryder will agree that it won't do our image any good if we file suit against you."

"And that's why you're prepared to back down?" Dev regarded him fixedly, as if trying to fathom an ulterior motive.

Jeffrey spread his hands. "A good businessman knows when to give way."

"We'd need time to replace everything—we can't just clear out the stock and leave the shop empty while we wait for new stuff to be made."

Maxine exchanged a glance with Jeffrey. "DeWilde's wouldn't be happy about your continuing to sell competing goods."

"Perhaps," Jeffrey said, "we could help find manufacturers for a speedy replacement of stock. I'm sure De-Wilde's Sydney has the right contacts."

Dev's eyes sought his mother's again. She nodded, and he turned to Maxine. "Okay, lawyer lady. We accept."

Maxine breathed a sigh of relief. "I've already drafted an agreement on my laptop. I'll print it out now and have you and your mother sign it. And Jeffrey, of course, subject to Ryder's approval."

When it was done, she gave them a copy of the document and slipped the other into her briefcase.

Jeffrey consulted his watch. "I'm afraid we should be on our way again, Maxine. We don't want to miss another flight."

He shook hands with Dev and Rooster and turned to Maggie. "I have a friend who may be visiting Australia shortly," he said. "May I recommend your guest house to him?"

Grace came back into the room, carrying her empty cup. "A friend?" Her voice held an odd note.

Jeffrey turned to her. "I do have some, you know—still."

Grace's blue eyes sparkled with what might have been anger. "Would this friend's name be Nick Santos, by any chance?"

A look of chagrin momentarily showed on Jeffrey's face. "Is it any of your business?"

Grace flinched infinitesimally, and Jeffrey's hand made a jerky little movement, then returned to his side.

Maggie hurried into the small silence that followed. "We've sorted everything out, Grace. It's such a relief! Thank you!"

She gave the other woman a hug, and Jeffrey frowned. "Grace?"

Maxine explained. "Mrs. DeWilde had some...suggestions that proved useful." Now the document was signed, surely Jeffrey couldn't resent Grace's input.

"Indeed?" The frown deepened and Maxine wondered if she'd have been wiser to accept the discomfort of taking the credit.

Grace looked reproachfully at Maxine, then guiltily at her ex-husband. "I believe," she said carefully, "that Maxine may have overheard some things I was saying to Maggie earlier."

"You do?" Jeffrey's sarcasm was evident. "By God, Grace, you are—" He seemed to struggle for words, his mouth trying to formulate them, and then to Maxine's utter astonishment he lost his composure totally in an explosion of laughter.

She found her bemused gaze colliding with Dev's, a silent message of surprise passing between them.

Grace's eyes lit with answering laughter, while her mouth twitched and then folded into a soft, demure expression. "Well," she said as Jeffrey sobered, "you never were terribly good at conciliation. I was afraid you'd drag poor Maggie and Dev into court over this silly storm in a teacup. Somebody had to find a way out."

"Incredible," Jeffrey said. "I think that's the word I'm looking for." He shook his head. "Oh, Gracie! How did we—"

Grace's eyes darkened to violet and shimmered with unshed tears as Jeffrey cut off what he was going to say, apparently recalling that they had an audience, and his face resumed its normal, somewhat austere lines.

Maxine felt a lump in her throat and swallowed hard. If two people who so obviously loved and understood each other and had so much in common couldn't find a way to live together, what hope was there for less compatible couples? Her eyes went involuntarily to Dev and she found him looking at her searchingly.

Instinctively she made a small, negative movement of her head and took a half step farther away from him.

Dev frowned, his hands jammed into his pockets.

Suddenly she couldn't bear to stay a minute longer. "I don't want to rush you, Jeffrey. But as you said, we've got a plane to catch."

"Yes, of course." Reluctantly he removed his gaze from Grace. "I'm ready."

Maggie stood on the veranda to see them go, and Maxine caught a glimpse of Grace hovering behind the screen door.

Dev came bounding down the steps. "I'll open the gate for you," he said, and got into the back seat.

It was a thirty-second ride to the gate, and for every one of those seconds Maxine was conscious of him behind her. The back of her neck prickled and she was sure he hadn't taken his eyes from her.

He got out to open the gate and she drove through, pausing to wind down the window. "Thanks."

He put a hand on the door and stooped to meet her eyes. "I'll see you in Sydney."

Maxine didn't answer. She knew he was waiting for her to give him some sign, but she didn't dare. Even while she fought a desire to put her hand over the lean brown one so close to the sleeve of her blouse, or to lift her face and invite him to kiss her goodbye, some part of her was screaming to her to get out of here before it was too late.

She touched her foot lightly to the accelerator and the engine revved up. "I'll send you the confirmation of the agreement as soon as we get it," she promised.

Dev looked at her hard, his eyes shrewd and his mouth straight. Then he nodded. "Right."

She pressed her foot down a little more and he stepped back, taking the hint. Maxine released the brake and the car sped forward.

Jeffrey slid a thumb under his seat belt, settling himself more comfortably as they headed for the open road. "That young man is very interested in you."

"I'm not interested in him," Maxine lied vehemently.

"No?"

Maxine shot a look at him. She didn't know him well, but her guess was that Jeffrey DeWilde wasn't given to making personal remarks to people who worked for him.

He looked thoughtful. "You spent some time with him this morning."

Maxine felt herself flush. "He showed me round the reptile section of the park. It was most informative," she added woodenly.

"I'm sure it was." The glance she threw at him showed he looked perfectly grave, but the grooves in his cheeks on either side of his mouth had deepened. "Will you be seeing him in Sydney?"

Hesitating, she was cross with herself for not being able to say an immediate *no*. "I work for DeWilde's Sydney," she said evenly. "I assure you I'm utterly committed to my clients."

"Good." Jeffrey seemed to relax somewhat. "Good."

Had he doubted her loyalty? Maxine hoped she'd redeemed herself—with a little help from Grace DeWilde—for having failed to ascertain Dev's real name earlier.

"You must be wondering," Jeffrey said, "about the Empress Eugénie tiara, and what it has to do with the Cutters."

Maxine didn't know how to answer that. She'd briefly been curious, but when her mind hadn't been determinedly concentrated on the outcome of their negotiations, she'd found it had an annoying tendency to wander to Dev Cutter—his teasing blue eyes, his hard, strong, but so gentle hands, his kisses.

"You're very discreet," Jeffrey congratulated her. "Of course, Ryder wouldn't have hired you if he hadn't been sure of that."

"In my job," she said, "discretion is essential." And single-mindedness and dedication and a whole lot of other things that would come under threat if she let a wild man with magical hands and a voice that could enchant untamed man-eating monsters get under her skin.

"Yes," Jeffrey said. "So I'm sure I can entrust the story to you. You may be able to help us."

"Us?"

"The family. It's...a family secret, you see."

Intrigued, Maxine said encouragingly, "Yes?"

"Many years ago—almost half a century ago—an uncle of mine disappeared from New York, where he was managing the American branch of DeWilde's. It seems clear now that he took with him some family jewelry, including a tiara that had once belonged to the Empress Eugénie, wife of Louis-Napoléon. Last year the tiara surfaced in New York and I was able to buy it back for the family. We traced the American who brought it into the States, and found it had been purchased about a year previously from a jeweler in Sydney."

Maxine was silent for a few seconds while she made the astonishing connection. "And you think the Cutters sold it?"

"The description Maggie gave fitted the Empress Eugénie piece."

"Wouldn't the jeweler have a record of the purchase?"

"The records were unfortunately destroyed by fire, and

the jeweler had retired, suffering from Alzheimer's disease. Nick struck a dead end.''

''Nick?'' Maxine put two and two rapidly together. ''Nick Santos? He's your private investigator?''

''Ah...I thought you might have overheard that when you came upon Grace and me on the veranda. He is. And Grace was quite right in thinking I intended sending him to the Cutters.''

Was this why Jeffrey was so keen to negotiate a settlement rather than alienate the Cutters? ''Will she warn them?''

''Oh, I should think so. Definitely. Grace has the knack of making friends, and she seems to have taken these people under her wing. The thing is,'' Jeffrey mused, ''I find it hard to believe that the tiara and the name DeWilde are totally coincidental, yet I fail to see the connection to my uncle Dirk. I thought that mentioning he'd been in Australia might lead to something, but Maggie didn't pick up on it. Although for a moment I thought she might.''

''You didn't tell her your uncle's name, did you?''

Jeffrey cleared his throat. ''Nick warned me when I told him we'd found Natasha that when a family like ours lets it be known they are looking for long-lost relatives, they lay themselves open to con artists. Some of these people can be very clever, very convincing.''

''You seem sure about Natasha.''

''Nick—and Natasha—insisted on DNA tests. The results support our belief that she's a DeWilde descendant.'' Jeffrey chuckled. ''Somewhat to her chagrin, initially. Fortunately she's come round to the idea. Anyway, Nick told me to be extremely cautious about what information I give to anyone who claims or hints at a relationship.''

''Maggie and Dev haven't...''

"Maggie was very interested in the DeWilde family history."

He'd told Maggie a lot about them, but Maxine realized that all of it had probably been published many times in newspapers and magazines. "It's an interesting story. She was quite open about her own family history, too. And no DeWildes featured."

"That's true. I'm inclined to believe in her integrity, but…my judgment of women is not especially reliable." His mouth took on a bitter twist. "Nick would be justifiably angry if I tried to do his job for him—he's already had some blistering words to say on the subject. I'll call him when we reach Sydney."

"He's in Sydney?"

"No, no. At the moment I believe he's following a lead in New York. When my uncle disappeared from there, it was rumored he had a lady with him."

"Not his wife?"

"Almost certainly someone else's. Nick is trying to discover who she was."

"Is it important?" Why would the DeWildes want to resurrect some old scandal?

"There are still some pieces of jewelry missing," Jeffrey explained. "We've recovered only two. I'm hopeful that the others may find their way home in time—with a little help."

"And this mysterious woman may be a clue. But isn't she quite likely dead by now?"

Jeffrey nodded. "Possibly. If so, she may have left some evidence—records. Perhaps a family. I wondered if Maggie—" He shook his head. "But if it's true both her parents were born and bred in the same part of Australia, that rules her out. And surely she wouldn't make that up, especially if she hoped to claim some connection with my family."

"I suppose not," Maxine agreed. The story was intriguing, full of tantalizing loose ends. "If there's any way I can help…"

"Dev didn't say anything that seems relevant to you now that you know about all this?"

Maxine thought for a minute, and shook her head. "Nothing I can think of."

"Well, perhaps you'd let me know if he does," Jeffrey suggested almost idly. "Supposing you do happen to see him again. Nick might be interested."

Maxine slowed the car momentarily and cast him a penetrating glance. "Mr. DeWilde," she told him, "you are a devious man!"

"My dear young lady," he said innocently, "what are you accusing me of?"

"I think you know very well. You're asking me to spy for you!"

"I merely said that if you *should* happen to see Dev Cutter—"

"I know what you said."

"Maxine," he soothed gently. "I wouldn't ask anyone to compromise their principles. But finding the jewels and returning them to the family where they belong has become very important to me. Your position as DeWilde's lawyer is secure so long as Ryder finds your work satisfactory, and I'm sure your advocacy for the firm will continue to be as excellent as he has found it in the past. But you did offer your help, and I'm bound to say that I personally would be grateful if you were able to pass on any information that might help in tracing the missing DeWilde jewels."

He sat back then as though he'd given his final words on the subject, leaving Maxine to think them over.

To earn Jeffrey DeWilde's gratitude would certainly do her no harm professionally; if she ever called in the favor, she knew he'd do his best to honor it. Maxine was well aware that career advantages weren't all due to hard work and sheer ability. Sometimes it helped to be in the right place at the right time—and to know the right people.

Jeffrey DeWilde was definitely one of the right people. And he wasn't expecting her to do anything shady or grant him sexual favors—both of which had been asked of her in the past by other men who'd dangled career advancement as bait.

She tried to tell herself it was all academic, anyway. Dev Cutter was never going to be a part of her life.

But even as she assured herself of that, she knew deep down that no matter how hard she might try to evade the mysterious threads of desire that drew them together, he'd be coming after her.

CHAPTER TEN

As it happened, he didn't need to. The following day she received a phone call from Ryder. "I want a couple of changes in that draft agreement," he said, brushing aside the regret she expressed at this matter interrupting his honeymoon. "I've discussed them with Jeffrey, and of course you'll take your instructions from him in my absence."

The changes would need Dev's signature—and Maggie's, as she was a partner. Maxine contemplated the problem, tapping a ballpoint pen against her teeth. Then she picked up the telephone.

She got Binnie first, and as she waited for Dev to come on the line, she found herself breathing faster, a fizz of anticipation running along her veins. She closed her eyes and took a deep breath.

"Maxine?"

Just his voice was enough to curl her toes. "I've heard from Ryder Blake," she said in her most businesslike tone. "He wants a couple of minor changes to the agreement that will need your signature and your mother's."

"What kind of changes?" Dev inquired cautiously.

"A time limit on your right to sell stock carrying the old logo. And a noncompete clause."

"What's that?"

"I'll fax you a copy," Maxine promised. She thought Ryder was being overcautious. "But we need those signatures."

"We'll think about it—after we've seen the alterations."

"Not for too long, I hope. I'm sure we'd all like to have this cleared up as quickly as possible, and Jeffrey has to get back to London shortly."

"I could come down on Friday and bring my mother. Will that do?"

"Perfect."

"I decided to sign that other agreement, too."

Her breath caught. "The TV contract?"

"Right."

A mixture of gladness and trepidation swept over her. "That's...er...nice."

"I hope so."

She ought to hang up, but instead she heard herself say, "How's Delilah?"

There was a short silence. Then Dev laughed. "She's fine—a box of budgies. I've been giving her lots of love and attention to keep her sweet."

Maxine closed her eyes and saw quite clearly Dev squatting by Delilah, stroking her pale belly with the hand she'd once nearly bitten off. "I'm sure she appreciates it," she said stiffly. "I'll get that fax through to you as soon as my secretary has it typed up."

I am *not,* she assured herself as she put down the phone, jealous of a crocodile!

HE PHONED BACK LATER in the day. "We need longer to replace our existing stock. This time limit you're asking for is too tight."

"You won't lose money," she reminded him. "De-Wilde's is willing to buy out the unsold items."

"We'd lose out on customer goodwill," he argued.

"They'll be disappointed if they can't buy their souvenirs before they leave the park."

"I'll talk to Jeffrey," she promised, thankful that Ryder had indicated he was happy to let Jeffrey deal with any further negotiations. "What time will you be in Sydney?"

"Bit of a snag," Dev told her. "I'll be tied up here until late in the afternoon. We'll be arriving after office hours."

"I'm sure we can arrange something," Maxine offered, "if you tell me what time your plane lands." It wouldn't be the first time she had worked after hours.

Jeffrey suggested he send a car to the airport to pick up the Cutters on Friday night and bring them to his hotel. "We'll conduct our business in my suite," he said.

MAXINE ARRIVED EARLY, but when she entered the revolving door into the carpeted lobby, Jeffrey rose from a deep sofa where he'd been leafing through a copy of a business magazine and greeted her, casting an impersonal but approving eye over her white silk blouse and slim dark red skirt.

"Sit down, Maxine," he invited. "I thought we might have a drink with our guests in the lounge before we go upstairs."

She did as instructed and deposited her briefcase by her feet.

"I'll be leaving Australia in a few days, but I've contacted Nick Santos. I gave him your name, Maxine, and would take it as a personal favor if you showed him every cooperation. As you've been dealing with the Cutter affair, he may want to ask you some questions."

"Is he coming over to see the Cutters?"

"Probably, although not yet. He has a strong lead in Quebec and wants to pursue that line first."

Maxine looked at him dubiously. "Will he be undercover?"

Jeffrey smiled. "Nick is rather distinctive, particularly outside his native America. I'm sure the Cutters would easily identify him from any description Grace might have given them." His gaze strayed to the door, and his expression changed as he got to his feet. "Speaking of whom..." he said with mild surprise.

Maggie entered the lobby, dressed in a smart, short-sleeved sky blue linen dress, closely followed by Grace, in a pair of creaseless silk-look trousers in palest apricot, teamed with a soft matching jacket and a deeper apricot shirt. She looked, as usual, cool and elegant and subtly expensive, but as Jeffrey headed toward them and Grace's eyes found his, she appeared a little embarrassed.

"Dev and Maggie insisted on my sharing the car," she explained, "since we were traveling together and I'd booked in here. It seemed silly not to—"

"Of course," Jeffrey said. "I wouldn't have had it any other way."

"I should have thought to ask Ryder when I told him I'd be coming to the wedding to recommend another hotel." Grace smiled rather bleakly. "But as this is the only one I know in Sydney..."

Jeffrey's mouth took on a wry twist. "Habit...they say it dies hard. I have the same problem."

Maggie explained that Dev was seeing to the bags, and he came in a few minutes later with a porter pushing a luggage carrier. It didn't take a genius to figure that the two overnight bags in Dev's hands were his and his mother's, while the expensive designer suitcase and matching overnighter on the trolley alongside a Styrofoam container belonged to Grace.

Dev's eyes went unerringly to Maxine, kindling into

familiar blue fire as he took in the demure blouse and skirt and examined her right down to her neatly crossed ankles and dark red pumps. Maxine felt suddenly breathless. She stood up, unable to tear her gaze away. His shirt was a paler blue than his mother's dress, making his eyes seem even more vivid by contrast, and he wore a green patterned tie and a pair of dun-colored cotton slacks with it. The man had no color coordination and no dress sense. And he looked more irresistible every time she saw him.

"You're staying here, too?" Jeffrey asked the Cutters.

"It seemed sensible. The TV company booked me in," Dev said. "They can get a discount in return for a credit at the end of the show."

"I thought we'd have a drink in the lobby bar first. Why don't you just check in and have your bags taken up? Grace—perhaps you'd join us?"

"How polite of you, Jeffrey. But you people have business to discuss." Grace made to turn away, until Jeffrey reached out and grasped her arm.

"This is not part of the business discussion," he said. "Please…"

Grace blinked up at him as though searching for a motive. Then she gave a tiny shrug. "If you insist."

After they had checked in and Grace and Maggie had freshened up in the ground floor ladies' room, Jeffrey had little trouble finding a table in the crowded bar, and a waiter appeared instantly at the merest lift of his eyebrow.

Jeffrey ordered a sandwich from the bar menu as well as a drink. "Does anyone else want something to eat?" he asked them all.

Maxine and Grace shook their heads, but Maggie asked for a salad, and Dev opted for a basket of potato wedges with sour cream and spices.

Jeffrey studied Grace as their drinks were put before

them. "You've had a restful few days? You look more…relaxed."

"I feel that way. Maggie's been a wonderful hostess."

"You were an easy guest," Maggie replied.

Dev's hand touched Maxine's where it rested on the arm of her chair. "What's he up to?" he muttered as the others talked on.

"Up to? He's just being a good host."

"This is supposed to be a business meeting. Why does he feel it's necessary to soften us up beforehand?"

"You're paranoid," Maxine told him. "There doesn't need to be a reason for having a friendly drink or two before we get down to talking contracts. Don't you want to unwind after your flight?"

Dev grunted. "I'll unwind when this agreement is finalized." The glass of beer he had ordered sat untouched on the table before him. He looked at her consideringly. "Would you care to unwind with me?"

"That depends," Maxine said carefully, "on what you had in mind."

He grinned. "We could work up to that."

"When the agreement's signed—" She recalled last time she had said something like that, and met his eyes apprehensively. "It's not a condition," she added hastily.

Dev nodded. "I guess I misunderstood."

"Yes. You did!"

"My mother's always telling me to think before I go off the deep end." He regarded her with curiosity. "You've got an impressive vocabulary, city lady. You learn those words at law school?"

Maxine blushed. "I shouldn't have lost my temper."

"Makes us quits, I reckon."

She had to laugh a little. "I guess it does." She sipped at her white wine. "You're doing a show tomorrow?"

"Yep. Gonna watch?"

"I don't watch TV much on Saturdays. What animal do you have with you this time?"

"A carpet snake. The hotel management won't let me have it in my room, even though it's completely harmless, but they've found a nice warm place for him. I'll check on him later."

The snacks were served, and Maxine declined a share of Dev's potato wedges. "How do you come to like snakes so much?" she asked him when he'd almost cleaned the plate.

"I have an eye for beauty." He leaned back and let his teasing gaze slip over her.

"Are you comparing me to a reptile?"

He laughed at her. "Don't you think they're beautiful?"

"Well...yes," Maxine admitted. "In a rather scary way."

"I rest my case."

She looked at him in indignation that dissolved in laughter. "You're not scared of me!"

"I've always been intimidated by lawyers."

"What?" she said scornfully. "The man who wrestles crocodiles?"

"The only reason I have to 'wrestle' them, if you want to call it that, is that I prefer it to using tranquilizers—it's less dangerous."

"*Less* dangerous?"

"For the animal. Reptiles have a very delicate metabolism. Crocs have died from being tranquilized. So I work without drugs and that means sometimes I have to dive into the water and grab them, or use my body weight to stop them thrashing around on land. They don't have a lot of stamina, and exertion and stress build up lactic acid in their blood. It's bad for them.''

"You must like the adrenaline rush or you'd find yourself an office job.''

"I do have an office,'' he pointed out.

"How much time do you spend in it?'' she challenged him. Not much when she'd been at the park.

"As little as possible.'' He grinned at her. "You're right. I like the great outdoors. Being shut up in a room all day would make me claustrophobic.''

Grace put down her liqueur glass. "Thank you for the drink, Jeffrey. I think I'll go up to my room now. I have an early flight.''

"You're leaving tomorrow?'' Jeffrey stood up as she moved, pulling back her chair for her.

"I have a business to run in San Francisco.''

"You haven't eaten—you should have something.''

"I'll get room service to send something up later.'' She leaned over and kissed Maggie's cheek. "Thank you for a wonderfully restful break. And you, Dev. Maxine—I'm so glad to have met you.''

"I'll see you to the elevator.'' Jeffrey placed a light hand under her elbow, ignoring her murmur that there was no need.

"They seem so suited to each other,'' Maggie said, looking after them. "Such a pity...''

WHEN JEFFREY RETURNED they had finished their drinks, and as no one wanted another, they all rode the elevator up to his floor and he let them into his suite.

Dev and Jeffrey looked over the agreement, and after a couple of minor adjustments both seemed satisfied. Relieved, Maxine made the necessary alterations to the document and got them all to sign three copies of it.

Jeffrey produced a bottle of champagne, which he'd apparently had delivered in anticipation, and poured them all a glass. "It's still early," he said. "Have you eaten? I could have room service send us up a proper meal. Or we could dine in the hotel restaurant."

"I don't need any more to eat, thank you," Maggie said.

Dev added, "Thanks for the offer. As a matter of fact, I was hoping that Maxine might let me take her out for a meal."

Maggie smiled, not noticeably surprised.

"Really?" Jeffrey bent a smiling glance of his own on Maxine. "What a good idea. Why don't you two go out on the town while Maggie and I finish up the champagne?" He picked up the bottle to refresh their drinks.

Maggie shook her head and laughed, draining what was left in her glass. "That's enough for me," she declared, and got to her feet. "I'm planning to go shopping tomorrow—make the most of my trip to the big smoke. I think I'll have an early night."

Dev said softly, "Maxine?"

There couldn't be any harm in having a meal with him. Besides, Jeffrey wanted her to go, though she knew he wouldn't press her to betray any confidence Dev might give her. And if it turned out that the Cutters were some kind of connection of the DeWildes, surely that could only be advantageous for them? "Yes, all right," she said quickly. "Thank you."

"Right," he said, jumping to his feet as if afraid she might change her mind. "We're off, then. Thanks, Jeffrey." He held out his hand and clasped the older man's. "Will you be okay?" he asked his mother. "Want me to come along and settle you into your room?"

"I think I can find my way without you holding my hand, son. I'm not doddery yet."

Jeffrey saw them all out, and they left him still holding the champagne as he closed the door. Maxine felt a flash of compassion as Dev steered her and Maggie toward the elevators. Despite his wealth and power, for a moment Jeffrey DeWilde had seemed a lonely figure. She didn't suppose he'd lift the phone and ask Grace to help him finish the bottle. And yet she had the feeling that one part of him would probably have liked to do just that.

Maggie got out two floors down with a cheerful wave. Maxine and Dev rode down to the lobby, and he took the briefcase from her. "Why don't we leave this with the concierge and you can pick it up later?"

Shortly they were walking down the street under the bright lights, his hand at her waist, heading for a nearby restaurant that the concierge had recommended as small and quiet, with friendly staff and good food.

They had to wait a little while for a table, but were soon settled into a semicircular booth that gave an illusion of privacy.

"This is nice." Maxine looked round at the understated red-and-black decor, the indirect lighting subdued enough to be restful but not so dim they couldn't read the menus the waiter had handed them.

"Yeah," Dev said, following her gaze. "Very tasteful."

"You say that as though it's not a compliment."

"Did I?" He shook his head. "No, you're right. It might be kind of anonymous and typical, but it's nice. Especially with you sitting there." He smiled at her. "I didn't think you'd come."

"You sort of put me on a spot," she reminded him.

"How? You could have said no."

The truth was, she hadn't wanted to say no. "I was hungry," she told him, making him laugh.

They laughed a lot during the next hour or two. It took that long to decide the choice of food and have three cups of coffee after they'd eaten, and squabble about who was going to pay for Maxine's share of the meal. They'd had quite a lot of wine—a bottle of white and half of a red. Maybe that, on top of the champagne, was why she felt so light-headed—in fact light all over—when they finally left the restaurant and returned to the busy, noisy street.

A car honked for some reason as it passed, and a crowd of young people swept by them with scant regard for other pedestrians. Dev pulled Maxine to his side out of their way and tucked his arm about her, keeping her close as they strolled back toward the hotel. "You like living in the city?" he asked, as if he couldn't believe anyone in their right mind could feel that way.

"I love it. It's alive! There's an energy, a vitality about it. There's so much happening, and people are going places."

He looked down at her. "Where are you going? Or have you already got there?"

"There's always another rung to climb up the ladder. I'm not sure yet just how far I want to go."

"You must be pretty high-powered to be working for DeWilde's."

"That was partly luck—in the form of Ryder Blake."

"He's a friend of yours?" Dev's eyes sharpened.

"We are friends now. But if you mean, did DeWilde's retain me as their lawyer because we were already friends, no. We met at a charity dinner when he was trying to get his new store off the ground."

"*His* store?"

"The Sydney store was Ryder's baby from the start.

He'd have liked to have established it on his own, and that's what he was trying to do when we met. He was so enthusiastic about the idea he fired me up, and I started giving him some free advice about the problems he was having securing the lease.'' Maxine laughed. "At the end of the dinner he said he'd like to hire me as his lawyer. Before we went home he took me round to this derelict old building so I could see what it was all about. The time was around midnight.''

"And then he took you home?'' Dev frowned.

"Yes.'' She looked into his eyes. "And left me at the door.''

"So he loves you for your legal briefs?''

"Don't be rude,'' she admonished him. "We like each other. And I like Natasha, too. When Ryder and I first teamed up, my partners weren't all that impressed with my new client, but they didn't know then about Ryder's connection with the DeWildes. When the corporation decided to pick up the lease and Ryder agreed to work for them, the store became part of the DeWilde empire, but he told London I was part of the deal.''

"And DeWilde's bought it?''

"Jeffrey trusts Ryder's judgment. He was satisfied.''

"I'll bet that impressed your partners.''

"Sure did.'' Maxine couldn't help a smile of sheer pride.

"Ryder Blake's a pretty good-looking bloke. And successful.''

"And married.''

"Not when you met him. He wouldn't be normal if he hadn't made a pass at you.''

"I'm sure Ryder's perfectly normal. But both of us value our professional relationship too much to put it at risk.''

Dev stopped and looked at her for a long moment. "Sounds as though you were made for each other."

"You think I'm a cold-blooded bitch." The thought crossed her mind that he was rather fond of cold-blooded creatures. Perhaps he could even grow fond of her.

"Uh-uh. I have reason to know you're not." For a moment his eyes lingered on her mouth before he started walking again. They were nearing his hotel. "I think you're a pretty single-minded lady."

"That's how you get ahead in this world. You must know that. It can't have been easy setting up your park."

"No, but I had my family on my side. Your people must be pretty proud of you."

"They don't—"

"Don't what?"

They don't understand, she'd been about to say. But that was a pathetic, whining sort of remark, and she swallowed it. "They don't live in Sydney. I haven't seen much of them since I moved here."

"You must miss them."

"Sometimes. Do you...do you have any brothers or sisters?" She'd gained the impression he was an only child, although she didn't recall anyone saying so.

"Nope," he confirmed. "But lots of cousins. The Cutter clan is a pretty big one, and then there are the Thompsons up north. I had holidays there sometimes when I was a kid."

"That's your mother's family."

"There's quite a few of them, too. Granddad was one of seven brothers. When they were teenagers I gather they were the terror of the entire district before they went off to the war. Mind you—" his voice dropped and sobered "—a couple of them never came back."

A bellman standing outside the hotel pushed the door

for them and they passed into the lobby. "I'll collect your briefcase," Dev said. "Unless you'd like to stay awhile?"

Maxine shook her head. "Thanks for the meal. And I'm glad we resolved the name thing without going to court."

"Do you have a car?"

"I own one, but I don't have it tonight. Around the city I usually use public transport."

He held the briefcase while the bellman got her a taxi. Then he opened the cab door for her and held it as she got in. "I'll be in Sydney until late tomorrow," he said. "Can we get together?"

Warning bells rang, but they were faint and faraway. She pulled a card from her purse and scribbled her home number on it. "Won't your mother want you with her?"

"I'd cramp her style in the shops. She hated living in the city, but visiting it is a different story. When she comes here she likes to make a day of it."

"Phone me after the show."

He pocketed the card. "Will you be watching?"

"Probably." She knew she'd be unable to resist. "I'd like to see this carpet snake."

He laughed, handed her briefcase over and shut the door, stepping back as the vehicle left the curb.

He hadn't even attempted to kiss her, and yet she felt warm and tingly all over, and deliciously, thrillingly alive.

CHAPTER ELEVEN

OF COURSE MAXINE WATCHED the show on Saturday morning. She could see why the producer had been so keen to sign Dev on again. After the anaemic-looking film critic and the reverential wine buff and the guest of the week—a bearded artist whose chief claim to notoriety was his use of cut-up nude photographs of men and women jumbled into random patterns that "symbolized a syncretism of the amorphous, overlapping and ambiguous nature of human sexuality"—Dev Cutter's rugged, tanned features, haphazard hairstyle and casual idiom were like a breath of clean, bracing outback air.

His clothes, of course, were still ludicrously in character but nothing could detract from the enthusiastic brilliance of his blue eyes.

He gently coiled the young snake into the crown of his Akubra hat, and pointed out for the camera the symmetry of its pattern. "This species preys on mice and rabbits," he told the audience. "They can grow pretty big, but they help get rid of pests and they're not venomous at all. You should never kill a carpet snake. Isn't he a beauty?"

The sound of that deep, smoky voice with its note of loving admiration sent warm shivers down Maxine's spine.

The camera panned up to Dev's face and his tender, absorbed expression, and Maxine's hands clasped tightly together in her lap. When he looked like that he really was gorgeous. A lovely man.

So when the phone rang immediately the show was over, she picked it up on the second ring and said with a breathless welcome in her voice, "Dev?"

"You were watching," he said.

"I was—I enjoyed it. You seem very…natural. Relaxed. And you're right. The snake is beautiful."

"I'll introduce you, if you let me come over to see you."

Maxine laughed. "All right. I'll look forward to meeting him."

"I was banking on that. Twenty minutes."

"TWENTY-ONE," SHE SAID, opening the door to him.

"You counted. Should I be flattered?"

"I'm obsessive," she told him. "So my friends tell me. Never late for anything." Grace DeWilde, she recalled, had called Jeffrey obsessive about his family's jewelry collection. She banished a faint, uneasy and quite unreasonable sense of guilt at the thought of Jeffrey and his oblique request to her. "You've changed."

"Since last night?" He looked at her quizzically.

"I mean, you've changed your clothes since you did the program." He was wearing a quite nice linen-look shirt with the sleeves rolled to the elbow, and light oatmeal trousers with tan leather moccasins.

"Are they okay?" he asked with a hint of anxiety. "My mother chose them."

"They're fine," she said. He looked stunning, in fact. "On the show…"

"Image," Dev explained. "They insisted. It was Binnie and Rooster's idea in the first place."

Maxine laughed. It would be, of course. "Do you *ever* actually wear…um…"

"That sort of clobber? Sure—when I'm up at Cape York or the Territory, camping out with a research team or chasing through rain forest and mangrove swamps one jump ahead of the hunters."

He came into her living room and swung a nylon bag down from his shoulder, placing it carefully on the barely off-white carpet before looking about him. She saw that the bag was open, and a light Styrofoam container nestled on top of his clothes.

Dev exclaimed softly, "Stone the crows!"

The apartment was full of glass and slender metal frames, glossy black leather upholstery and avant-garde pictures. A few elegant ceramics shared a wall of shelves with orderly rows of books, CDs and videotapes. It was boldly contemporary, exceedingly chic, and Maxine was very, very proud of it.

"You don't like it?"

"Looks like something out of my mum's *House and Garden* magazines. I'd be scared to sit down in this place."

"The chairs are quite comfortable," Maxine said crisply, against a childish sense of disappointment.

He looked at her quickly. "Don't get me wrong," he said. "It's, uh…pretty stylish. Fantastic. I just meant—um—they look a bit fragile." He perched on the edge of one of the black leather chairs, an abbreviated hammock shape slung on curved metal strips not more than two fingers in width.

"Relax," Maxine advised him. "It won't break."

He eased himself back, and a look of surprise came over his face. "You're right, it's pretty comfy." He shifted his shoulders and stretched out his legs. The chair rocked slightly on the strong but flexible metal supports. "Just one thing wrong."

"Wrong?"

He tucked his hands behind his head and grinned up at her. "It's only big enough for one."

"That's big enough," she told him. "Can I get you a drink or something?"

"In a minute." He dropped his hands. "Do you want to say hello to the carpet snake, or was that just a ploy to get me here?"

"Dream on. Is he in there?" She looked down at the bag.

"Yeah." He leaned forward to open the container and remove the snake from the linen bag resting on a bed of moss. He lifted it gently and it curled around his arm. Maxine dropped to her knees on the carpet and touched the snake, tracing the dark and light brown patterns along its length.

"He's not full grown, is he?"

"Not half. He's just a tiddler." Dev unwound the snake deftly and dropped it into the bag head first, then laid it back in the container.

Maxine sat back on her heels. "He'll be comfortable there?"

"He was fed just before we left. He's pretty contented just now."

Dev replaced the lid on the box, and as he straightened his hand circled Maxine's wrist.

She remained passive in his grasp, both wary and expectant. When he looked at her, she met his questioning gaze with a straight stare, and he gave her wrist a tug, at the same time leaning back in the chair.

She found herself coming up onto her knees, then he

tugged again and she tumbled into his lap, her legs hanging over the side of the chair.

"Ah!" Dev sounded deeply contented, wrapping his arms about her as her head lay against his shoulder. "It is big enough for two after all."

"I told you it was strong. Is this to prove a point?"

She felt him laugh, his chest moving under her breasts. "Yeah—the point is that you and I have got something going here, dragon lady."

"Dragon lady?" She raised her head and regarded him with indignant suspicion.

He gave her a slow smile. "I like dragons—beautiful, mysterious creatures, strong and fierce and brave—"

"Brave?"

"Yeah, brave. Have to be to stand up to those clanking knights in armor with their swords and lances and magic cloaks and stuff."

"Okay." Maxine nodded. "Brave."

"And gallant, and protective."

"Hey, that's the knights!"

"Nah." Dev shook his head. "The dragons stood at the mouths of the caves, remember, protecting them."

"The caves?"

"Well...maybe protecting what was in the caves."

"I see. And you know what that was, I suppose."

"Probably the little dragons, all huddled down there in the darkest corner they could find, scared out of their tiny dragon minds."

"Uh-huh. And what about the poor princess tied up outside the cave? The one the knight was supposed to rescue from the dragon?"

"Just part of the food chain."

"The..." Maxine stifled a choke of laughter. "The food chain?"

"A dragon's got to eat," Dev explained patiently. "And feed the little dragons. Of course, the princess wouldn't understand that, any more than the mice and rabbits our friend down there gobbles up understand that he has a right to eat, too. Unfortunately death is a side effect of the cycle of life. And a nice tasty princess who happens to wander through the forest is—to a dragon—just a snack."

"When your mother read you fairy stories, did you prefer the dragons to the princesses?"

"Still do. Princesses always seemed a bit boring to me. Most of the time they sat around moping in towers waiting to be rescued and married—when they weren't acting as bait. Dragons are much more exciting. Only I didn't know then—" he raised his hands and tipped her head until his lips were only inches away from hers "—that one day I'd meet a dragon lady with a sweet mouth that would set me on fire."

It must have been his eyes that had ignited, she thought hazily, because they blazed so fiercely that she had to close hers, and then his lips moved softly down her cheek to find her mouth, and she thought, No, it was his mouth...or mine...or both.

And then she stopped thinking at all as he kissed her deeply, fully, and his hands cupped her breasts and shaped her waist and pushed up her skirt to find the smooth skin of her thighs underneath.

Her palms flattened against his chest as she became conscious that they were going rather fast and that she, for one, hadn't planned for this to happen.

He withdrew his hand and muttered, "Don't go away." Holding her around the waist, he lifted his head to look at her. "Sorry, was I taking too much for granted?"

Slowly, Maxine shook her head. "I guess you were

entitled to think...I mean, I wasn't exactly fighting you off.'' Her breasts tingled from his touch and felt heavy and full. She could still taste him in her mouth. She wanted him to touch her again.

All her life she'd known that delayed gratification was the answer to her yearnings, the only way to ensure that she got what she really wanted. And she wasn't about to throw away her hard-won discipline, her long-held principles now. ''Let me up, Dev,'' she said.

Reluctantly, he let his arms slide away and watched her move off him and stand upright. ''Whatever you say goes,'' he assured her. ''I wouldn't force you to do anything you didn't want, Maxine.''

''I know.'' And she did know, she realized with surprise. One of nature's gentlemen, was Dev Cutter. She knew with utter certainty that she could trust him not to bully her, not to coerce her. Whatever she did with this man, it was her choice, her responsibility. And her loss if the consequences were disastrous.

''Have you had lunch?'' she asked him.

''I thought we might go out for it, if you'd like that.''

And he'd want to pay. Anticipating this, she'd gone shopping early, before the TV program started. ''We could eat here,'' she suggested tentatively, wondering if it would be safer to go out, after all. ''I can fix something.''

''You cook?'' His grin came and went.

''Of course I cook.'' No need to tell him she hadn't actually cooked what she was offering now, she advised her overactive conscience.

He eyed her slender figure dubiously. ''Two slices of tomato and a sliver of ham rolled round an asparagus spear, garnished with a single spring onion—that sort of thing?''

"Certainly not!" She could imagine what he'd think of fashion-statement cuisine. "I have a whole roast chicken and a potato salad in the fridge, and I can make a green salad in five minutes."

"You're on," he said, and stood up. "Can I help?"

"Do you know your way around a kitchen?"

"As a matter of fact, I make a mean salad myself. Should I have brought a bottle of wine along?"

"There's one in the fridge," she told him. "My kitchen's so tiny I don't think there's room for two—"

"Like that chair?" His eyes dancing, he assumed a calculating look. "We could—"

"No, we couldn't!" Maxine said crushingly. "I'll give you the cutlery and plates and you can set the table and pour the wine."

He did it quite well, and she placed a generous quarter of chicken on his plate, a rather smaller portion on hers, and handed him the bowls of green and potato salads to put on the table, then a basket of crusty French bread.

She asked after Archie, and Marmaduke the emu, and—wryly—about Delilah. And they discussed names for the two little tree pythons.

"Flora and Fauna," Maxine suggested.

"Done to death."

"Monty and...?"

"We've got a Monty Python already."

"I might have known. You think of something."

"How about Buttercup and Dandelion?"

"You said they won't stay yellow," Maxine objected.

"Okay. Grasse and Greene. Both of them with an *e*."

Maxine moaned. They went on tossing suggestions back and forth and decrying or considering each other's choices, and couldn't agree on any.

Dev told a joke he'd heard from Rooster, and Maxine

made him laugh with a story about her expedition to buy vegetables that morning, when a garrulous elderly lady standing next to her had inspected everything in Maxine's basket and told her exactly how bad her choices were. ''She even squeezed my tomatoes and told me they weren't firm enough for a good salad! And then she reached over and got some others out of the bin and swapped them!''

''And was she right?'' Dev laughed at her indignation.

''I don't know! The point was, she was so...so...''

''Cheeky.''

''That's an understatement.''

''But you didn't tell her to beggar off and mind her own business?''

''How could I? She was *old!*''

He grinned at her, shaking his head.

''I had a horrible feeling someone was going to jump out from behind the cabbages and shout, 'Smile, you're on *Candid Camera.*' ''

It was all light and fun, skating over the surface of the tension that shimmered between them, a tension that manifested itself in the way their eyes locked now and then in tiny, fraught silences; in Maxine's hasty withdrawal of her fingers from the bowl of potato salad when she handed it over to him for a second helping, so that he almost dropped it; in Dev's overcasual pose when he leaned back in his chair and pushed away his plate.

''I'll get coffee.'' Maxine stood up. ''Or tea?''

''Neither, thanks.'' Dev swirled the remains of wine in his glass. ''I'm okay with this. Don't let me stop you if you want one, though.''

''I won't bother. Is there any more of that?''

''Sure. Sorry.'' He emptied the bottle into her glass, but instead of sitting down to drink it, she took the glass and wandered to the window overlooking the street. The apartment was on the second floor of a recently built block. In the narrow space between the building and the high wall separating it from the street was a row of young trees, but they weren't very tall and she could see over them.

Cars passed in a steady stream, and on the other side of the road a row of shops attracted customers who hurried in and out of the doors like ants to their nest.

Dev got up and came to stand behind her, his arm sliding loosely about her waist. She fought the temptation to lean back against him, and allowed herself to lose.

His chin nuzzled her hair. "Pretty busy street," he commented. "How do you sleep?"

"The windows are double-glazed. And there's always something to look at down there—something going on."

"They're just people."

"Interesting people. See that man wearing the dark suit and red tie? He's a film director—he lives in the neighborhood. And that blond woman carrying the wine bag and baguettes? She's an artist, quite well known. Exhibits regularly at a gallery in George Street. The man with the ponytail and the wispy beard—I'm sure I've seen him somewhere. And that couple coming out of the café now—they look so…"

"Trendy," Dev said in her ear.

Maxine moved her shoulder a little irritably. "So what? I bet they both have exciting jobs."

"And live in a place like this?" He must have felt her stiffen. His arm tightened about her. "Okay, there's nothing wrong with trendy. Or exciting. I'm probably jealous."

Maxine couldn't help a small giggle. "Of their exciting jobs?"

"Sure. I bet they haven't waded through any rain forests and mangrove swamps lately, getting attacked by leeches and giant mosquitoes and sandflies. They probably go to work in a Porsche—two Porsches, his and hers—not a four-wheel drive. And they have drinkies every Friday night in some posh city watering hole."

"Not the pub at Goanna Gap, that's for sure," Maxine agreed dryly. "They'd get run out of town."

"No, they wouldn't. You got the bum's rush because the locals thought they were sticking up for me and my mum." Dev turned her to face him, his expression grave. "They didn't scare you, did they?"

"That lot? Not likely."

"That's my girl." He smiled and lifted his nearly empty glass to her, waiting.

When she touched her delicate crystal goblet to the one he held, he said more seriously, "Will you be?"

"Be what?" Uncertainly, she met the grave question in his eyes.

"My girl. My dragon lady."

And he would be her wild man. Maxine looked away, thinking. Or at least trying to think, against the tide of longing that seemed about to sweep her away. She'd only known this man a week. It wasn't like her to be so overwhelmed, so unsure of her ground. "It's a bit soon," she said, "to be making promises."

He grimaced. "I guess. Will you see me next week, anyway, when I'm back in town?"

"Saturday afternoon?"

There was the tiniest pause. "Yeah. Saturday afternoon. I can take a late flight home."

It wasn't too late to change her mind and refuse to see him again. That was what she should do, if she was sensible. But maybe she was tired of being sensible, circumspect—and lonely. "All right." Maxine lifted her glass to her lips and recklessly drained it. She detected a distinct odor of burning bridges in the air.

CHAPTER TWELVE

DEV PHONED HER EVERY night. The calls weren't long enough, but she had videotaped the show on Saturday and played the tape over and over until she knew every nuance of his beautiful voice, every faint quirk of his mouth, even the shape of his hands. She was acting like a besotted teenager, and she didn't care.

For the first time in years she was consumed by something other than her work. It felt remarkably good.

Time out, she told herself. Everyone needed it sometime, and this was hers. For once in her life she wasn't thinking of the long-term future, but simply savoring the moment.

The following Saturday he brought along a pale green, spiny-backed lizard. "It's a genuine dragon," he told her.

"I know, a forest dragon," she said, touching the scaly skin with one finger as he held the creature. It was hardly longer than his forearm. "I watched the show. 'Gentle and completely harmless,'" she quoted him. "He's beautiful."

"She."

"She?" Maxine looked up at him.

"Both of you." Dev smiled at her. "And both beautiful."

Watching the little dragon explore the apartment, Maxine was enchanted. Dev suggested they put it back in its container while they went out to lunch, and she said indignantly that he was cruel and heartless to propose leaving the poor thing locked up and alone. She made them lunch instead.

Dev didn't have much time to spare. Maxine drove him and his green dragon to the airport and saw them off, feeling dissatisfied and frustrated.

ON THURSDAY WHEN HE phoned, he told her, "I could come down tomorrow, get there in the evening and stay at a hotel overnight."

"You could?"

"Are you busy?"

"Friday evening? No. I could meet you if you like," she offered. "Pick you up from the airport."

SHE WAS EARLY, arriving before the plane came in, anxiously scanning the lists of incoming flights.

Minutes later she watched him come toward her, an overnight bag swinging from one hand.

She stood and waited for him, her hands worrying the strap of the tan leather bag over the shoulder of the short-sleeved mint green jacket she wore with a paler green, fitted sleeveless dress and tan shoes.

He stopped in front of her, and then reached out to grasp a handful of the thick hair she had left loose in his honor. And just stood looking at her as if he didn't really believe she was there.

Maxine nervously moistened her lips and gave him a tentative smile. "Hi."

Dev smiled back. "Hi." And he bent forward to brush his lips lightly against hers. "Thanks for meeting me." He relinquished his hold on her hair and hooked an arm about her waist.

"No animals?" she queried.

"I'm borrowing a platypus from a local wildlife park. I might do that again instead of bringing animals from Queensland. Some of them don't travel well. We'd be able to provide more variety and give the local park a bit of a plug. They don't mind free publicity."

"Do they mind that the TV channel is using you and not them?"

"They probably do, a bit. But we help each other out all the time. One day they'll be on the receiving end of a favor."

"Do you want to go to your hotel first?"

"Not necessarily. Have you eaten? How about a meal first?"

She took him to a Middle Eastern restaurant, where they ate exotic food sitting on huge cushions at a low table. The lights were dim and the music mysterious, and the smell of incense and Turkish cigarettes mingled with spicy aromas wafting from the kitchen.

Afterward Maxine drove to a vantage point for a view of the city lights, the landmark Harbour Bridge, and the ghostly sails of the Opera House rising above the shimmering multicolored reflections in the darkened water.

"Don't you think this is beautiful?" she asked him.

"Sure, it's beautiful. From a distance." Dev reached for her hand, taking it from the steering wheel and holding it lightly, his thumb massaging her wrist. "I like the nearer view a whole lot better, though."

She wrinkled her nose at him in the shadowed light of a nearby street lamp. "Pure corn, Cutter. Can't you do better than that?"

"I can try." He tugged at her hand and she went willingly into his arms, meeting his kiss with her lips parted and her head against the seat back.

It was a long, lingering, frankly sensual kiss, and when

he eased back into his own seat he was breathing hard and Maxine felt dizzy, the lights of the city swimming before her dazed eyes.

"I'll take you to your hotel," she said finally, and turned on the ignition. Her innate caution revived, telling her this was too soon to get in any deeper.

Dev looked at her sharply as he fastened his seat belt, but all he said was a dry, "Thanks."

She drove him to the door of the hotel. He tipped her face to him and kissed her too briefly, then reached over to the back seat for his bag. "You could come to the show tomorrow if you like. I'll get them to hold a seat for you. Just give your name at the studio door."

"Yes," she said. "I'll be there."

"Good." He kissed her again, taking longer about it, reluctant to leave. A taxicab swept onto the concourse behind them, bathing them in harsh light, and Dev lifted his head and released her. "See you tomorrow."

THE DUCKBILLED PLATYPUS was a hit with the studio audience. And so was Dev.

"But what is it," the show host asked, "a mammal or a bird? Surely not a reptile?"

"They actually belong to a pretty rare group of mammals called monotremes." The animal flapped about and scrabbled with its webbed feet as Dev lifted it, but when he stroked its sleek fur, it quieted.

After the show he returned the platypus to the keeper who had brought it to the studio, talked for a few minutes to a group of youngsters, one of whom asked him for an autograph, and then took Maxine's arm. "Come on, let's get out of here. You're going to show me Sydney."

The day was fine and not too hot, and she took him to Watson's Bay for lunch at Doyle's on the Beach, and

Maxine encouraged Dev to order the dish that had made
the restaurant famous—golden-battered fish fillets served
on a mountain of fried potato chips.

"Try the chili plum sauce," Maxine advised as Dev
poured tartar sauce over one of his fillets.

"Yeah? Is it good?" he asked dubiously, but he tried
it, anyway. One thing about Dev, she reflected, he wasn't
afraid of new experiences.

Maybe she was, though. This was a new experience for
her, falling so heavily for a man who was totally the opposite of her ideal.

Ryder Blake, now. He was more her type—a very at-
tractive man, yet even when she had briefly considered
the possibility that their friendship might become something deeper, Ryder had never made her feel the way she
felt when Dev was around.

Dipping one of her shrimps into the chili plum sauce,
she watched him tuck into the meal and smiled. "I'm
beginning to think you must have gone away hungry last
week."

He looked up. "I did…but not for lack of food."

She'd walked right into that one. Maxine glanced away
from him to the blue, sail-speckled harbor and thought,
I'm hungry, too.

She had been hungry for a long time, she realized. Hungry for love, for understanding, for real closeness with
someone—someone who mattered, and who would feel
she mattered to him.

How had she not known about this emptiness at the
center of her life? She had everything she'd wanted—a
great job, enough money, a car that she didn't owe too
much on, the kind of home she'd always dreamed of,
friends she could call on for support and a sympathetic
ear when things went wrong at work, or for company

when she felt like taking in a show or having a small party. At Easter and Christmas she visited her family; last year one of her sisters had come to Sydney with her husband, and Maxine had shown them the town. She lacked for nothing.

Why did it suddenly all seem less than satisfactory— *not enough?*

"What are you thinking about?" Dev asked, shoving away his plate at last and evidently gauging something from her pensive expression. "How bad can it be?"

"It's not bad." She smiled absently at him. "I was thinking…that I've got everything I ever wanted."

"You're lucky."

"What about you? Are you happy, Dev?"

"Right now," he said, smiling at her in a way that made her heart turn over, "extremely." He leaned forward and took one of her hands in his. "So, if you've got everything you've ever wanted, what's the big worry?"

"Maybe we should…think about things."

"Things? You and me?"

Maxine nodded. "We're very different. We…don't want the same things from life."

"We both want to be happy, don't we?"

"That's the point—we're happy now—we like our lives the way they are."

"Sure we do. And I'd like mine even better if I knew I'd see you every time I came down to Sydney. Do you have a problem with that?"

"Not…right now." Except that there was no future in it. But then, he hadn't said anything about permanence. He knew as well as she that this—whatever they had between them—couldn't last, that their life-styles and their aspirations were poles apart. She was being unnecessarily scrupulous. Surely with his adventurous life-style, chasing after wild animals in the far north, he didn't want to be tied down? His remark about seeing her when he came to Sydney might have been meant to warn her not to take him too seriously, that all he was asking for was a convenient affair.

Maxine's life plan had left her scant opportunity and even less inclination to be drawn into potentially time-consuming and emotionally messy love affairs. Why shouldn't she indulge herself for a while? She was secure enough in her job to spare a little time for looking after her emotional life, surely?

She was an adult, she could handle it. Many women in her situation would have said she'd hit on the ideal set-up. During the week she'd be free to pursue her career without being trammeled by the demands of a man who expected her to spend time with him, and every weekend a handsome hunk would bring a day or two of love and laughter into her life.

"There's not much sense," Dev said, "in trying to anticipate problems that may never happen."

"Is that your philosophy?"

"Part of it."

It could be a good one. Every step of her life so far had been meticulously planned; she'd worked toward her goals and achieved them. How would it be to embark on uncharted seas for once, the destination unknown and the path unseen? "I don't have much sense of adventure," she confessed.

He might not have known exactly what she meant, but his reply was instant. "I've probably got enough for us both."

They finished lunch but stayed at the table, talking, and then strolled for a while along the beach hand in hand.

And all too soon it was time to get Dev to the airport for his flight back to Queensland.

He kissed her goodbye and she found her lips lingering wistfully, needing more of him, not wanting to let him go.

"Next week," he said huskily, his eyes dark and demanding as he reluctantly eased his hold on her. "If I can, I'll try to wangle an extra day. Friday night to Sunday—how does that sound?"

It sounded great. "Do you think you can?"

"I hardly ever take time off. The park's really getting off the ground now, and we can afford more staff. We just took on extra weekend workers. Yeah, I think I can. Rooster and Binnie are already on at me about having a girlfriend in Sydney, of course."

Would they guess it was her? "I thought your girlfriend was Delilah."

"Hah. Binnie's little joke."

"Well, you seem...fond of her."

"Like I told Jeffrey, I don't take her to bed."

He hadn't taken Maxine to bed, either—yet. She couldn't help coloring as she met the tender teasing in his eyes.

THE WEEK DRAGGED. Maxine tried hard to keep her mind on her work, unable to blot out everything else as she always had before. She stayed by the phone every night waiting for his call. And he did call, to tell her about his day and ask about hers, and describe Rooster's latest scheme for publicizing the park and Binnie's transparent efforts to get him to let slip who he was seeing in Sydney.

He told her there'd been a fire in Goanna Gap and the hairdresser's shop was gutted, but the volunteer fire brigade had saved the adjoining buildings, and the hairdresser was temporarily conducting her business at the library. "Mum says the customers have to get in line to use the only hair dryer they saved, but there's plenty to read while they wait."

"Was the shop insured?"

"Yeah, but since she lived at the back of it, all her belongings are gone, and they weren't. She'd just started in business a year ago, so all her money was tied up in the shop. While the place is being rebuilt, she's moved in with a neighbor, and their garage is already full of clothing and furniture and stuff that people have donated."

The next evening he told her somebody had brought an injured young wallaby to the park; Binnie was hand-feeding it. And the hairdresser who'd lost her shop was having a problem with the insurance company. They didn't seem to want to pay out.

"Why not?"

"Dunno, exactly."

"If you find out," Maxine offered impulsively, "and ask her for a copy of the policy, I may be able to help. There isn't a lawyer in Goanna Gap, is there?"

By the weekend he'd found out what clause in the small print the insurance people were sticking over, and he brought the hairdresser's copy of the policy with him. Maxine read it over lunch and was pretty sure the woman had a good case for compensation and the insurance company was being unreasonable. When they had eaten, she drove to the deserted offices of Bartlett and Finchley, where Dev helped her look up law books late into the night, proving himself a surprisingly good researcher.

On Sunday he went home with a sheaf of notes and photocopies. "No charge, of course," Maxine assured him. It made her angry to think that a woman who had worked hard to build up her own business and lost it through no fault of her own should be victimized this way.

THE BRUNCH SHOW'S HOST had been nominated for an award. The cast was invited to support their colleague at the awards dinner, and Dev asked Maxine to accompany him. "Dress up," he said. "It sounds like the sort of thing you'd enjoy."

When he turned up to escort her, Maxine opened her door, put a hand to her heart and moaned, feigning a swoon.

In evening clothes, with his hair freshly styled by the barber at his hotel, Dev was stunning.

He raised dazed eyes from the gold chiffon dress that hung from narrow shoulder straps and swirled lightly about her body, and grinned at her. "You're pretty gorgeous yourself."

She hoped so. She'd done her best, and spent ages trying different hairstyles before settling on leaving it loose because she knew he liked it that way.

That evening she met several people she'd only seen on TV before. Dev seemed to make a point of introducing her to celebrities. The host didn't win, but no one seemed particularly downhearted about that. The man shrugged off commiserations and Gil, the show's producer, poured more sparkling wine all round. Maxine found herself wishing for the whole thing to be over so she and Dev could be alone.

He'd insisted on a taxi tonight, and Maxine recklessly drank more of the wine on the table than she might have otherwise. On the way to her apartment Dev pulled her into his arms and kissed her, and she responded freely, ardently, her body pliant and eager, her lips yearning, passionate.

He bundled her out of the cab and went with her up the stairs, his arm about her waist. But when they entered the apartment and she turned to him, he switched on the light and took her shoulders gently and held her away from him, regarding her flushed face and bright eyes intently. His mouth curved in a smile. "Ms. Sterling, I do believe you're the slightest bit tiddly."

Maxine smiled at him brilliantly. "Only the slightest," she said. She didn't recall when she'd ever had a little too much to drink. Truth to tell, she didn't believe it was the wine that was affecting her as much as the man who was now looking at her so quizzically, his blue eyes both tender and laughing. She put her hands on his chest. "Dev...?"

He groaned. "Don't look at me like that!" Suddenly he pulled her close, his arms wrapped about her as he kissed her thoroughly, wild and sweet and sizzling. And then he let her go so abruptly she swayed on her feet. He steadied her, nodded a little grimly as though she'd just confirmed his suspicion that she was less than sober, and flung open the door, hurling at her a hoarse, "Good night, Maxine."

And then he was gone, leaving her staring at the closed door while his footfalls receded down the stairs.

"I WASN'T DRUNK," was the first thing she said to him when he turned up the next day. "I never get drunk!"

"I know you weren't." His voice was low, soothing— and full of laughter. "So shall we skip the sculpture exhibition and the jazz concert and just go to bed together, instead?"

Maxine glared, wanting to throw something at him, but her chairs had no cushions, and there wasn't a weapon handy that wouldn't do any damage. "I'm taking you to the exhibition," she said loftily. "The gallery owner is a client, and as I wasn't able to make the opening last night, the least I can do is show some interest this morning. And the concert will do you good—instill a bit of culture into you."

Dev laughed, unoffended. "Is it part of your job to support your clients after hours?"

"It doesn't hurt to go that extra mile. Besides, you never know what new contacts you might make at a function like that."

She didn't find any useful new contacts but did run into some friends, who eyed Dev with interest and invited him and Maxine to join them for lunch at a nearby restaurant. Maxine mentioned the concert in the Opera House forecourt, and in the end they all went, opting for a picnic lunch while they listened. It was a pleasantly relaxed afternoon, and as she drove to the airport, Dev remarked, "I liked your friends. A nice couple."

They were, and they'd enjoyed his company, she'd been delighted to see.

She accompanied him to the concourse and kissed him goodbye, reveling in the scent of his skin and the feel of his mouth on hers before he released her.

"I have to go," he muttered on a note close to anguish. "I'll ask for a hotel booking again next weekend, okay?"

Maxine looked away from that blue, intense stare for a moment and moistened her lips. Then she looked back at him with a faint smile and shook her head, just barely. "You don't need to do that. You can stay with me."

Dev drew in a deep breath and let it out. His big hand came out and cupped her chin, and he kissed her fiercely, longingly, and then tore himself away. "My plane's leaving," he said.

"I know." She gave him a little push. "Go."

She left the concourse feeling both elated and frightened by what she had done. She had truly let herself in for it, practically promised to make love with him.

There was still time to change her mind. Dev wouldn't hold her to it. Nothing irrevocable had happened...yet.

THE FOLLOWING FRIDAY evening she drove to the airport with her nerves leaping. In the big impersonal public area she waited, feeling more jumpy by the minute. She'd rifled through her wardrobe before settling on a simple dark crimson sheath dress with a dramatic, wide gold zipper down the front and a large gold ring at the closure. It looked great on her, but she hoped it wasn't too obvious.

Dev came striding into the concourse, looking about for her with an expectant but slightly tense expression, as if afraid she might not have come after all. He wore a white shirt and what looked like brand-new jeans, and his hair was ruthlessly combed back, but he still had to flick that stubborn strand away as his eyes searched the crowded, noisy area. She felt her heart do something strange, as though it had turned to runny chocolate, soft and gooey, warm and sweet. Then he saw her, his eyes lighting up.

"Dev," she said. And walked straight into his arms.

"HAVE YOU HAD ENOUGH?" Maxine pushed the remains of the apricot cheesecake toward him.

"More than." Dev sat back and finished off his wine. "Did you make that?"

"'Fraid not." Maxine shook her head. "The delicatessen down the road." She had grilled the T-bones, though.

He had read her mind. "The T-bone was delicious."

Maxine laughed. "I'll make coffee."

This time he didn't argue, but while she was waiting

for it to brew, he came into the kitchen and slipped his arms about her, pulling her back against him. "I missed you," he murmured into her hair.

She laid her hands over his. "I've only been gone two minutes."

"*I've* been gone a whole week." He nuzzled aside her hair and kissed her nape, sending a delicious shiver of delight down her spine. "You smell wonderful."

She'd used a new perfume that was guaranteed to send men wild. She leaned her head back against his shoulder. "Coffee will be ready soon."

"What'll we do until then?"

Maxine smiled. "I don't know. Do you have any ideas?"

"One." He bent to find her lips with his and turned her into his arms.

Maxine let her hands slide about his neck and kissed him back with frank enjoyment. But when he made to insert his thigh between hers, she drew away, slightly breathless. "Coffee."

"If you insist." He sighed and loosened his tight hold on her waist, but his hands shaped her hips and caressed her behind briefly before he let them drop completely away from her.

"Maxine?" he said to her back as she poured the coffee.

"Yes?" She picked up the mugs and turned to face him.

"I won't hold you to a thing. If anything happens this weekend it'll be because we both want it."

"I know that."

"Right." He nodded and took his cup before leading the way into the other room.

There was a two-seater that matched the single chairs,

and Dev eyed it dubiously and then sat down, waiting for her to join him.

Maxine laughed at him. "It's quite safe." She settled beside him. "Trust me."

"I thought that was my line."

"Along with, 'Of course I'll still respect you in the morning'?" Maxine teased.

He laughed. "You've heard them before."

"Not often." She looked at him and then away.

"That's about what I thought," he said quietly.

So he didn't assume she did this all the time. Somehow she didn't think he did, either.

They drank their coffee and Maxine took both cups into the kitchen. This time he didn't follow. When she came back, Dev was standing at the window with his hands in his pockets.

It was dark outside, but there were still people about in the street. She came to stand beside him, and he put an arm about her shoulders, drawing her close. "It was a great meal."

"Thank you."

He tipped her face with a hand under her chin and kissed her lightly, then drew back as if testing her reaction. Apparently reassured, he kissed her more deeply, and as she responded he groaned and held her closer. One hand groped for the cord that would close the blinds over the window, but it stuck, and she giggled as he let her go with a muffled expletive and did the thing properly.

"Don't laugh," he growled. "This is supposed to be romantic, not funny."

She laughed openly at that, and Dev lunged for her, dragging her close again, and smothered her laughter very effectively with his open mouth on hers.

Maxine swayed toward him, intoxicated by the feel of

his aroused body against hers, his tongue exploring her mouth, the scent of his skin—part woody, part musk.

One hand found her breast and settled there, holding it gently, and this time she didn't object when his thigh nudged at hers. But the dress was snug about her hips and thighs, and his hands roamed down her back until they found the hem and pushed it up, his fingers on her skin. His hand stayed there, supporting her, big and warm. After a little while he drew back, easing himself upright, and while one hand moved caressingly over her behind he hooked a finger of the other into the gold ring at the top of her zipper.

"I brought a bedroll," he told her, looking into her eyes. "I could sleep on the floor."

"Do you want to?"

He eased the zipper down an inch or so. "What do you think?"

"I think," Maxine admitted, "that I'm past thinking."

Her arms were hooked about his neck. He smiled at her, and she smiled back. He brought the zipper down another inch. "I'm used to sleeping rough."

"I'm not. If you think I'm going to share your bedroll—"

Dev laughed softly, his eyes lifting from the zipper he was opening with such painful slowness, to study her face. "What's the alternative?"

The zipper had reached her waist. He slipped his hand inside the dress, lightly touching her ribs. Maxine felt her eyelids flutter, her lips part as she drew in a shaky breath. "Alternative?" she repeated hazily.

His fingers skimmed her breasts, encased in the sheerest lace and satin. He was barely touching her, but her body reacted instantly, her heart hammering. "I have a perfectly good bed," she whispered.

"Is that right?" he drawled. The light in his eyes was devilish, and she thought there might be more than one reason for his nickname. He withdrew his hand and she almost cried out a protest, but he'd hooked his finger into the shining ring again, to gently slide the zipper to its limit at the lacy edge of her bikini panties. He looked down, and the muscles of his face went taut. She saw him swallow, his throat working. His eyes looked heavy-lidded. "Is your bed big enough for two?" he inquired interestedly.

Maxine gave a choked little laugh, and he looked back at her face, his own eyes filled with laughter mingled with lambent passion. She said, "Why don't we try it and see?"

IT WAS BETTER THAN SHE HAD ever imagined. Dev's love-making was slow, and sensuous, and tender, and then fast and fierce and raunchy. His wonderful, work-hardened but sensitive hands brought her to a sobbing, unrestrained climax, then soothed her into a delicious lassitude. And then he did it all over again, differently. Each time he had joined her with his own hoarse, unguarded cries of sheer delight, his body shuddering against hers while she wrapped her arms about him. She hadn't felt so good in years. In fact, she didn't remember when she had felt so incredibly relaxed, replete, content.

She drifted into sleep finally with the bed in chaos, her head on his shoulder, one leg bent across his body.

When she woke it was just beginning to get light and Dev wasn't there. He'd covered her with the sheet, and the pillow that had ended up at the bottom of the bed last night now lay neatly beside the one under her head.

The sheet alongside her was still warm. Groping for a robe, she pulled it round her and got up, and found Dev in the darkened living room. He'd opened the blinds and was watching the sun streak the sky with early morning flame. He had nothing on and looked like a silhouetted Greek statue. Only better.

"Dev?" She walked toward him, loosely tying the robe. "Is something the matter?"

"I'm used to getting up early, that's all. Sorry, I didn't want to wake you. Well, I *wanted* to, but I figured you might prefer to sleep."

"I missed you," she said, echoing his words of last night. And felt a tremor of unease. She couldn't afford to become dependent on this man. They were having an affair, she reminded herself. A temporary indulgence that wasn't meant to last.

"Come here."

She hardly hesitated before walking toward him. He reached for her and brought her close, his cheek rubbing against hers.

"Ow," she said sleepily.

Dev drew back. "Sorry." He touched his hand to her skin. "I'll go and shave."

He went into the bedroom and came out with a men's toiletry bag in his hand. "Wait for me."

Maxine curled into the chair he'd sat in the first time he came here, and waited for his return.

He came back and put the bag on the table next to the leather chair and pulled her to her feet and kissed her.

In no time it was more than kissing, and he sank into the chair, holding her on top of him, her legs straddling his. He opened the robe she wore and touched her all over, his hands roaming her back, shaping the swelling curves below and stroking her thighs, then gliding up past her hips and closing on her breasts.

She slid closer to him until his erection was warm and

firm against her belly, and he said, "I'm not sure if I can hold out much longer."

She smiled at him and teased, "No stamina, Cutter?" But she was almost as impatient as he, and when his mouth searched out her breasts, she flung back her head and moaned, a hot cascade of frantic need almost drowning her. Minutes later she eased herself over him, settling on him with a sigh of satisfaction.

"You feel wonderful," he said, and folded her close, finding her mouth again.

He felt wonderful, too, but she was too busy kissing him to say it aloud. He had to know it, though, because her body was telling him in so many different ways, sending messages to his mouth, his hands, and that part of him that was buried deep inside her. She was rocking gently against him, and the chair responded to the movement. She heard him groan deeply, and increased the rhythm, goading him deliberately, making the leather sling beneath him sway more and more, bringing him to the edge and beyond, and then she was flying with him, flung into ecstasy with her arms spread like wings and her legs on either side of him as he held her breasts cupped in his big, cherishing hands and nuzzled his hot face between them.

CHAPTER THIRTEEN

THEY ATE BREAKFAST in one of Maxine's favorite neighborhood cafés. Afterward they took the ferry across the harbor to Manly and strolled on the Corso among the Saturday shoppers and had a late lunch at a trattoria, feeding each other pasta.

They rode the sky train to Darling Harbour and shopped at a delicatessen in Chinatown, returning to the apartment with packets of exotic foods that they didn't eat, instead ending up in bed and snacking at midnight on toasted cheese sandwiches. At sunrise they were on Circular Quay while the glassy waters of the harbor and the white multiple roofs of the Opera House were briefly washed with gold.

She showed him what she loved about Sydney, and what she loved about him. And he watched her face and sometimes laughed at her and sometimes quizzed her silently, and sometimes gave a lopsided little smile, his eyes softening with tender humor.

They acted like lovers. They were lovers.

SHE KEPT HER WEEKENDS free for him, lived for them. Even her work was no competition. One day she realized that her work had become so narrowly focused that most of her cases were routine, devoid of challenge. There were few interesting highlights like the DeWilde name issue.

The biggest buzz she'd got lately was the day Dev told

her that the insurance company had paid Goanna Gap's hairdresser, and the woman sent her a parcel of shampoos and hair products.

When Dev mentioned in passing that a local farmer was having problems over his lease, she pricked up her ears. "Is he a friend of yours?"

"Known him all my life. Ted's a good bloke."

"Does he have a good lawyer?"

"He doesn't have the money yet to pay any lawyer. The publican's opened a fund for his legal costs. I wasn't hinting, Max. You can't take on the legal problems of every lame duck in Goanna Gap."

Maxine hesitated only briefly. "Tell him to get in touch with me."

"I don't think he'll be able to afford your price, even with help from the town."

"I won't charge him for initial advice. If he can fax me the details, I'll see what I can do. We can talk about fees later if I do any actual work for him. Or I could recommend someone in Brisbane for him if that's more helpful."

"If you're sure you want to do this, I know Ted will appreciate that."

The warmth of his approval was enough to make the effort of helping worthwhile.

THE WEEKEND HIS CURRENT TV series finished, Dev stayed over until Sunday. They woke late and lazed, lunched and then made love one more time in Maxine's bed. Finally Dev got up and showered, then started to pack his overnighter while Maxine used the bathroom. By the time she got back with a terry robe loosely belted about her waist and started pulling clothes from her wardrobe, he was zipping up the bag.

"You don't have to drive me to the airport," he said, eyeing her languorous movements with amusement. "Why don't you crawl back into bed?"

"Not unless you're going to crawl back with me." She held up a hanger to consider a pair of jade-green harem-style trousers and a matching jacket.

Dev laughed. "Don't tempt me."

Maxine turned to lay the outfit on the bed and gave him a wickedly flirtatious look, madly batting her eyelashes. "Could I?" she asked throatily.

He grabbed the robe's belt by the ends and hauled her to him, his eyes alight with laughter and lust. The laughter died as he brought his mouth down to hers and kissed her long and lingeringly.

He held her loosely in his arms and looked into her face. "Marry me," he said.

Maxine stiffened, her eyes going wide. Then she laughed. "You're not serious." He couldn't be.

Dev scowled. "I'm not joking, Maxine."

She swallowed. "You can't mean it. We...we've only known each other a short time."

His face cleared. "Okay, I'll ask you again when we've known each other a bit longer."

"Dev—" It wouldn't be fair to let him think she might say yes in a few more weeks, a few more months. "This has been...fantastic. Let's not spoil it. Don't start asking for too much. You must realize it would never work."

"Why not?"

"Because...well, because we're incompatible."

He cocked his head and his brows drew together. "These weekends prove that, I suppose?"

Faint panic rose inside her. "Our life-styles are too different!"

"Differences make life interesting, don't you think?"

"Listen." She lifted her chin and met his eyes squarely. "I'm not a very nice person."

Dev shook his head, looking puzzled. "Why do you say that about yourself?"

"It's true. I've worked hard to get where I am, and I intend to go higher in the profession. I'm ambitious."

"That makes you a nasty person?"

"It makes me an unsuitable person——for you."

"You mean, I'm unsuitable for you," he contradicted.

"I know you're dedicated to your work. I respect that."

"But...?" His voice lost its smoky texture and became harsh.

"I thought we'd just...be together on a casual basis for a while. I had no idea you thought this was anything more than...than that."

"Casual?" He sounded hostile. "I don't recall mentioning anything about *casual*."

"You didn't need to say the word—"

"I didn't even *think* it!"

Maxine stared at him uncertainly. "Maybe not, but—"

"But you did?" His scowl was positively ferocious now. "I don't know what sort of relationships you're accustomed to, city lady, but in my family we don't go in much for *casual*."

"Neither do I!" Maxine snapped, insulted. "I never wanted to get involved with a man like you!" The panic intensified, fueled by insidious temptation. "I won't!"

The warmth died and his eyes hardened. "A man like me? And what sort of man would that be, huh?"

Pushed into honesty, she said, "A man who's happy to spend his life in a place like Goanna Gap."

He looked at her thoughtfully, his eyes still smouldering with temper. "Goanna Gap is a pretty good town."

"I'm sure you think so." She couldn't help the irony in her voice.

"Yeah." His head lifted. "Matter of fact, I do. That the kind of place you came from?"

Maxine's breath caught in surprise. "Why do you say that?"

"Call it a lucky guess," he drawled.

A clever guess, she amended mentally. "Yes," she admitted. "I grew up in a place not much different from Goanna Gap. And I couldn't wait to get away from it."

"Was it that bad?"

"Bad enough."

"What did they do to you?"

"*They* didn't *do* anything. In fact, you could say that was the problem." Her mouth curled. "Nobody did anything much. The local farmers scraped some kind of living between droughts and floods, and complained about the weather and the government and how hard done by they were, and the shopkeepers griped about the lack of money in the town and moaned about the good old days, when things were better. The good old days that never really existed except for brief periods of prosperity between the bad years. They were born and lived and died in that place—it was all they ever knew."

"And you hated it," Dev said quietly.

"Yes, I hated it. The girls I went to school with dreamed of marrying out of the district and going to the city and living differently, but most of them had a white wedding at eighteen to a local boy—sometimes a pretty hastily arranged one. By the time they were twenty-five they had three or four children and were out helping their husbands keep the damned farm going, and looking gaunt and hard-lipped and defeated. And nothing changed. Nothing ever changed!"

"But you did."

"Yes. It wasn't easy, but I did. I got a scholarship to university and worked like a dog to keep myself out of that place. I'm never *never* going back!"

"Maxine, it isn't always that way—"

"It *is* that way!" she cried. "I've seen it over and over again, and I won't fall into that trap. You can't force it on me!"

He looked at her hard. "Nobody can force it on you. I wouldn't even try." He sounded suddenly bleak and weary. His lips compressed as though he was trying to bite back the words that sprang to his tongue. "I have to go," he muttered abruptly. "No—" he said as she made to pick up her clothes. "Forget it. I'll find myself a cab."

HE DIDN'T PHONE that week, and when she telephoned the park she got first an answering machine, and then Binnie, sounding very secretarial and efficient. "No," Maxine said, defeated. "No message."

On Monday she was listlessly trying to concentrate on a partnership agreement when her secretary tapped on the door. "There's a man here to see you."

For an instant her face lit with hope, but the man who brushed by the secretary with a curt word of thanks was quite different from Dev. He was very big and very dark, and the expensive suit clothed a body that looked as though it were made of honed steel; he had the bearing of a man who lived with danger.

"Yes?" she said, rising from her desk and adjusting her face to a cool, inquiring mask.

"Ms. Sterling?" He cast a lightning-fast glance over her, and she had the chilling feeling that he'd summed up her entire character in that fleeting second. "I'm Nick Santos."

She'd known before he opened his mouth. As Jeffrey had said, Nick Santos could never have approached the Cutters undercover if Grace had described him. His powerful personality must be something of a handicap in his line of work.

She told him she was busy, unable to spare time at the moment, and he came right back with a demand for a time, a place for them to talk. She suggested the Waterfront Restaurant at the Rocks. "It's rigged to look like a sailing ship," she said, "with four masts. You can't miss it. I'll come as soon as the office closes."

When she met him and he had found them a table and ordered drinks, he didn't waste time on remarks about the weather or the view. Stretching out one long leg with a slight grimace as though it hurt him, he said, "Jeffrey told me you'd be willing to cooperate." His unfathomable near-black eyes held a hint of resentment.

"Jeffrey told *me* I was under no compulsion."

He digested that silently. "Okay. Shall I tell him you've changed your mind?"

"I didn't say that!"

"So, what are you saying, Ms. Sterling?" His voice was velvety smooth like a dark liqueur, and hid a subtle bite. "I don't have a lot of time. If you want to please Jeffrey and keep on the right side of your most important client, you'll do what he asks."

"What makes you think DeWilde's is my most important client?"

The waiter brought their drinks, and Nick took a couple of gulps of his before replacing the glass on the table. "You were an up-and-coming, ambitious young lawyer among hundreds of others in the profession—your firm's newest, youngest probationary partner—when you met

Ryder Blake. You rode on his coattails into an association with the DeWilde Corporation.''

Maxine bristled, but she couldn't really argue with his brutal assessment.

''You've picked up other big clients since—good, solid businesses—but none as important as DeWilde's.''

Startled, Maxine tried to keep her expression neutral.

''DeWilde's Sydney will be needing its own corporate lawyer before long. Ryder will probably make you an offer you can't refuse. It would be a smart career move. You've made them before—you're a climber, Ms. Sterling. You started without money, connections or a useful family background, but you know how to get ahead. And you know better than to get offside with the wrong people.''

''Have you been investigating me?'' Maxine was outraged.

''Just a background check. When I'm instructed to work with someone, I don't want any nasty surprises cropping up.''

From the slight emphasis he had given to the word *instructed,* she guessed he hadn't been too thrilled at Jeffrey's suggestion. It figured; she had him pegged as a loner, not a team player. ''I'm a lawyer,'' she said, ''not a detective.''

''But you've met the Cutters. I want you to tell me all you know about DeWilde Cutter and his mother. Especially anything that might connect them with Jeffrey DeWilde's family.''

''Like a birthmark or something?'' she asked snidely. She could tell him that Dev Cutter had no birthmarks, but that he bore the marks of a crocodile's teeth, and he had a long, thin scar on his left thigh, disappearing into the thick curls of hair at his groin—a knife wound that he'd got at twelve years old, gutting a fish the wrong way. "Damn near gutted myself—or worse," he'd told her, laughing. "Gave my mother a hell of a fright. I bled like a stuck pig."

Nick Santos evidently didn't think her remark was worthy of a reply. "Jeffrey said you'd spent time with the crocodile hunter."

"He isn't a hunter! He's a conservationist!"

The dark eyes regarded her curiously. "I stand corrected, counselor. When with a lawyer, choose your words carefully."

"I really can't tell you any more than Jeffrey would have," Maxine said stiffly. "We went to the Cutters' wildlife park together."

"Were you together all the time?"

"No."

"Sometimes you were with one or the other—or with Robina and Ross Cutter—when Jeffrey wasn't?"

"Well…yes, but—"

"Then you could have information that Jeffrey doesn't."

"I doubt it. I don't know anything useful."

"You're good at your job, Ms. Sterling. I'm damn good at mine." He paused, and added on a faintly acrid note, "Usually." His gaze dropped for a moment before returning to her. "So you just answer my questions and let me decide if the answers are useful, okay?"

"If the Cutters were after the DeWildes' money—"

"Do you think they are?"

"No! But Jeffrey said you'd warned him—"

"Sure I warned him. Listen, Ms. Sterling. When I complete this investigation, I might have some conclusions to present to Jeffrey DeWilde. Until then I'm keeping an open mind. Okay, so you've answered my first question.

Why do you think they're not after the DeWilde millions?''

''You're asking for an opinion?''

''We're not in a court of law. You're an intelligent woman. I'd like to hear your opinion.''

He seemed to mean it. ''All right,'' she said. ''For what it's worth, I think they're genuine, honest people. Even if—''

''If?'' His alert, dark eyes scanned her face. As she hesitated, he said softly, ''This can't do them any harm, supposing you're right and they are honest. Did either of them confide any secrets to you?''

''No.''

''Then you can't betray any confidences. What were you going to say?''

''Maggie,'' Maxine said slowly, ''might have been… avoiding something. I don't know what. She was talking quite freely and suddenly seemed to decide not to anymore.'' She shrugged. ''It was nothing, really. We were strangers, after all—she was probably just guarding her family's privacy.''

Nick nodded. ''What else do you remember?''

He kept her there for over an hour, and by the time he paid the tab and she was about to leave him at the harborside she felt as if he'd wrung every bit of information from her.

She was already turning away when he asked, ''When are you seeing him again?''

Maxine straightened as if she'd been shot. ''What?''

''When are you seeing DeWilde Cutter again? You two are an item, aren't you?''

Color rushed into her cheeks. ''I thought you said a background check—how dare you spy on me!''

''Didn't,'' he said laconically. ''But you've just told

me what I wanted to know. I'll be in touch. And this is where I am tonight, in case you recall anything else." He handed her a card with the address and phone number of his hotel scribbled on it in bold block letters.

She felt like tearing it up, but she swallowed her anger and pushed the card into her handbag instead.

When she reached her apartment, the light on her answering machine was blinking. She pressed "play" and ran through the messages, none of them from Dev. Hope died hard.

She wandered around, putting away her briefcase, changing her clothes, trying not to think about him. And kept looking at the telephone, willing it to ring.

In the end she picked it up and dialed.

Binnie answered. "Maxine? No, sorry, Dev's away, chasing a croc that's got into trouble with some sugarcane farmers. Aunt Maggie? She had to go to a meeting in Goanna Gap. She's chairperson of the library committee and they've got this big fight going on about a cut in funding. She'll be home late. Can I do anything?"

Maxine thought a moment. "Does the name Nick Santos mean anything to you?"

"No...don't think so. Just a minute—I'll ask Rooster."

Maxine waited until she reported back. "He says he thinks Mr. DeWilde mentioned someone of that name. Is it important?"

"Never mind," Maxine said. Evidently Binnie and Rooster weren't privy to whatever Grace might have told Maggie about the detective. "I'll phone your aunt tomorrow. Good night, Binnie."

Dismay filled her as she put down the phone. Dev was away? And Nick Santos was prowling about, determined to uncover any secrets that Maggie might have.

So what? her rational self said. If Maggie was innocent

of any wrongdoing—as Maxine was ninety-nine percent sure she was—what harm could Mr. Santos do?

She had no idea, but he'd made her feel like a witness for the defence—and she was supposedly on his side. Maggie was too soft for her own good, Dev had said once. And Rooster and Binnie were no match for a man as wily and determined as Santos.

She took out the card he had given her and fingered it, frowning. "This is where I am tonight," he'd said. No prizes for guessing where he'd be tomorrow.

She chewed on her lip, then lifted the telephone. Had he had time to return to his hotel?

The receptionist put her through to his room, and the ring burred several times. She was about to hang up when the ringing stopped. "Santos."

"It's Maxine Sterling," she said. "What time is your plane to Brisbane?"

The small sound he made might have been the beginning of a laugh. "You want to come?"

"Yes. As DeWilde's lawyer, I think I should."

He seemed to be thinking. "Okay," he drawled finally. "I'll get you the flight number. Just a minute."

DEV WADED IN WAIST-DEEP greenish water, keeping his movements slow and creating as little disturbance as possible, his eyes hunting through the murk for any sign of movement. A shadow stirred on the bottom, little eddies of mud floating in the water. Dev stopped moving and his narrowed eyes fixed on the spot.

On the bank two men watched, one smoking, another cradling a precautionary rifle.

Dev let the mud settle. He could see the shape of the croc now, the tail toward him. Ideal. Less than two meters long, as he'd expected. He grinned. They'd told him "a ten-footer.'' People always exaggerated a croc's size. Silently he signaled to the men on the bank. The one with the cigarette removed it from his mouth and straightened, killing the lighted end with his fingers. The gunman readied the rifle.

Dev took a few more unhurried steps, gulped in a breath and dived, feeling first the cold shock of the water, then the hard, scaly length of the croc as he wrapped his arms about it behind the head.

It bucked and fought, a mass of frantic, armor-encased muscle, but he found his footing on the slimy bottom and hung on as he stood up and staggered toward the shore.

"Take her tail!'' he instructed as he reached the shallows. "Get her away from the water.''

The man with the gun backed up before them while the other man skirted the croc's jaws and took the weight of the thrashing tail, making it easier for Dev to carry the animal away from the bank and lower it to the ground, his legs pushed under her hind ones, keeping her feet off the ground.

"The rope!'' he gasped, lying sprawled along the scaly, hard back of the crocodile. "Between her jaws.''

Gingerly the other man swung the looped rope three times before it caught the upper jaw.

"Good,'' Dev approved. "Right. Okay, sweetheart. Here we go. You won't like this, but no one's going to hurt you.''

He could feel the croc's muscles bunching under his thighs as it prepared to roll. "Come in behind me,'' he ordered the helper. "We need more weight.''

When she settled, he cautiously tightened the rope and knotted it. Eventually they got another loop of rope over both jaws, pulled it tight and wound it round a few more times for good measure before fastening it.

The bunched muscles heaved, the heavy, ridged tail swung in a deadly arc, and Dev tightened his thighs on the croc's body. "Yeah," he said softly. "I know you're really scared, but I'm not leaving you for the shooters to get, honey. You may not believe me now, but the last thing I want to do is lock you up. All I want is for you to be safe. Safe, happy…and free."

He waited until she lay still again. Crocs were strong and fast, but easily exhausted. "Okay," he said to the other men. "Let's get a bag on her and put her on the truck."

Twenty minutes later he was transporting the crocodile to a new locale, far away from the farmers who had invaded her territory and objected to her dining on their chickens and young stock.

MAXINE WAS TRAVELING in a different seat row from Nick Santos, but she caught up with him as they left the aircraft. The slight hesitation she had noticed in his stride didn't slow him down much.

"Do you have a car waiting?" she asked him. "You know it's nearly two hours' drive to the wildlife park?"

"Sure I know. You have baggage to pick up?"

"No." She wondered if he would have waited if she had. As it was, within fifteen minutes she was sitting beside him in a rental car that seemed too small to accommodate his long legs.

"Have you driven on the left before?" she asked him. He hadn't offered her the driver's seat.

"I've driven all over the world."

Silly question, she told herself, fastening her seat belt. He looked as though he'd done pretty much everything in his time, for all that he probably wasn't much over thirty.

"Are they expecting you?" she asked him.

"You didn't tell them I was coming?"

"No." She'd considered phoning again to warn Maggie. But Maxine worked for DeWilde's. All she'd been able to think of was that she ought to be here, keeping some kind of watchful eye on developments. She'd phoned her boss and told him she wouldn't be in the office tomorrow, using the magic word "DeWilde's" to ensure his assent.

"Remembered whose side you're on, did you?"

The man was uncanny. "I hope it won't be necessary to take sides, Mr. Santos. You did say you knew how to keep an open mind."

He cast her a glance and his mouth curved down, but except to check with her that he was taking the right turn when they left the highway, he scarcely spoke another word until they drew up outside the park.

The sign had been changed, Maxine noted, the rustic-style lettering bearing no resemblance to the DeWilde signature.

Rooster was on gate duty, and his friendly greeting to Maxine made her feel guilty. "Mr. Santos would like to see your aunt," she told him.

Rooster's appraisal of the big man held curiosity, but he gave a welcoming nod. "In the shop, Maxine. You know where it is. Dev's not here."

Maggie looked apprehensive when Maxine introduced Nick, but she left Binnie in charge and said, "You'd better come over to the house. We can talk there."

She offered them tea and scones, and Nick surprised Maxine by accepting. With Maggie he suddenly seemed younger—respectful and almost boyish. Maxine eyed him with suspicion. The man was a chameleon.

"I'll come and help," Maxine offered as Maggie headed for the kitchen.

Instead of staying in the sitting room, Nick followed them to the kitchen and looked around. "This is nice— homey. Can we have our tea here?"

Maxine guessed that he was making sure she didn't have time to speak alone with Maggie. Did he trust any-*body?* "Mr. Santos is a private investigator," she said. "Acting for DeWilde's."

"Yes?" Maggie looked even more wary. "Well, why don't you both sit down while I make the tea?"

When they were all seated at the table, Maggie regarded Nick over the rim of the teacup and asked, "How can I help you?"

Nick was already biting into a fresh buttered scone. He put down the uneaten half, fished an envelope out of his pocket and pulled several photographs from it. "Do you recognize any of these, Mrs. Cutter?"

Maggie put her cup carefully down on its saucer and took up one of the photographs. "Oh," she said faintly. "Oh, yes. This one. It's my tiara." She looked at Maxine and handed the photograph to her.

"Excuse me?" Nick said.

"Well…" Maggie looked at him uncertainly. "It looks like it."

She turned at a sound on the porch, and then the screen and the door were thrust open and Dev came into the room, removing the Akubra hat from his head. His clothes were very similar to his TV attire, only considerably less clean. He hadn't shaved and his eyes were bloodshot, as though he'd had little sleep.

"Hello, dear!" His mother jumped up. "You're back early."

He wiped a hand over his forehead, and his eyes found Maxine. He didn't react at first, but then he stiffened as he saw the man sitting beside her.

"This is Mr. Santos," Maggie told him. "Maxine brought him."

"Maxine?" His eyes sought hers again. "You're here in your official capacity, then."

"She's representing DeWilde's legal interests." Nick stood up and held out his hand. "You must be DeWilde Cutter."

Dev slowly took the proffered handshake and nodded curtly, his blue gaze summing up the other man. "Jeffrey sent you." He turned to his mother. "I need a shower. Don't answer any questions until I get back."

He looked at Maxine again, and her heart sank at the coldness in his eyes. Then he headed for the door to the passageway.

Nick took another scone. "These biscuits are delicious, Mrs. Cutter. You make them yourself?"

"For the café. Most of the cakes and things are delivered, but I always think scones should be homemade."

"You recognize any of these other pictures?"

Maggie shook her head. "No. Only this one."

Nick shoved the others back into the envelope and slid it into his pocket. Maxine glanced at him with suspicion as he leaned back and eased his leg. He met her look with a bland stare and took another bite out of his scone.

Dev returned in less than ten minutes, freshly shaved and wearing a khaki shirt and trousers, his hair still darkened with water and slicked back from his forehead. He didn't even look at Maxine as his mother handed him a cup of tea.

Nick flicked him a glance and then concentrated on Maggie. "Jeffrey says you seemed reluctant to explain just how your son came by his name."

Maggie bit her lip. "Well, you see…it was the only thing I felt I had to give him."

Nick said nothing, waiting for her to go on.

"The only thing?" Maxine asked. She put down the picture of the tiara. It was a magnificent piece of jewelry, the diamonds and pearls glowing against a background of black velvet.

"I'm not talking about material things," Maggie said, following her gaze. "Money or heirlooms. I mean the things most parents are able to give their children—a background, an ancestry. Knowledge of where they came from, who their parents were, and their grandparents—"

"I don't give a damn," Dev said. "But my mother felt I was entitled to something."

"Are you saying Dev was born out of wedlock?" Maxine asked gently. It was hardly a stigma these days.

Maggie shook her head. "Phil and I were married, and Dev is our son. I named him for my father. That was all I ever knew about him, really. His name."

Maxine recalled the night she and Jeffrey had spent here. Maggie had spoken openly and at length of her childhood—her parents and grandparents and the district they'd grown up in. It didn't make sense, unless... "You were adopted!"

Maggie nodded reluctantly.

"It's nothing to be ashamed of," Dev told her.

"I'm not ashamed, son." She turned to Nick. "I didn't find out until I was twenty-one. My...adoptive parents were afraid I'd be taken away from them because the adoption wasn't strictly legal."

In the 1940s, Maxine thought, there'd have been records. "But your birth would have had to have been registered." These days it was difficult for anyone to go through life without a birth certificate. Maggie would surely have had to produce it when she married.

"My parents headed for a new opal field in New South

Wales about 1947, taking their two boys. When they got back to the Territory they brought a baby girl with them. I was registered there as their own child.''

Nick broke his watchful silence. ''But they knew your real parents.''

''Yes. When they decided I should know all this, I made them tell me everything. This couple was staying at my mother's boarding house. A Mr. and Mrs. Freeman. But they left—and didn't take their baby.''

Nick straightened slightly in his chair.

''My mother—my adoptive mother—had been helping Mrs. Freeman look after me. She—Mrs. Freeman—seems to have been delicate or incompetent. Maybe both. My mother, I think, was half sorry for her and half exasperated. Life on the opal fields was pretty hard, and the poor woman was out of her element in a strange country, and very unhappy.''

''She wasn't Australian?'' Maxine asked.

Maggie shook her head. ''My mother thought she was French, but she spoke of being a child in Quebec. So perhaps she was French Canadian.''

Nick gave a faint nod as though she had confirmed something.

''She seems to have just run away one day. Some time later her husband said he was going to find her. My adoptive mother was afraid if she told the authorities I'd been abandoned, they'd put me into an institution or give me to someone else.''

Nick nodded. ''So these people you call your parents upped stakes and took you with them—along with a valuable piece of jewelry.''

''My father—Mr. Freeman—gave it to them as insurance for me.''

''Insurance?'' Nick's eyes narrowed.

"He left the tiara as a kind of pledge against his return, and told them if anything happened and he didn't come back after all, they were to use it to provide for me."

"So why didn't they?"

"They were good people, Mr. Santos, who loved me. They kept it for me instead."

Nick's eyes flickered under her stern, proud gaze.

"I always knew the boys were to have the property, and the tiara was my inheritance. My mother kept it in her glory box."

"She kept it *where?*" Nick sat forward, seemingly as stunned as Maxine supposed he ever allowed himself to be.

"Her glory box. They've gone out of fashion now, but girls used to be given a glory box when they were in their teens, often on their sixteenth birthday, to save up linen and stuff against the day they'd get married. And after marriage they made useful storage chests. Everyone had one when my mother was a girl."

"And that's where she kept the Empress Eugénie tiara—" Nick couldn't quite hide his disbelief "—for how many years?"

"She died in 1982. Not long before my father." Maggie's eyes darkened with remembered sorrow.

Nick shifted restlessly. "So there's no one left alive who can verify this story?"

Maggie shook her head. "What did you call the tiara?"

"The Empress Eugénie tiara." He flicked a finger at the photograph lying on the table. "And you sold it to a jeweler in Sydney?"

Maggie's eyes widened. "You know that?"

"I traced the tiara back to there, but I couldn't find the name of the woman who'd sold it to him."

Dev stared accusingly at his mother. "You went to *Syd-*

ney? So that's why I couldn't find out who bought it! I tried every damned jeweler in Brisbane.''

Maggie gave him a smile. "It's too late now."

Nick shot Dev a look of inquiry.

Dev said grimly, "She wouldn't tell me the buyer's name. Just turned up with the money and said, 'Here it is. Now you can start building your wildlife park.'''

"Dev was furious at first." Maggie smiled again. "He would have gone to Sydney and demanded the tiara back if I'd told him where I'd sold it.''

"That piece is worth one hell of a lot of money," Nick said. "The jeweler's records were lost, but at a guess you probably got a fraction of what it's worth.''

"I got a lot of money," Maggie said tranquilly. "Enough to start off the park.''

Nick cocked his head as though he couldn't quite make her out. "Do you still have the receipt?" he asked after a moment.

"I can show it to you if you like."

Nick nodded. "Later."

Maxine too had been trying to work something out. "You said your father's name was Freeman."

"Yes, but…" Maggie looked at Nick and said almost defiantly, "Maybe you'll think this is pure fantasy, but for some reason my father was living under an assumed name. I'm certain his real name was Dirk DeWilde.''

CHAPTER FOURTEEN

"WHY DIDN'T YOU TELL Jeffrey this?" Maxine asked. "You let him think the Thompsons were your natural parents."

"Good question," Nick drawled. "If you believe you're a DeWilde, why lead Jeffrey up the garden path? Or did the idea come to you after he'd left here?"

Dev pushed back his chair. "What are you suggesting, Santos?" His eyes were blue glass chips, his jaw thrust forward.

Nick waved a placating hand. "I'm not accusing your mother of anything. Just asking questions, okay?"

Maggie looked embarrassed. "I did wonder, when Jeffrey said his uncle had come out here. I'd always wanted to know about my origins and it was tempting to hope that I'd found a clue, but...claiming a relationship to an ordinary, everyday family is one thing. Claiming to be related to someone who owns a string of luxury stores worth millions—well, I don't want to look like some bludger wanting a handout from the rich relatives. Especially as he'd mentioned they'd already discovered a new relative down here. It would seem I was jumping on the bandwagon. I wasn't sure enough, and...I suppose I was afraid he wouldn't believe me."

Nick sat back in his chair and stared at her. His lips twitched, and Maxine could have sworn he was choking back laughter. "Do you have any sort of proof?"

"Just a minute." Maggie got up and left the room, returning seconds later with a thick, leatherbound volume in her hand. She opened it up at the front, and Maxine guessed it was a Bible. "I don't suppose it's proof exactly," she said, "but it's the only evidence I have. My birth mother left it behind when she took off. So my...Mrs. Thompson kept it for me." She laid the volume open on the table and Nick bent over it. Maxine shifted so that she too could see the words inscribed on the flyleaf.

"*Marguerite DuBois,*" Nick read the top line aloud. "*Her Bible.*" His finger moved down and across the page. "*Marguerite DuBois—Dirk DeWilde—*" He traced down again to the next entry. "*Marguerite Marie-Claire Freeman...*" And a date.

Maxine looked up at Maggie. "It's a record of your birth."

"Yes." And below that Maggie had recorded her own marriage and the birth of her son, DeWilde Thompson Cutter.

Nick was looking more enigmatic than ever. "You got a copier here?" he asked Maggie. "Could I have a copy of the page?"

"Yes, all right. I'll do it now."

Nick got up and followed her, and Dev looked across the table to Maxine. "Is the hotshot private eye more your type?"

"Don't be stupid!"

Dev pushed back his chair and stood up. Maxine eyed him apprehensively.

"That's what you think, isn't it?" he asked her. "That I'm stupid. Too thick to be more than a temporary distraction for a clever city lady like you."

"I never meant to be insulting, Dev."

"Sure—you can be insulting without even trying. That's quite a skill, lawyer lady."

"I wish," she said between her teeth, "you would stop calling me that!"

"That's why you're here, isn't it? As DeWilde's lawyer. You and their tame detective."

Maxine couldn't help a breath of laughter. *Tame* was the last adjective she would have applied to Nick Santos.

Dev jammed his hands into his pockets as though he needed to keep them from doing something violent, and started pacing about the kitchen. Maxine felt as if she were locked in the small space with some dangerous animal that might spring at any moment. Strangely, the thought was not nearly so frightening as it was exciting.

She clenched her own hands under the table. "I came because I...because Binnie told me you weren't here." She'd compromised her role as DeWilde's legal representative to protect his nearest and dearest, and he wasn't making this any easier.

"Oh, great!" he said. "Sorry to disappoint you, but I am here now. Just as well, too. That guy's probably a direct descendant of Torquemada."

"He didn't threaten your mother in any way—"

"He *is* a threat. A walking, talking, breathing threat."

The thing was, she knew what he meant. Nick was a coiled spring, a volcano waiting to erupt. She sensed the powerful tension inside him—a tension that only needed the right catalyst to explode into dangerous action.

"If you want my advice," Dev continued, "you won't choose him for your next *casual* encounter."

Maxine's cheeks flamed. "I didn't ask for your advice—and I can't imagine why you think I'd want it!"

"Well, maybe you need it."

"Oh, go to hell!"

They were glaring at each other when Maggie and Nick reentered the room. Nick held a piece of copier paper and Maggie was saying, "I don't think my brothers will remember anything—they were very young—but I can give you their phone numbers."

"What?" Dev growled suspiciously. "What else do you want?" he snarled at the investigator.

His mother looked at him in surprise. "Nick would like to know more about the opal field and my mother's boarding house." She turned to the other man. "It's pretty much a ghost town now, I believe. I don't even know if the boarding house exists anymore."

"Thank you, Mrs. Cutter," the American said courteously. "I appreciate your help. And I'm sure Mr. DeWilde will, too. And…Dr. Cutter." He turned to Dev. "Thanks for your time."

In the car on the way back to the airport Maxine said, "You called Dev 'Doctor.' Why?"

"Just being polite."

"What?"

He glanced at her. "You don't know, do you? He took a doctorate after getting a double degree in veterinary science and zoology at the University of Queensland."

Numbly, Maxine shook her head. No, she hadn't known.

"He's pretty well regarded in scientific circles. But he only seems to use the letters after his name when he writes papers for obscure scientific journals, you know the kind of thing. *The Morphology of Crocodilus Porosus,* stuff like that." He looked at her a little longer this time, reading the stunned look on her face. "You learn something new every day."

How stupid she'd been! Dev had mentioned camping out with a research party, and she'd assumed he'd gone along as a guide of some sort. She hadn't even bothered to ask, blinkered by her own arrogant assumptions. Her cheeks burned.

Not that it really made any difference. Letters after his name didn't make Dev any more—or less—a man. A man she loved but whose life-style she couldn't share.

After a while Nick said, "He's jealous as hell. Why don't you put the poor guy out of his misery?"

And me out of mine, Maxine thought, closing her eyes. "It's not that simple." She wanted nothing more than to ask him to turn the car around and take her back, but she recalled the hard chill in Dev's eyes and didn't dare.

Nick grunted, and they both lapsed into silence, the car eating up the road as his foot increased the pressure on the accelerator.

Maxine wrenched her thoughts round to the reason for their journey. "Do you think Maggie is Dirk DeWilde's child?" she asked.

Nick took a minute to reply, and at first she thought he hadn't heard. Then he seemed to come out of whatever grim reverie brought that shuttered, bitter look to his face. "Probably."

DEV WAS ADMIRING the sunset from the veranda of the shabby two-room shack that had once belonged to the one-time buffalo and crocodile hunter who had tamed Delilah. The old man had willed it to him, he supposed, in return for his promise to care for the crocodile. Hearing the sound of a vehicle approaching over the rutted, unsealed road, he quelled a feeling of irritation. Hardly anyone knew about this place and usually he could rely on being undisturbed with his notes, tape recorder, and a generous supply of tapes and batteries, to continue his detailed year-by-year study of life in the nearby billabong.

A four-wheel drive vehicle nosed its way out of the trees and came to a halt beside his own battered Land Rover. The windscreen was filmed with reddish dust and the canopy was up. The engine died and he heard the creak of the handbrake being pulled on. After a short pause, a sneaker-clad foot and a pair of long feminine legs appeared, and Dev's heart seemed to stop.

Maxine jumped lightly to the ground and stood looking at him, her head tilted, the fading sun bronzing her hair, her face innocent of makeup but with a dusky rose flush shading her cheeks, and her eyes regarding him with a mixture of bold inquiry and trepidation. Her breasts under the workmanlike olive cotton shirt that she wore with her sensible khaki shorts rose and fell softly with her quickened breathing. "Hello, Dev," she said.

His first thought was that he must be hallucinating, his nighttime dreams invading the day. That was it—he'd been alone in the Cape York wilderness for too long and was experiencing the well-known phenomenon of "going troppo."

Maxine moved, at first uncertainly. But then, with a firming of her gorgeous dragon lady's mouth, she took two steps toward him and placed her hands on her hips. "You could at least say hello before you throw me out."

Dev found his voice—or it found him. "What the flaming hell are you doing here?"

Maxine blinked, and the color faded from her cheeks. Her voice was husky as she replied, "I...hoped we could talk."

Talk. He didn't want to talk. He wanted to grab her and sweep her up into his arms and take her inside, lock all the doors and make love to her forever and ever.

But forever wasn't what the dragon lady wanted. She'd sear him with her kisses and shrivel him up in her sweet fire, and then she'd leave him and return to her cave in the city. He should tell her to go away, back to Sydney where she belonged—where she had so determinedly made a place for herself that she found comfortable and safe.

But she looked so right here. And she'd come damn near three thousand kilometers to find him. Why?

Dev cleared his throat. "You'd better come in."

MAXINE ALMOST FAINTED with relief when he asked her in, however grudgingly.

He gave her hot, strong tea without milk. "No milk delivery here," he growled, handing her a thick china mug.

"This is fine." She took the mug and folded her hands around it, hoping Dev hadn't noticed them trembling. She'd been so afraid that he'd simply tell her to turn right round and go away, to leave him alone. He had come here to work and she was intruding.

Dev started to clear papers and notebooks from the scarred table, but she stopped him. "I'm disturbing you," she said.

Dev gave a crack of laughter. "The understatement of the century."

He'd given her the wooden kitchen chair with a shabby, dished cushion softening the seat. Now he lifted a sheaf of papers and a dictionary from a sturdy stool and put them on top of others on the table, hooking the stool with his foot to sit down opposite her.

"I'm sorry," she said. "I didn't know."

"Didn't know what?"

"About your doctorate, your research work. Not until Nick told me."

"Nick Santos?"

She glanced at him and wondered if she'd made a tactical error. "He's very thorough. It's his job."

"Does it make a difference?" His voice seemed full of ironic mockery.

Maxine shook her head. "Not really. It didn't change the situation."

He hadn't poured a drink for himself. He sat at the other side of the table, staring at her fiercely, as if she might disappear if he removed his gaze for a moment. Which meant, she hoped, that he didn't want her to.

"Did Santos send you here?" he demanded. "Or Jeffrey?"

"No one sent me. This has nothing to do with the DeWildes." She sipped at the hot tea and tried to find words for what she wanted to say. Despite constant rehearsal during the grueling flight, and later—while reading her map, revisiting Binnie's detailed instructions, and coaxing the rented four-wheel drive over roads that made her ribs clash together and jarred her teeth—she still didn't know how to start. Veering into inconsequence again, she looked down at the table. "You've been very busy."

"This—" he indicated the notes "—is only the end of it. The rest is sitting for hours recording animal behavior, with mosquitoes down my neck and centipedes crawling up my trousers, my legs cramping, and sweat soaking my shirt."

Maxine nodded. Was he warning her off? Did he know it had been on the tip of her tongue to ask if she could help? Even mosquitoes and centipedes would be bearable if she was at his side. "Still, the work must be... interesting." She winced at the banal words.

Dev placed his folded arms on the table. "There's a lot to learn about animal behavior in the region. It's not impossible there are still undiscovered species here. What's even more interesting," he said, "is what the hell you're doing here, if it's not for DeWilde's."

Maxine drank some of the tea, working up courage. "When I got back to Brisbane, after the last time…the last time I saw you, there was a message from one of my sisters. My other sister's husband had turned over a tractor and got pinned under it."

"I'm sorry." Dev frowned, searching her face. "He died?"

Maxine shook her head. "He might have preferred that. He's a farmer, and a bit of an amateur sportsman. His spine was crushed—the doctors say he'll never walk again."

Dev drew in his breath. "Tough. You went home?" he asked quietly.

"Yes. To Ramblers Creek, that little place just like Goanna Gap that you guessed I came from. I took some leave that was owing, went up there and tried to…to help. But you know…they didn't need me."

Dev frowned. "Just knowing you cared enough to be there would have helped." He paused. "Did you want them to need you?"

"It's not that." She had never wanted to be indispensable to her family, or to depend on them. She loved them, but it had been her choice to distance herself from their everyday lives. Only, maybe her sisters' choices had not been so limited, after all. "You remember what happened after the fire at the hairdresser's in Goanna Gap? How the town rallied round? My sister's neighbors started getting up two hours earlier every morning to come and milk the cows before they started on their own. They're still doing that. Other farmers finished the barn my brother-in-law was building, mended fences, drenched his herd. The local

vet treated a sick cow free of charge. And the
women...there was so much food brought along there's
enough in the freezer now to last them for months. People
offered to take the children, they...well, you know the
kind of thing.''

Dev nodded. ''Country people are like that.''

''I'd forgotten,'' she said. ''I remembered how hard it
was to not fit in—not conform to the prevailing pattern,
and how suspicious my family was of my wanting to go
to university. I was terrified they'd drag me back there
after all and I'd be trapped in that place forever. But I
didn't remember the generosity, the loyalty. And I never
realized...'' She put the cup down and stared into the tea
leaves that remained, then raised wondering eyes to his.
''They were actually proud of me!''

''You didn't know that?''

Maxine shook her head. ''When I've been home before,
it was for family holidays, so I hardly saw other people.
This...was embarrassing. My sisters and brother kept telling people, 'Max is a big lawyer in Sydney, you know—
she's the clever one.' And people would say, 'Good on
ya, girl! Your mum and dad are really proud of their lawyer daughter.' Or, 'Yeah, I remember you from school.'
They were nice to me.''

Dev laughed. Relieved, Maxine smiled back at him.
''Like you said, I'm a snob. What made me think that it
matters how people speak, or that I had a right to judge
how my sisters and my schoolmates want to live their
lives?''

Dev shrugged. ''I don't know, dragon lady.''

Maxine bit her lip. ''Dragon lady,'' she repeated softly.
''The thing is, you see—in the fairy stories the dragon
always dies in the end. With a lance through its heart.
That's how I felt all the way back to Sydney that day with

Nick, knowing I'd given away the chance to…be with you. As if I had a lance in my heart.''

Dev straightened, his palms flattening against the table. His eyes flared.

"And," Maxine said, "I got to thinking…that maybe living in a place like Goanna Gap wouldn't be so bad after all.''

Dev hadn't moved, and she didn't dare look at him anymore. The silence stretched, and she closed her eyes, thinking, *He doesn't want me anymore, only he doesn't know how to tell me.* She'd practically proposed to the man, but he'd had plenty of time for second thoughts since he'd asked her to marry him. Plenty of time to decide that a woman who thought some people were better than others because they spoke like BBC announcers and wore suits to work wasn't worth wasting a second thought on. He probably thought he'd had a lucky escape.

She opened her eyes and pushed away the chair to stand up, unable to bear the silence and stillness any longer, turning toward the door with some vague idea of gaining fresh air.

Dev spoke at last. "Goanna Gap is no place for a high-powered legal practice.''

Maxine trembled. He was trying to let her down lightly. Dev Cutter wasn't a man who liked hurting people. She ought to retreat now, before she made a complete fool of herself. Instead she found herself pleading, "There must be people there who need the services of a good lawyer. Your friend Ted was pretty pleased with what I did for him.''

"He was bloody grateful. But there are no big corporations around Goanna Gap. You'd get bored. Besides,'' he said, "you love Sydney.''

"I love *you*,'' Maxine whispered.

Dev seemed to stop breathing. He went very still, and finally inquired in an oddly flat voice that made her heart sink, "Is that what you came all this way to tell me?"

Maxine nodded.

He got up so suddenly that the stool rocked and tipped over, but he ignored it.

Maxine waited for him to come to her, gather her into his arms. But he strode out onto the small veranda with its sagging tin roof, as if he couldn't bear to be in the same room with her. He leaned a hand on one of the posts, looking out across the grassy clearing toward the trees.

After a long moment she followed him as far as the doorway. A large, long-legged bird flapped upward out of the trees, then dipped and disappeared.

"You love Sydney," Dev reiterated without looking round. "I can even understand now why you love it—you taught me that. You don't really want to give all that up and live in Goanna Gap."

"I'd miss Sydney," she admitted, "but it's not the only city in the world. Brisbane's not far from Goanna Gap."

"You've got a career to think of."

"Career goals can change. People mature. The fact is, I've got to where I wanted to be, and the next step is working for DeWilde's or a firm like it. More of the same, but it's like a pyramid—the higher you climb, the narrower it gets. That's why I went after you and the wildlife park so aggressively. It wasn't often I had such an interesting fight on my hands. I didn't help out Ted and the hairdresser only for altruistic reasons. I actually *liked* getting my teeth into something different. It was stimulating. Running my own law practice would give me a new challenge."

There was a long silence. Maxine held her breath.

"If you set up a practice in Brisbane," Dev said slowly,

"I could commute from there, maybe. We could have a house in the city," he added, and turned at last to face her. "Would you mind if it's a house, not an apartment?"

She went dizzy with relief. He was considering the options—they could work something out. "You'd hate it there." He'd stifle in the city.

"I hate living without you," Dev said. "Anything else I can stand."

Her heart turned over with love. "Oh, Dev." She flung herself into his arms, and they closed about her so tightly she could hardly breathe.

"No," she said against his shirt. "We'll live in Goanna Gap, even if I do work in Brisbane. It makes more sense," she insisted over his objection. "You start work earlier—"

"You'd be exhausted, traveling to and fro nearly every day."

"I'd get used to it. Maybe I could rent a small apartment, stay in town a few days a week."

"Maybe."

She lifted her head and smiled at him. "You can stay with me sometimes. It would be like having a love nest."

He didn't smile back. "I want it legal, Maxine—I want to marry you."

"I want to marry you, too," she whispered.

"My mother would be disappointed if she had no grandchildren," he warned her.

Maxine sensed that he was still holding back. His body trembled against hers and his eyes told her he wanted her desperately, but was determined to see this discussion through first.

"I'd want to bring them up in Goanna Gap. Where there's room to run and play, fresh air and space."

Dev swallowed. "I won't let a family wreck your career."

"I could go part-time. There'd be enough work in Goanna Gap for that—at least. Children grow up." She looked at him a little anxiously. "They'll have to leave when they finish school, to further their education."

Dev gave her a reassuring smile. "We won't hold them back."

She took him by the shoulders, looking earnestly at him, begging him to trust, to believe in her. "I love you. I discovered that was more important than being De-Wilde's lawyer, than having my own apartment in the clty, than proving I can make it on my own. I've done that, and now it's time to move on. There'll be other opportunities for me, different challenges. And...I hope there'll be you."

"Always," Dev said at last. "You'd better understand that, dragon lady. This is forever. Happy ever after. There's no going back." And at last he bent his head and kissed her.

HIS BED WAS IN THE BACK room, an old-fashioned double bedstead surrounded by mosquito netting. By the time they got there, both their shirts were unbuttoned and Maxine's hair was tumbling about her shoulders.

Dev shucked off his boots and then knelt to remove Maxine's as she sat on the edge of the bed. The mattress was surprisingly comfortable, the bed wide and inviting. "Have you had women here before?" she asked suspiciously.

"Dozens," Dev answered cheerfully, pulling off her sneakers and allowing his hands to slide up her calves and under her sensible shorts.

She lifted her bare feet and gave him a shove, throwing him off balance.

Laughing, he leapt up and advanced on her. "But not all at once."

Maxine's fist thudded against his chest, and when he grabbed it and pushed her onto the bed, she glared at him and struggled until he wrestled her into stillness, his heavy body pinning her against the sheets.

Her shirt had fallen open. He looked down at her and the laughter in his face faded. "You're the first," he confessed. "The first, last and only one. Love me, dragon lady. Let me love you."

Maxine lifted her hands and drew his head down until their lips met, and Dev settled into her arms as if he had never left them.

Outside, the sun sank behind the trees and threw flame across the sky and over the surface of the billabong, where the dragonflies shimmered just inches above the water, watched by frogs with bulging eyes and pulsating throats, sitting on lily pads. A winged beetle whirred by and a long tongue shot out and the beetle disappeared. The frog splashed from its floating perch into the depths.

A wallaby hopped to the edge of the billabong to quench its thirst, keeping a wary eye out for the crocodiles lazing on the muddy bottom. Above the murky water a slender red-and-black banded snake hung from a tree, hoping for a meal of tasty frog.

Inside the hut, geckos ambled across the walls and froze into stillness, waiting for the mosquitoes that would come with the night. The cycle of life went on.

Cocooned in the white screen of their mosquito net, a man and a woman lay entwined in each other's arms, enacting another part of nature's intricate, complex and infinitely varied dance of life. Passion flared and blazed and set them afire for each other, as they touched and kissed and murmured and discovered new heights of pleasure in the texture of satin-smooth feminine skin against roughened masculine fingertips; in the taste of the man's eager, exploring tongue in the woman's soft, welcoming mouth; in the contrast between her lush curves and his lean, muscled body; in the way her breasts fitted perfectly into his palms, the velvety centers tightening into hard little dark-rose buds; in the gentle friction of his hair-dusted thighs settling into the cradle hers made for him; in the hot, slick excitement of his thrusting entry into her body, so that they became no longer man and woman but one transcendent, elemental entity.

And at last the fierce, sweet conflagration of their love and need consumèd them both, so that for a few minutes they were annihilated in its dark, mysterious flame.

EPILOGUE

<small>MAGGIE READ ALOUD:</small>

"Dear Maggie and Dev,
I am glad you have forgiven DeWilde's for causing you so much trouble. And delighted that the affair has led to the discovery of a new branch of the family. May I warmly welcome you both to the DeWilde clan, and extend an equally warm welcome to Maxine as Dev's future wife.

I hope that before too long I may be able to visit Australia again and that we can get to know each other better. In the meantime, please accept the enclosed as a gift to commemorate these happy milestones, and some compensation for the sacrifice of your inheritance from my Uncle Dirk. The tiara's rightful place historically is with the other jewels in the DeWilde collection, but this minor piece fashioned in the 1930s by our own jewelry designers seems particularly suited to you. One might say it was made for De Wildes.

I have asked Ryder Blake to deliver it in person to ensure its safe arrival.

Yours sincerely,
Jeffrey DeWilde."

"What is it?" Binnie asked as Maggie folded the letter and picked up the distinctive dark blue DeWilde's jewelry box Ryder had handed her. On the sofa, Dev leaned forward, his hand tightening its hold on Maxine's.

Maggie lifted the hinged lid, and Binnie gasped as her aunt drew out a gold chain necklace. The chain held the curved body of a jeweled crocodile, its green enameled scales studded with tiny diamond brilliants, the eyes gleaming red stones.

"Wow!" Rooster said.

Ryder had remained standing when he presented the package to the family. "It's quite a spectacular piece," he said. "A real eye-catcher. If you want to display it, you'd be wise to contact a good security firm."

"Display it?" Dev queried.

"All the DeWilde stores have a piece of display jewelry. Perhaps you'd like to carry on the family tradition."

Maggie looked across at Dev.

"We'll think about it," he said. "Why don't you put that on, Mum?"

Maggie shook her head. "Jewelry's not my style. But I'd love to see it on Maxine."

"No, it's yours," Maxine protested.

"A family heirloom," Maggie told her firmly, "and you're family now. Try it."

Dev got up and took it from his mother, fastening the chain around Maxine's neck.

"It looks good," Ryder said judicially. "Exotic and intriguing—not many women could wear it, but you have the height and the coloring for it. Suits you, Maxine."

She touched the cool scales. "It looks like Delilah, only more colorful." She had helped Dev feed the crocodile this morning, and hoped that eventually they might be friends.

"It looks like a million dollars," Dev said, and drew her to her feet. "Come and see."

He took her to a mirror hanging over a half-round table that held a bowl of flame-red proteas.

Watching as Dev hooked his arms about Maxine's waist from behind, Ryder mused that while DeWilde's was going to miss her services, he was glad she had found happiness with a man who was strong enough to accept her almost frightening ambition, and even, perhaps, to temper it. The DeWildes were an interesting family. He had married one himself, and he wondered if he should give his friend Maxine some advice about what she might be taking on.

But, he reflected as Maxine turned and laughed up at her fiancé, touching Dev's cheek with her hand, perhaps she didn't need any advice. Judging by the way Dev Cutter was looking down at her, with all his heart unashamedly in his glittering blue eyes, Maxine knew how to handle her DeWilde man just fine.

Weddings By DeWilde

continues with

ROMANCING THE STONES

by Janis Flores

Available next month

Here's a preview!

ROMANCING THE STONES

"GIVE ME THE STUFF, or I'll cut you."

Dr. Kate DeWilde froze as the knife flashed silver under the fluorescent lights of the clinic. The blade came so close to her face that she flinched despite herself.

She knew the teenager standing in front of her meant what he said; desperation was evident in every taut line of his body.

"You don't want to do this, Emilio," she said, willing her voice not to shake. "Taking drugs from me won't help you. You need—"

"Shut up!" Sweat beaded his forehead and matted his black hair. He used the hand that was holding the knife to wipe his face. "I need to think."

Kate couldn't just stand there. Her heart pounding, she said, "While you're thinking, why don't you let me take care of that injury?"

They both looked down at his left arm, which hung straight by his side. From what she had gleaned when he first burst into the clinic, he'd been involved in a gang fight. Blood from a wound he'd sustained flowed off his fingers and fell, drop by crimson drop, to the scuffed linoleum floor. Like a blossoming scarlet flower, the puddle of blood by his feet grew wider and potentially more lethal with every drop.

Emilio took a step toward her, his handsome young face twisted with anger and pain. He swayed, and Kate knew he was about to pass out. But he still had too tight a grip on the knife for her to make a grab for it, so she remained in place, her brain racing, trying to decide what to do.

In another second or two, he was going to either drop the knife or else surrender it to her, Kate thought. She was just holding her hand out to him when she saw a movement out of the corner of her eye.

Emilio saw it, too. They both turned as a man burst into the clinic. The front door was still banging against the wall when the stranger launched himself over the counter and grabbed Emilio. Startled, the young Latino shouted a curse in Spanish as the weight of the intruder bore him back against the cabinets. He grabbed his assailant as they crashed to the floor.

Now that Kate had a chance to see who it was, she gasped, "You!"

"Yes, me," Nick Santos said grimly. He still had a grip on Emilio, who in turn was glaring murderously at him. Nick checked him out for additional weapons, then kicked away the knife, which had fallen to the floor. That done, he turned to Kate. "Where's the phone? I'll call this in and—"

"Call it in? You mean to the police?"

"No, to the local talent show—what do you think?" Nick said impatiently. "Of course I'm going to call the police. The last time I checked, threatening someone with knife was a crime."

"If you bothered to look, I'm sure even you could see that he's injured."

Nick glanced once more at Emilio, who was still losing blood. Then he caught sight of himself. Crimson stains smeared his white shirt, and there was blood on his suit jacket. He muttered an exasperated curse.

"I do now," he said. "Wouldn't you know, this is a new shirt."

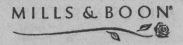

MILLS & BOON®

Weddings ✦ *Glamour* ✦ *Family* ✦ *Heartbreak*

Weddings By DeWilde

Since the turn of the century, the elegant and fashionable DeWilde stores have helped brides around the world realise the fantasy of their 'special day'.

Book 11: ROMANCING THE STONES—Janis Flores

Nick Santos was close to solving the mystery of the missing DeWilde jewels, but Kate DeWilde was proving to be a major glitch in his progress. Falling for his boss's daughter had put a definite crimp in his investigative style—doing as she asked would mean kissing the case of a lifetime good-bye...

Book 12: I DO, AGAIN—Jasmine Cresswell

Michael Forrest represented everything Julia Dutton wished to avoid in a man—but his high voltage sexuality was irresistible. Was Julia brave enough to commit to a man who offered only a few short months of ecstasy? Meanwhile, the missing DeWilde jewels were coming home to Jeffrey—via his ex-wife. Would the collection, his family and his marriage finally be whole again?

Coming to you in March 1997

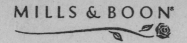

MILLS & BOON®

Weddings By DeWilde

If you have missed any of the previously published titles in the Weddings by DeWilde series, you may order them by sending a cheque or postal order (please do not send cash) made payable to Harlequin Mills & Boon Ltd. for £2.99 per book plus 50p postage and packing for the first book and 25p for each additional book. Please send your order to: Weddings by DeWilde, P.O. Box 236, Croydon, Surrey, CR9 3RU (EIRE: Weddings by DeWilde, P. O. Box 4546, Dublin 24).